Michelle Willingham

To Tempt a Viking

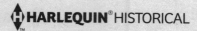

HARLEQUIN® HISTORICAL

Recycling programs
for this product may
not exist in your area.

ISBN-13: 978-0-373-29773-3

TO TEMPT A VIKING

Copyright © 2014 by Michelle Willingham

This edition published by arrangement with Harlequin Books S.A.

For questions and comments about the quality of this book,
please contact us at CustomerService@Harlequin.com.

Printed in U.S.A.

*His eyelids were heavy
and he closed them, surrendering
to the temptation of unconsciousness.
Sleep was what he needed now.*

But a moment later Elena's arms were around him and she was supporting his shoulders.

"Ragnar!" She shook him lightly, demanding that he open his eyes.

His vision flickered, but he managed to look at her.

"Don't leave me," she demanded. Her eyes welled up with tears and she commanded again, "You can't leave me here alone."

"Just...resting," he told her. Sleep would make it easier to bear the pain. The darkness was tempting him to let go, to fall into nothingness.

"Your lips are blue," she told him. "If you go to sleep now you might never awaken."

He didn't answer her, for his body had been transformed into lead and the last bits of consciousness were sliding away. Though a part of him understood what she meant, he lacked the strength to fight it.

"Don't you dare die on me!" She wept, shaking him again. "I can't survive out here alone. Do you hear me?" she demanded. "If you die, I'll die, as well."

He tried to form the word no, to tell her he wasn't going to die at all. But before his lips could move her mouth came down on his in a searing kiss.

* * *

To Tempt a Viking
Harlequin® Historical #1173—February 2014

Forbidden Vikings

Resist them if you can!

Styr Hardrata has traveled to Ireland
with his wife, Elena, to save their marriage.
They have grown apart and, when he is captured
and she kidnapped, both find themselves
faced with irresistible temptations....

Fearsome warrior Styr is captured
by the beautiful Irish maiden Caragh in
TO SIN WITH A VIKING
Already available

Lonely Elena is stranded with her husband's
best friend, Viking warrior Ragnar Olafsson, in
TO TEMPT A VIKING
February 2014

Read both stories in this powerful new duet
of forbidden passion by Michelle Willingham

Dedicated to all mothers who love their children
with special needs.
Your courage and steadfast love are inspiring.

Author Note

To Tempt a Viking is the second book in my Forbidden Vikings series (Book One was *To Sin With a Viking*). This duet is centered around the idea that sometimes arranged marriages don't work...and what will happen when a husband and a wife meet their true soul mates?

Elena Karlsdotter has always dreamed of a loving husband and children, but after being barren for years she blames herself for the failure of her marriage. Her husband no longer desires her, and she's afraid to let him go, but when she's stranded with her husband's best friend, Ragnar Olafsson, she comes to realize that the man of her dreams has been there all along. Fierce and strong, Ragnar holds dark secrets of his own, and Elena helps him to heal old wounds.

I hope you'll enjoy these Irish Viking stories. Incidentally, the epilogue of this book is based upon a true story about friends of mine who struggled for years to have children.

My other Viking stories include *The Viking's Forbidden Love-Slave, Pleasured by the Viking* and "The Holly and the Viking" in *Warriors in Winter.*

Visit my website at www.michellewillingham.com for excerpts and behind-the-scenes details about my books. I love to hear from readers and you may email me at michelle@michellewillingham.com or write via mail at P.O. Box 2242, Poquoson, VA 23662, U.S.A. I can also be found on Facebook at www.facebook.com/michellewillinghamfans and on Twitter at www.twitter.com/michellewilling.

Chapter One

Ireland—AD 875

There was nothing worse than being in love with your best friend's wife.

Ragnar Olafsson tightened his fists over the oars, pulling hard against the waves of the sea. He shouldn't have gone with them to éire. But when Styr had asked him to come, he'd agreed in a weak moment. Though he'd buried all traces of his obsession with Elena, the idea of never seeing her again was worse than the torment of seeing her with her husband.

Never once had he let either of them know of his fascination. No one knew of the raw frustration gnawing within him when he watched Styr take the woman he loved into his hut. It was a dark torture, seeing them together.

And yet, he couldn't bring himself to let her go.

As he rowed, Ragnar kept his gaze fixed upon Elena. Her fair hair held glints of red, like touches of fire upon gold. She was like a beautiful goddess—he worshipped her from afar.

She considered him a friend, but nothing more than that. It wasn't surprising. A woman like Elena deserved a strong marriage to a high-born warrior. Her match with Styr had been arranged years ago and Ragnar wasn't the sort of man to steal a woman away from a friend. Especially not his best friend.

She'd made her choice and Styr had done everything to make her happy. For that reason, Ragnar had stepped aside.

He'd tried to find another woman over the years. Although he was a strong fighter and several maidens had cast their eyes on him, none of them compared to Elena. Perhaps no one ever would.

He studied her as she stared off at the grey waters. Something had changed in the past few months. She and Styr were hardly speaking to one another any more. Her barrenness was eating away at her spirit, drowning her in misery. When she stared out at the sea, her face was unnaturally pale. There were no words to mend the broken pieces, nothing Ragnar could say to her.

As the boat neared the shore, the waters were shallower than they'd guessed.

'We'll stop here,' Styr ordered. Glancing at the others, he moved to stand beside Ragnar. For a moment, his friend stared out at the shoreline. 'Will you stay behind with Elena?' he asked. 'I don't want her near the front, if there's danger.'

'I'll keep her safe.' He would bathe his sword in the blood of any enemy who dared to threaten Elena. Though she didn't belong to him, she was his to guard. He wouldn't hesitate to offer his life, if it meant saving her.

Styr rested a hand upon Ragnar's shoulder. With a dark sigh, he admitted, 'I am glad you came with us. A journey like this could only be endured with friends.'

'None of the men has slept in three days,' Ragnar agreed. 'We all need a good meal and rest.' Their vessel had been tossed upon the waves as if the gods had wanted to claim them as a sacrifice. They'd fought the hard winds, trying to battle the storm. And they'd won, at the cost of sleep. His body and mind were so strung out, he could hardly piece together any thoughts other than the desire to collapse upon the sand.

'A pity you haven't a woman to warm your bed,' Styr added with a shrug.

Ragnar sent him a wry look. 'The last I heard, there are women in éire. I might find one yet.'

He'd had a few women over the years, but none of them compared to *her*. Though he'd tried, time and again, to purge Elena from his mind, there were many nights when he awakened, covered with sweat…his shaft hard with visions of the woman he loved.

By the blood of Thor, he had to stop thinking of it. Elena belonged to Styr and there was never any hope that it would change. Once she quickened with her husband's seed, she would find her happiness. Ragnar tightened his hand upon his sword and reached for a shield to distract his mind.

Styr took his own shield, adding, 'I'm glad you're here. I need strong fighters among my men.' To emphasise his point, he lightly punched Ragnar's upper arm.

Ragnar responded by seizing Styr's wrist and holding it fast. 'I've bested you a time or two.'

'Because I allowed it.' But his friend sent him a dark

smile. Styr was like a brother to him. He had taught him how to fight, after Ragnar's father had neglected to do so. They had trained together in secret, until Ragnar could wield a sword as well as him. In truth, Ragnar was the better fighter, but Styr would never admit it.

Ragnar said quietly, 'I'll always guard your back.' And so he would. Despite his traitorous feelings, he would never betray his greatest friend.

After dropping their anchor, they waded through the waist-high water. Elena remained on board the ship, as if uncertain whether or not to approach.

'You can stay on the ship if you want,' Ragnar told her. 'We'll see if it's safe.'

She appeared troubled but shook her head. 'No, I want to go with the others. Perhaps if they see me, they won't think you're attacking.'

Her reasoning made sense, for invaders rarely had a woman among them. But still, he intended to keep her behind the others.

Ragnar helped her down, trying not to let his hands linger upon her slender form. She wore a cream-coloured gown with a softer rose apron, pinned at the shoulders with golden brooches. Her hair was in tight braids, pinned to her head, and she winced as she made her way through the frigid water.

'We'll build a fire for you, soon enough,' he promised.

Ahead, Styr had his battleaxe firmly in his grasp and all of them studied the settlement. It was unnaturally silent, which set Ragnar on edge. The scent of outdoor fires lingered and he saw evidence of a tribe that had fled. A pot of liquid boiled, the steam rising in the cold air…but there was no one to tend it. A length of cloth lay discarded on the ground, as if its owner had fled too quickly to take it.

'Stay back,' Ragnar warned Elena. As he trudged through the water, his vision seemed to blur, his footing growing less stable. The lack of sleep from the violent storms was starting to affect him. He pushed back against the spinning sensation, ignoring his body's demands for rest.

Something was wrong within the settlement. There were no people and no animals. With each step forwards, his mind dulled. He couldn't seem to grasp a clear thought and, when he blinked, the world seemed to tip on edge. Ragnar took a moment to steady himself, claiming a deep breath. He would not allow exhaustion to overcome his strength.

When he glimpsed movement, he turned back to Elena. 'You should return to the boat,' he commanded. 'Stay there until we know what's happening.' He didn't want her caught in a battle if the Irish misunderstood their reasons for coming here.

She shook her head. 'If I stay there alone, I'm unprotected.' Ragnar started to argue, but she insisted, 'I'm not going back. I'll stay here, at the water's edge, but I need to be on land.'

'Behind me, then,' he acceded. Before they could venture another step, he stopped to look at her. Her seagreen eyes held him captive, her skin as pale as milk. So many nights he'd dreamed of sinking his hands into her fiery hair, claiming her soft lips in a kiss.

'Is something wrong?' she asked, her face flushed

at his stare. It was as if she could read his forbidden thoughts.

Ragnar focused on the sand ahead. 'No. Nothing at all.' He scanned the ringfort for movement. In the distance, he spied shadows moving behind one of the huts. The silence was unnerving, as if they were the prey of some unknown attacker. They continued walking through the water until they stood upon dry land.

Ragnar moved several steps towards the shadows, gripping his shield in his left hand, a short sword in the other. More than ever, he was starting to believe that Elena should have stayed on the ship. She remained behind him, on the edge of the sand. Waves washed around her ankles, while she waited with her hands gripped together.

'Stay back,' he warned. 'Call out if you see anything.' She nodded and Ragnar hesitated. Instinct warned him not to leave her…and yet he wasn't about to risk endangering her from an unseen attacker. 'Will you be all right?'

'Yes.' But her voice held no confidence at all. She reached to her belt and gripped the hilt of a dagger.

Ragnar moved cautiously towards the shadows, while the others followed Styr. Their gait was heavy, as if the weight of the past few days remained upon their shoulders. All could fight, if necessary, but fatigue had set in.

He kept walking, his mind focused upon any threat, when suddenly, he heard Elena's scream cut through the stillness. He spun, raising his sword…and found her surrounded by four men.

By the gods, where had they come from? Like ghosts, they'd emerged from the mist that surrounded her.

A dark violence awakened within him. The blood rage pushed away the exhaustion and he raced back to Elena, his sword in hand. He lunged at one of the young men, only to have his sword blocked by a shield. Renewed energy coursed through his veins as he fought with all of his strength. Two men attacked him and he used his shield to deflect a blow, slashing his sword down with his right hand.

He let the battle madness sweep over him, releasing the rage inside. When metal clashed against wood, he slid into the familiar fighting. Everything else faded away except the primal need to protect her.

Another enemy crept up behind him and he saw the wild look in Elena's eyes. He didn't care that he was outnumbered. He would not let anyone harm her—not while he had breath in his body. With a crushing blow, he used his shield to knock down the third man, slashing a savage blow to the other.

One of the men grabbed Elena from behind, twisting her wrist until her dagger fell to the sand. He dragged her backwards and Ragnar fought with all his strength to break free of the Irishmen.

But he didn't know if he'd reach her in time.

Blood thundered in his veins as Ragnar released a battle cry. He cut through the men surrounding him, his blade slashing towards his enemy. Dimly, he was aware of Styr charging forwards as well.

Two men tried to cut them off, but he and Styr divided their enemies. When his attacker struck out,

Ragnar threw himself to the sand, rolling free while a sword sliced the place where his head had been.

More of the Irish charged forwards and while he continued to fight, Ragnar saw a young man seize Elena, holding a blade to her throat. There was desperation in the young man's eyes, of a captor who had never killed before. That made him even more dangerous.

With a renewed surge of aggression, Ragnar pushed his way free, just as Styr raced towards his wife. Before Styr could tear Elena's captor apart, everything changed.

Another woman emerged, shouting at both of them. In her hands, she held a thick staff as her weapon.

Ragnar ignored her, all of his attention focused on Elena. The young man was distracted, giving him an opening to free her. He inched his way closer, waiting for the right moment.

For an instant, the young man faltered, as if considering whether to let Elena go. He seemed to recognise that if he did, Styr would split his head open with the axe.

But Ragnar could attack from behind, catching the young man unawares. If he struck true, he could free Elena before anyone knew what had happened.

Closer…

He lifted his sword, prepared to strike. Before he could move, the woman brought her wooden staff across Styr's head, catching him on the ear. His friend dropped to the ground.

Thor's blood. Ragnar didn't think, but lunged, just as another man raised his blade for the kill.

'Styr!' Elena cried out in anguish, just as Ragnar

blocked the blow. She was reaching towards her fallen husband, while the other woman was speaking foreign words that sounded like an apology.

The young man dragged Elena back, stepping towards the water. Deeper he moved, until she was submerged to her waist. He could drown her if he tried.

Ragnar shouted to the others, knowing that all of them were needed to protect Elena and Styr. His friends kept their weapons drawn, their shields at the ready as they approached. Upon the sand, he saw the dark-haired woman binding Styr's wrists and ankles with long strips of leather. An older man helped her drag him away.

'Ragnar,' Elena pleaded. 'Save him.' Her voice was barely above a whisper, her sea-green eyes holding her fear of death.

He was torn between saving his best friend…and saving Elena. Gods help him, this was a decision he'd never wanted to make.

'What should we do?' his friend Onund asked.

In the end, there was only one choice. He had to save the woman he loved, even at the cost of the man who was like a brother.

'If anything happens to her, Styr will hold us all to blame.' Ragnar raised his sword and shield and started towards the water.

Chapter Two

Elena watched in disbelief as Ragnar laid down his weapon and shield upon the sand. What was he doing? He was stronger than any of these men and she didn't doubt he could kill them all. Why would he surrender?

Unless he had another plan she didn't know about.

Ragnar moved in closer, the water pooling against his leather boots. He wore chainmail armour and an iron helm while his rough brown hair hung down past his shoulders. Dark green eyes gleamed with purpose, his face holding the merciless cast of a warrior who intended to slaughter his enemies.

And so he would. Elena had seen him training alongside her husband and had witnessed his skills firsthand. There was no fighter stronger than Ragnar Olafsson, and he moved with a speed no man could match.

'Let her go,' Ragnar called out to her captor. 'We'll return to our ship.'

He spoke to the Irishman as if he believed the man could understand the Norse language. His words were calm, his hands raised up in surrender. But beneath the gesture lay an unspoken threat.

For Ragnar would never bargain with an enemy. Her heart pounded faster as the other Irishmen began to close in.

What was he planning to do? Sacrifice himself? No. He wasn't the sort of man to play the martyr.

Onund stared at Ragnar with fury. 'You might intend to surrender, Ragnar, but we won't. We outnumber them!' the man snapped, refusing to lay down his weapons.

A flare of irritation slid over Ragnar's face and it was then that Elena understood his deception.

The Irish might have taken them by surprise, but the same could be wrought upon them, if they believed in the surrender. Ragnar was granting their kinsmen time to gather together. Couldn't Onund see that?

'If we attack, he'll slit her throat. And they'll kill Styr as well.' Ragnar lowered his voice, and Elena could no longer hear his plan while her captor dragged her into deeper water. They had almost reached the ship and she didn't know what Ragnar intended to do.

He had never once taken his gaze from her. The hard look in his eyes spoke of a man determined to get her back. Her mind flashed to the strange way he'd stared at her earlier. It had shaken her senses, for his look had held desire. As if he wanted her…intimately.

The memory of it made her heart pound faster, for she'd never seen him look at her that way before. His green eyes permeated her defences, reaching deep within. She didn't understand her own reaction to him and her skin prickled from more than the frigid water.

A horrifying thought occurred to her. Ragnar didn't

want Styr to die, did he? Her husband was now a prisoner of the Irish and somehow they had to rescue him.

But what if Ragnar wasn't intending to save him? What if he turned his back on Styr?

Never could she imagine Ragnar as a traitor, but she couldn't let go of the unbidden fear.

At last, the others followed his lead, setting down their shields and returning to the water. One by one, they followed, while the Irish closed in behind them.

'Some of you should stay behind for Styr,' she called out in warning.

But the instant she spoke, the Irishman plunged her head beneath the icy water. In shock, she lost her breath, her hands clawing at the surface. He jerked her from the water, her hair sodden and blinding her. Harsh words were spoken, his voice issuing warnings she didn't understand. And before she realised what was happening, he'd hauled her back on to their ship. She never had the chance to fight back, for the cold had penetrated her body, seizing her with shock.

Her consciousness grew hazy and she was only dimly aware of the blade at her throat while he gripped her wrists and found a length of rope to bind her. At last, he secured her to the front of the boat.

Before long, her kinsmen emerged from the water, four Irishmen behind them. They didn't try to fight, but allowed themselves to be taken. She strongly suspected they would wait for the right element of surprise.

And yet there was no one to help Styr. With a sinking heart, she stared back at the shoreline. Her husband was already gone and there was no way to know if she'd see him again. Although they'd grown distant over the past few months, she knew it was her own fault for turning him away. He was a good man, a warrior who deserved better than a barren wife like herself.

The knife of self-pity slid into her and she forced it back. It would do her no good now. She needed to gather her courage and do what was necessary to survive. It was their only hope.

When Ragnar climbed aboard, he kept his eyes upon her as they bound him. She couldn't guess his plans, but the message was clear. He had every intention of freeing them from captivity.

The Irish had taken the oars, but with only four of them, the ship didn't move very fast. Her captor, whose name she learned was Brendan, took command of the sails, letting the wind pull them far away from land.

Only when Ragnar was shoved a few feet away from her did she dare to whisper at him, 'What will become of Styr? You left him behind with no one. He could already be dead.' A chill crossed her at the thought and hot tears rose to her eyes.

'If they'd wanted him dead, they wouldn't have taken him prisoner,' Ragnar pointed out. 'They'll try to use him as a hostage. But we'll return before any harm can come to him.'

She didn't know what to believe. For all she knew, they might torture Styr or kill him as an act of vengeance. 'What if you're wrong?' she murmured.

'I'm not. Trust me.'

She locked her eyes with his, silently pleading with him to strike sooner. 'You can't abandon him.'

His demeanour shifted into a man who resented her accusations. There was no softness, no mercy upon his face at all. 'I swore to him that I would guard you with my life. And so I have.' He leaned in, his dark green eyes demanding her attention. 'We're going to take back the ship, this night.'

'Your hands are bound,' she argued.

'Are they?' His voice held such indifference, she began to wonder if she was wrong to doubt him. Upon her face, she felt the warmth of his breath. His long brown hair held hints of gold, his face rigid like a conqueror's. The look had returned to his eyes, one that made her falter. It reached beneath her desperate fear, sliding through her veins until he held her captive.

Trust me, he'd demanded. She wanted to believe in him, for he was their best hope of returning to the ringfort. But once again, he was watching her in a way that made her pulse quicken. It only deepened her discomfort.

A moment later, one of the Irishmen grasped him and shoved him back. Though his words were incomprehensible, she couldn't tear her gaze from Ragnar. If he had somehow freed himself, he'd done a good job of disguising it.

The winds had swelled again, the skies growing darker. She was growing hungry, but no one offered food or water. When the Irishmen explored the ship, they quickly found Styr's store of supplies below deck. They devoured the food savagely, eating every bite of dried meat and preserved fish without offering them a single morsel. Only the bag of grain remained. Glancing at the Irish, Elena suddenly noticed how thin they were. It was as if they had been starving, their faces were so gaunt.

For the second time, she wondered if it had been wise to surrender. These men had not the strength of the Norsemen. But in their eyes, she saw that they were bent upon survival now, as if all traces of humanity were gone. Like animals, they fought amongst themselves for the choicest pieces of food.

Her earlier frustration with Ragnar diminished. Men who cared for nothing but their own lives would do anything. They would kill with no remorse.

Their leader, Brendan, was hardly more than an adolescent. But in his eyes, she saw determination. Whatever he planned to do with them, he would not be swayed from his course.

Though it had been hours since she'd been dragged back to the ship, she'd been unable to get warm. Her body was freezing, while her wet hair was clammy against her skin. Fear magnified the discomfort and her mouth grew dry with thirst.

'Could I have some water?' she asked Brendan, even knowing he did not understand her words. She glanced over at the men, who were drinking wine, nodding to them to convey the meaning.

His mouth closed in a grim line and he ignored her question, adjusting the mainsail instead. When she studied her friends and kinsmen, she watched to see if Ragnar was right. Had they managed to free themselves? They sat motionless, their arms behind their backs. None would look at her.

Perhaps…

Ragnar spoke to the men, his voice a calm echo against the sea. 'At moonrise.'

She took a breath, glancing at the Irish to see if

they'd understood him. They were too busy gorging on food, but Brendan's brow furrowed. Without a word, he unsheathed his blade and crossed the boat until he sat behind her. She felt the kiss of the blade upon her throat, and the young man stared back at Ragnar in a silent challenge.

Ragnar intended to gut the Irishman, before the night was over, for daring to touch Elena. He'd sliced through his bonds, using a hidden blade that he'd passed to his kinsmen, one by one. Now, the blade was his again and he was waiting for the right moment to strike.

They had been sailing for hours and several of the Irish had fallen asleep—all, save the man holding Elena captive. Brendan seemed to sense that the moment he let her go, his life would be the forfeit.

The sun had descended below the horizon, and the moon was beginning to rise. Ragnar eyed the other men, silently warning them to be ready. He kept his gaze fixed upon Elena, watching for the moment to seize her. She appeared tense and, upon her throat, he saw the barest trace of blood.

His fist clenched upon the dagger, while he vowed his own vengeance upon the man who kept her captive. Elena's shoulders were held back, her body stiff as if she didn't dare move.

Ragnar needed a distraction, a way of diverting Brendan's attention away. Taking a hostage or possibly attacking without warning. His brain went through a dozen possibilities, all of which were feasible, but held an inherent risk.

Gods above, why couldn't this be any other hostage but Elena? If it were, he'd simply drag her away, slicing her attacker's throat. But the threat was too strong. Elena meant everything to him and he would do nothing to endanger her life.

He saw her glance up at the crescent moon, which had slid out from behind a cloud. At the sight of it, her face went white. Ragnar wanted to say something, to reassure her that all would be well.

'Elena.' He couldn't stop himself from speaking her name, despite the risk. *Don't be afraid. I'll free you.*

The Irishman spoke words that sounded like another warning, but his voice cracked at the end, undermining the threat. Reminding him that he was hardly more than a boy.

'The ship is moving closer to the shore,' Ragnar told her.

'I—I can't swim very well.' Her fear was tangible, but she cast a look at the dark water. The wind was strong now, pulling the vessel east. Ahead, he spied a large outcropping of rock, a tiny island not far away. She could reach it, if she tried.

'I won't let you drown,' he swore.

She seemed to consider it, seeking reassurance from him. Though he knew she belonged to Styr, he wished in that moment that he could hold her. Give her the comfort she needed.

And then, as if the gods had willed it to be so, he spied the perfect diversion.

Brendan Ó Brannon had never been so terrified in all his life. He held the knife to the *Lochlannach* woman's throat, all the while wishing he'd never left the shores of his homeland. At the time, he'd believed he was protecting his sister Caragh. He'd thought he could force the invaders to leave, bringing their ship miles away from home before he and his friends could abandon the ship at night, swimming to shore.

But these men hadn't slept. They'd never taken their eyes off him or the woman he held hostage. With every minute that passed, his impending death came closer.

A hollow sorrow filled him up, with the knowledge that he'd never see his sister or brothers again. All because he'd tried to be a hero. What did he know of defending them against fierce *Lochlannach* invaders? Nothing at all. He was only seven and ten, barely a man. He'd acted without thinking and worse, he'd left his sister Caragh alone. She had no one to take care of her and he doubted if he would make it out alive.

One man, in particular, made him nervous. He stared hard at him, as if he intended to murder Brendan the moment an opportunity presented itself.

Silently, Brendan prayed that he could somehow get out of this. He considered letting the woman go, throwing himself overboard, no matter how far from shore they were. His chances of survival were better.

But he held on to her, for she was the only person keeping him and his friends alive. Soon enough, they would reach the southernmost tip of the eastern coast of éireann.

The moon was clouded this night, making it difficult to see. His body was exhausted and he fought to keep his hands from shaking.

A shout came from one of his men, alerting them

to another ship. Brendan kept his blade at the woman's throat as he turned to look. Just as his friend had warned, a large merchant ship was bearing down on them.

But the men weren't Irish.

His mouth went dry, his palms sweating. It was the *Gallaibh*, the Danes who were as fearless as the Norse. His grandsire had spun tales of the bloodthirsty invaders who would kill anyone who breathed.

God help them all. If they survived this night, it would be a miracle.

'Turn the ship!' Brendan commanded. If they could get closer to shore, they might have a chance of escaping. But he wasn't accustomed to the *Lochlannach* vessel and he didn't know how to steer it. Instead of moving in the direction of the shore, it seemed that an invisible force was turning them towards the path of the Danes.

Fear ripped through him and he caught a glimpse of archers taking aim. His stomach twisted and he stared back at the water, wondering if he had the courage to seize his escape. Drowning was better than facing a dozen arrows.

His gaze fixed upon his hostage. The woman was hardly older than his sister Caragh. He took a breath, wishing he'd never taken her. She didn't deserve to fall into the hands of the Danes, who would rape her before they killed her. He'd made countless mistakes this day, but there were precious seconds left.

With his knife, he cut the ropes securing her to the front of the boat, then sliced through her bonds. She stared at him in surprise, rubbing her wrists. Without asking why, she stumbled back towards her kinsmen.

To his friends, Brendan ordered, 'We'll have to jump. If they get too close, we won't survive.'

'If we abandon the ship, we'll drown,' a friend countered.

Brendan's heart beat faster, a thin line of sweat sliding down his neck. 'Once we make it to shore, we'll journey back to Gall Tír on foot.'

If they made it to shore. The Danes were even closer now and he heard them shouting words in an unfamiliar tongue.

'It's too far,' his friend argued.

'We don't have a choice. If we stay here, we'll die tonight.' After they abandoned the ship, he could only hope that the *Lochlannach* would remain on board and let them be. But from the mercenary look in the Viking leader's eyes, Brendan wasn't at all convinced that the man would let them go. His stomach lurched at the thought of their impending fate.

Without warning, the *Lochlannach* rose from their places, closing in on him. It was clear that they'd freed themselves from the ropes some time ago and had been waiting for the right moment to attack.

The archers drew back and the first storm of arrows struck the ship. Brendan threw himself to the deck and heard the dull thud of an arrow piercing flesh. When he saw the face of his dying kinsman, he cringed, keeping low on the ship.

The Norsemen were shouting, and all around him, he heard the sounds of men jumping overboard. He heard the screams of those who were shot by the archers before their bodies landed in the water.

The woman lay against the bottom of the boat, while her kinsmen defended her. He saw the *Lochlannach* leader stiffen when an arrow pierced his leg. The woman cried out, and a moment later, she emerged from her hiding place, jumping off the ship. The man followed, though Brendan doubted he would make it to shore with his injuries.

Fear rose in his throat and he closed his eyes, prepared to face his death. All around him, he heard the sound of the Danes closing in.

Let my death be swift and painless, he prayed. *And let my sister be safe.*

Elena's heart slammed into her chest, her pulse beating so fast, she was dizzy from fear. The icy water struck her like a fist, her gown weighing down upon her. Though she moved her arms and legs, it was not enough to swim—more like treading water.

Now that she was free of the ship, it seemed that the outcropping of rock was impossibly far away. Her breathing quickened and she fought with her arms and legs, struggling to keep her head above water. Behind her, she heard the shouts of men and the clash of swords.

Her face dipped beneath the wave and she choked upon the salt water, coughing as she struggled again to reach land. In the darkness, she could barely see anything around her and she doubted if she could make it to the small island.

Fear penetrated her to the bone. *You're not strong enough to reach land. You're going to drown.*

Her resolve was weakening, but she continued churning her arms, until there was a sudden splash. A strong arm grasped her around the waist, pulling her to him. When she looked up, she saw Ragnar holding her. He propelled them through the water with immeasurable strength, like a ship cutting through the waves. She gripped him around the neck, thankful that he, too, had escaped.

'Swim!' she heard Ragnar say. 'Don't look back.'

She was desperately afraid, her mind seizing with shock. Her face dipped below the water again, but a strong arm dragged her up. Ragnar urged her to keep moving, holding his arm at her waist. They swam together while behind them, they heard the shouts of the Danes taking command of the ship.

Freya, protect me, she prayed, as they fought to reach land. The crescent moon slid from behind a cloud, reflecting its light upon the surface of the water. She stared at the light, her fear closing in again.

She had to live. Despite her terror, she would fight to survive. Even if they were the only two left alive.

Chapter Three

Her arms were leaden, her body freezing from the icy water. But with Ragnar at her side, she took courage. He was speaking words of encouragement, though his pace had slowed.

When at last her feet touched the bottom, Elena breathed a sigh of relief. Her body was exhausted and trembling, but they were both on land.

Ragnar's steps were heavy, his body leaning upon hers as she strode through the water. She couldn't understand why he was struggling to walk, until the moonlight gleamed upon him, revealing the arrow protruding from his upper thigh.

'You're hurt,' she breathed, offering him her support as they stumbled to the sand.

Ragnar didn't answer and she felt the urge to panic. How badly was he wounded? A dark fear rose up that she couldn't survive on her own.

A moment later, she pushed aside the errant thoughts. He wasn't dead yet, and if she tended his wound, he might live.

Her mind sealed off all thoughts except those that

would aid her. She needed to take out the arrow, bind his wound and get them a fire and shelter. There was enough wool in her gown to tear off for a bandage.

'Ragnar,' she said. 'Look at me.'

He did, but there was so much pain in his gaze, she feared the worst. His hose and tunic were soaked with seawater, the chainmail armour gleaming against the moonlight. She needed to take off his armour to examine his wound.

'I'm going to help you over to those rocks,' she said. 'Can you manage to walk that far?'

He gave a nod, as if it took too much energy to speak. Blood streamed down his leg from the arrow in his thigh, but at least it wasn't pumping out. She eased him to sit down and helped him remove his armour and the padded tunic beneath. Then she used the knife at his waist to cut long strips from her skirts. The thought of pressing more salt water against his wounds was excruciating, so she looked around for an alternative. There were patches of moss and she dug at the stones, trying to find something to make a barrier against the wet wool.

'We need a fire,' Ragnar reminded her, reaching inside his tunic. 'You might…build one.'

'Soon,' she promised. 'I'm going to take out the arrow.'

'I might bleed out if you do,' he said quietly.

'I can't leave it, can I?' She placed her hands on his shoulders, kneeling down before him. 'You kept me protected. I'll do everything I can to help you.'

For a single moment, she caught a glimpse of a fierce longing in his eyes, before he shielded it and looked away. She didn't know how to respond, for fear that she'd misread him.

Elena took a deep breath and reached for the arrow. It would pain him more if she told him when she was planning to take it out. Though she'd never before removed an arrow from a man's skin, it didn't look too deep. She questioned whether to force it all the way through the skin or whether to jerk it out. Both would cause pain, but pushing it through would likely be easier.

'I don't want to cause you pain,' she said steadily. 'But this must be—' with one huge push, she forced the arrow through the opposite side '—done,' she finished, snapping off the tip and sliding the shaft free. He let out a gasp of pain, but she packed the wound with moss and bound it tight with the first strip of wool.

'I thought you would give me more warning than that,' he breathed, fighting against the pain.

'Anticipated pain is worse than reality,' she responded.

'And you've had an arrow tear through your flesh before?' His voice was harsh, but it was done now.

'It wasn't that deep,' she offered. 'The bleeding isn't as bad as I thought it would be.' Thank the gods for that. If it had gone any deeper, she doubted if she'd have had the strength to force the arrow through the other side. His rigid muscles would have made it impossible.

Once Ragnar was bandaged, she left him sitting against the rocks. There was a tremor in his body, as if he were unable to stop himself from shaking.

He was right; they did need a fire to warm them.

But first, she had to find flint. It was too dark to see the stones, however.

Her mind stumbled with panic, the freezing air and the darkness starting to undermine what little courage she had left. They needed shelter and warmth to protect them this night. Their survival depended on it.

Elena forced herself to think of the smaller details, knowing that a fire would help them both more than anything. She still had Ragnar's knife. 'I'll try to find flint among the stones,' she told him.

'Wait.' He reached into his tunic and pulled out a stone that hung from a leather thong around his neck. 'This is flint.'

She tried to loosen the knot while her hands rested against his throat.

'You weren't hurt, were you?' he whispered. His voice resonated between them and a spiral of warmth rippled through her. She grew aware that her hands were around his neck, almost in an embrace.

'No.' To calm her beating heart, she murmured, 'Don't speak now. Just rest while I build a fire.'

When the knot wouldn't untie, she lifted the leather thong over his head, taking the flint and his blade. The scent of his male skin was unlike her husband's, but it held the familiarity of a close friend. How many times had she relied upon Ragnar over the years? They'd been friends all her life, and if she had to be stranded with anyone, she was grateful it was him.

She renewed her courage and slipped into the comfort of routine, gathering dried seaweed for tinder and driftwood along the beach. It was clear that in the morning they would have to move inland to get food. They couldn't survive here without fresh water or shelter. Yet she didn't know if Ragnar could manage to swim again.

Don't think of that now, she ordered herself. Dawn was soon enough to worry about the rest of it.

When she'd arranged the wood and tinder, she struck the flint with his blade, until she caught a spark and blew it to life. Slowly, she fed the fire until the warmth blazed.

Her clothing was sodden, but it felt good to sit beside the flames. When she looked back at the water, there were no ships anywhere—only the cool lapping of waves against the shore of the island. 'What do you think happened to the others? Do you suppose they're alive?'

'I overheard the Danes talk of selling them as slaves.' He grimaced, adjusting his position against the rocks. 'If they didn't murder all of them.'

Elena rubbed her upper arms, trying not to imagine it. The idea of being the only survivors from their voyage was impossible to grasp. Even the thought made her fears well up inside, before she pushed them back.

'You're cold, aren't you?' she remarked, moving beside him. Though she'd bandaged his thigh wound, his clothing was as wet as hers. 'Do you want me to help you get closer to the fire?'

Ragnar shook his head. 'I'll be all right.' He closed his eyes, adding, 'In the morning, we'll go to the mainland.'

'Do you think you can manage the crossing?' She worried about whether he had the strength when he was struggling to walk. Her own swimming was barely strong enough to keep her above water. Though he was stronger than most men, the salt water against his wounds would make it brutally painful.

'I don't have a choice, do I?' Though he kept his words neutral, she sensed his pain and wished there was something she could do to alleviate it.

She reached out to take his hand. 'We're going to live, Ragnar. And I owe you my thanks for saving me from the Danes.'

He squeezed her hand, but his gaze remained distant. Though he gave no answer, she understood that he'd sworn to protect her. Nothing would make him forsake that vow.

'Will you come and sit beside me?' he asked.

Something within her stirred at his request. It was dangerous to be so close to this man. Although he was a close friend, instinct held her back. Elena took a few steps away, needing the space.

'I should gather more wood,' she argued, fumbling for an excuse.

'It's going to be all right, Elena,' he assured her.

She wanted to believe it. But they were miles from anywhere, and her husband was a prisoner. Their men were held captive, taken as slaves or killed. She felt herself hovering on the brink of tears. As she gathered up more twigs and small bits of driftwood, she glanced up at the crescent moon once again.

A ripple of uneasiness filled her, but she brushed the feeling aside. Right now, she had to concentrate on surviving the night ahead. Doggedly, she continued searching for wood, letting the mindless task blot out the horrifying fears. The night temperature had begun dropping and she returned to the fire, stacking the sticks and twigs she'd gathered.

'Do you think my husband is alive?' she asked Ragnar, thinking of Styr.

'I've no doubt of it.' He leaned against one of the stones, gritting his teeth when he moved his leg.

Though it should have made her feel better, the longer she sat by the fire, the more despondent she grew. In the space of a few hours, she'd lost everything—her husband, her people, their ship and even a shelter. Silent tears welled up and spilled over, against her will.

'Come here, Elena.'

She ignored him, needing a good cry. She deserved it, after all that had happened.

'Are you really going to make a wounded man drag himself across the sand to get to you?' Although his voice held teasing, there was enough determination that made her aware that he'd do it.

'I'll be fine.' But she obeyed, returning to sit beside him. When his arms came around her, she wept in earnest. His kindness was her undoing, for she didn't know how to gather up the pieces of her life or how to begin anew from here. Her husband, as well as their kinsmen, could be dead. They had no ship and they were stranded in a foreign land, far away from home.

Ragnar said nothing at all, but held her tightly and his presence did bring her comfort. She wasn't alone, despite all that had happened. That, at least, was a consolation.

His skin was warm from the fire and she rested her cheek against him, closing her eyes. 'Sleep,' he urged. 'I'll just lie here and count the hours until I stop hurting.'

Although he was trying to make light of the injury, she knew he was in a great deal of discomfort. 'I wish I had something to take away your pain.'

An enigmatic smile crossed his face. 'It would be worse if you were not here at all.' With a heavy sigh, he added, 'In the morning we'll decide how to get to the mainland.'

She lay beside the fire, but sleep would not come. The heavy weight of her wet clothing was making it difficult to dry off. Elena unfastened the brooches at her shoulders and peeled off the wet outer apron, leaving on the cream-coloured gown. She set it upon the rocks to dry, though she doubted this was possible by morning. Still, she might sleep better without the heavy layers of wetness.

She huddled upon the sand, leaving the fire between them. Ragnar's face was as exhausted as hers, his dark green eyes solemn. 'You can sleep beside me without fear, Elena.'

She hesitated, for never had she slept beside any man except Styr. But then again, there was no shelter here. Sleeping alone would be uncomfortable for both of them.

But did she dare sleep beside Ragnar? Her reluctance must have been evident, for he shrugged and leaned up against one of the rocks as if it were no matter.

With a sigh, she realised that she was being foolish. Sleeping beside Ragnar would mean nothing at all. He would never threaten her marriage, not when her husband was his closest friend. Her apprehensions were groundless.

Silently, she rose from her place on the sand.

Dawn came far too soon. Ragnar had hardly slept at all, but the warmth of Elena's body was pressed against his back. His wounds ached, but he didn't move at all, not wanting to disturb her.

Her hair was still damp, in a tangled red-and-gold mass around her shoulders. The braids had come undone and the strands held the wildness of bent curls. Her pale gown outlined her slender body with curves and he forced the sinful thoughts away.

Not yours, he reminded himself.

Her eyes opened and she yawned, sitting up. 'Did you sleep?' Eyeing his wounds, she added, 'Are you in much pain?'

He was, but he welcomed the dull ache. To lie beside Elena had been a dream he'd never imagined and his torn flesh had reminded him of the boundaries between them. If he had died last night, he could think of no better place to spend his last hours.

His leg burned, but he forced himself to answer, 'I'll be all right. We need to reach the mainland today.'

She knelt before him and unwrapped the bandages. At the sight of his wounded flesh, she blanched. 'It doesn't look good.'

He shrugged. 'I'm alive.' *For now*, he thought, but didn't say so. If he developed a fever, that could slay him quicker than the arrow wound.

'You need a better healer than me,' she argued. Rising to her feet, she took a deep breath and glanced around her. 'But it's too far for both of us to swim to the mainland.' She stared at the small copse of trees. 'There may be some fallen wood we could use for a raft.'

'You aren't strong enough to pull a log into the water,' he argued. Already Elena appeared exhausted, her green eyes clouded with unspoken fear.

'No, but I can find smaller branches and tie them together. We could hold on and then try to swim.'

'And what are you going to tie the wood with? Grass?'

In answer, she lifted her skirt, baring her legs to the knees. 'I'll cut off more of my dress.'

The image of her long bared legs was enough to send a sharp flare of heat coursing through him. 'If you think it will work,' he said. He'd never seen beyond her ankles, but now she'd revealed shapely calves. He could only imagine the rest of those long legs, for she was a tall woman.

And another man's wife.

His best friend's wife.

Ragnar leaned his weight against the stones, pushing his way up to a standing position. The sky was a hazy rose and gold, and mist frosted against the edge of the mainland. His stomach twisted at the thought of food and he hoped they would catch fish or other game.

But he wasn't much use to Elena. Not like this. The barest pressure of weight upon his leg was agonising, and he gritted his teeth, forcing himself to limp towards the other side of the island. It was a small outcropping, hardly more than a copse of trees and large boulders. There was no food, no water and their only hope for survival was to make the crossing.

He glanced at the grey salt water, knowing that it would burn his wounds with unholy fire. Elena's suggestion, that they bind fallen limbs together, was a sound one. The pain had been bad enough when the arrow was still inside him, but more flesh was exposed now that she'd taken it out.

When Elena emerged from the woods, she dragged four stout branches along the sand, each the thickness of his forearm. She had gathered up her hair, twisting it in a knot and securing it with a small stick while she worked. She used his knife to cut off more material from her skirts. As she bound the limbs together, his traitorous imagination conjured up the vision of her bared legs tangled with his own, his body lying atop hers.

Ragnar closed his eyes, furious with himself for even thinking such dishonourable thoughts about her.

'Let me help you,' he said to Elena. He needed the activity to distract him. Anything to keep his gaze away from her bared flesh.

Limping towards the pile of limbs, he sat down and wove the fabric under and over each branch, securing it tightly. Elena worked opposite him, mirroring his method, until at last it was ready.

The morning light reflected upon her skin and, though she appeared tired, there was determination in her eyes. She was staring at the arrangement of wood, frowning. 'It won't float with your weight.'

He shrugged. 'There's not enough wood for that. But if it gives us something to hold on to, that will be enough.'

She studied their raft, then glanced overhead at the sparse trees that shaded them. 'I wish you had a battleaxe as your weapon. It would be more useful, cutting branches and trees.'

'I prefer a sword.' He liked the balance of the weapon and it suited fluid battle motions where he could slash at his enemy. 'Styr's weapon is the axe.' The moment he spoke her husband's name, a flash of sadness came over Elena.

'I want to believe he's alive,' she murmured. 'That somehow he'll come for me.' But she shook her head, rubbing her arms against the chill.

'If he doesn't, I'll take you back myself.' His words were little reassurance, for neither of them knew what had happened to Styr. He might still be a prisoner, or he could be dead.

'You can't make the journey with that leg. It's too far.' With a sigh, Elena began pulling the small makeshift raft across the sand.

Before she could go any further, Ragnar limped towards her and caught her arm. 'I may be wounded, Elena, but I'm not dead. The wound will heal.' He didn't want her to think of him as helpless and he let his hand slide down her arm to grip her hand. A trail of gooseflesh rose over her skin at his touch. 'You won't be stranded here. I swear it by the blood of Thor.'

Her hand gripped his and, when she met his gaze, there was a flicker of hesitancy before colour spread over her cheeks. 'I'm glad you're here.'

He wanted to pull her close, to taste the lips that had haunted him for so long. But she only turned back to her discarded apron, pulling it over her head and fas-

tening the brooches at her shoulders. She had the innocent demeanour of a maiden, but the body of a woman
who had known a man intimately.

Without a word, he began dragging the raft towards
the water, suppressing a gasp when the salt water lapped
against his bandaged wound. The vicious pain was the
reminder he needed to stay away from Styr's wife.

Elena joined him, holding on to the bound limbs
while they made their way towards the mainland. Ragnar kicked with his good leg, grateful that the tide was
coming in, aiding them in their journey. But by the
gods, the salt against his open wound was shredding
apart his control.

The bound wood did give them a means of staying
together, without the risk of drowning. As she struggled
to swim, he bit back the pain and fought to help her.

'You look as if you're hurting again,' she com-
mented, churning her left arm in the water while she
held on with her right.

'It's like hot knives searing my skin,' he admitted,
keeping his voice light. 'Not very comfortable.'

She sent him a sympathetic look. 'When we reach
land, it will be better, I promise.'

If he didn't drown first. He bit his lip hard against
the pain, forcing himself to continue.

The waves pushed them closer and Ragnar concen-
trated on the strand ahead of them. With every stroke,
it seemed further away. The cold water numbed his
skin and he felt his eyes beginning to close, his fingers
slipping from the wood.

'Ragnar!' Elena shouted at him, pulling him back
to the present moment. 'Stay with me. You can't let go

now.' She made her way to his side, holding his waist. 'We're not so very far.'

He knew it, but his body was rebelling against the sea water, his mind fighting to help her. The cold embedded within his veins, making it more difficult to move.

'I need you,' she whispered. 'Please.'

It was her voice that forced him onward. She spoke words of encouragement, urging him not to give up. And although they had been in the water for what seemed like an hour, eventually he felt his feet sink into sand. He bit hard to keep his teeth from chattering, and Elena remained at his side, holding on to him. He stumbled through the waves, but she helped him to remain balanced.

They staggered through the sand, his vision blurred and his ears ringing. He damned himself for the weakness, fighting to remain conscious. Elena needed him and he would not fail her.

'Listen to me,' she insisted. 'We're here. We're safe now, but you can't stay on the sand. Just a little further.'

She held his waist, letting him lean on her as she tried to get him past the water's edge. But when her leg accidentally bumped against his wound, he couldn't suppress the hiss of pain.

She apologised and pleaded, 'We're almost there. Only a few steps more.' The world tipped, but she held tight, keeping him on his feet.

'I'm not going to die,' he told her, but his words sounded thick and slurred.

'I won't let you.' She eased him to sit down with his back against a hillside. Ragnar leaned back, resting his head upon the amber grass while he stared up at the clouded sky.

'You're too cold,' she said. 'I have to get you warm.' She moved beside him wrapping both arms around his waist. Though her skin was cool, her presence slipped beneath the pain of his wounds, offering comfort.

He wanted to tell her what she meant to him, to spill out the words he'd kept buried for so long, but honour kept his lips silent. He would accept the warmth of her embrace, knowing that it could never be more than that.

He was angry with himself for leaving Styr behind, though he'd had no choice at the time. The Irish might kill his friend, for Styr had no value as a hostage and he would never be any man's slave.

Ragnar glanced over at Elena, who was busy gathering tinder for a fire. Her skirts were cut short to her knees, while her red-gold hair was still bound in a knot at her nape. She moved with efficiency, but as she stacked the wood and arranged the seaweed, the earlier tremors became impossible to stop.

So cold. He couldn't feel his fingertips or his toes and his muscles felt stiff and ungainly.

'You're so pale,' Elena said, hurrying to strike a spark. 'Don't worry, I'll get you warm again, as soon as I can start the fire.' But her own hands were shaking, as if she, too, were suffering from the intense cold of the sea. After several attempts, the spark kept dying out.

His eyelids were heavy and he closed them, surrendering to the temptation of unconsciousness. Sleep was what he needed now.

But a moment later, Elena's arms were around him

and she was supporting his shoulders. 'Ragnar!' She shook him lightly, demanding that he open his eyes.

His vision flickered, but he managed to look at her.

'Don't leave me,' she demanded. Her eyes welled up with tears and she commanded again, 'You can't leave me here alone.'

'Just...resting,' he told her. Sleep would make it easier to bear the pain. The darkness was tempting him to let go, to fall into nothingness.

'Your lips are blue,' she told him. 'If you go to sleep now, you might never awaken.'

He didn't answer her, for his body had transformed into lead, the last bits of consciousness sliding away. Though a part of him understood what she meant, he lacked the strength to fight it.

'Don't you dare die on me,' she wept, shaking him again. 'I can't survive out here alone. Do you hear me?' she demanded. 'If you die, I'll die as well.'

He tried to form the word 'no', to tell her he wasn't going to die at all. But before he could speak, her mouth came down on his in a searing kiss.

Chapter Four

Elena couldn't say why she'd kissed Ragnar. It was either that or strike him. Anything to shock him into awakening. As she'd hoped, his eyes had sharpened, his body jolting at her touch.

'Why did you do that?' he demanded.

It had been only a short kiss, one hardly more than the touch of her lips on his. But he was staring at her with fury and she let go of him, edging her way back on the sand.

'You weren't responding. I thought if you closed your eyes, you wouldn't wake again.' But her face was on fire now and she regretted her actions. Worse, she'd never seen him this angry before.

'Don't ever kiss me again,' he warned.

'I'm sorry.' She hadn't expected him to react so strongly. 'It was just a way of getting your attention, to make you open your eyes.'

'The next time you need my attention, use your fist. Not your mouth.' He grimaced, easing up to a seated position near the fire. 'Styr is my friend and your husband. You would do well to remember it.'

'I haven't forgotten.' But her face was burning with humiliation. She hurried to finish building the fire, wishing she'd never done anything. 'It was meaningless, Ragnar. Truly.'

But nothing she said would dispel the anger and frustration in his eyes. She hadn't truly considered the consequences and his violent response unnerved her.

'It will never, ever happen again,' she swore.

'See that you keep that vow.' His voice was cold, almost cruel.

Elena backed away, wishing there were words enough to apologise for what she'd done. Why couldn't he understand that it was only an impulse, one intended to awaken him? Instead, he acted as if she'd tried to seduce him.

The forbidden thought of this man claiming her swirled inside her. Of his mouth opening against hers, taking her down against the sand.

She closed her eyes against the dark heat that poured over her. No, she would never fall under such a spell of madness.

Finally, Ragnar said, 'We'll need food and shelter. Go and look around at the terrain. But stay nearby, in case you have need of me.'

Elena didn't point out that his injuries would prevent him from defending them. Instead, she welcomed the chance to leave, to escape her embarrassment and make herself useful. She hurried from the shore, shielding her eyes against the sun as she searched for a way to make shelter.

She crossed over the rise of a hill and saw a wide oak tree with many branches. The leaves might shelter them from the rain, but there was still too much exposure from the wind. Her mind turned over the problem while she gathered as many fallen branches as she could find. She began to organise the branches by length and width, laying them out in neat stacks.

Some were tall enough to make a lean-to shelter, but nothing larger than that. She was grateful that it would only be temporary, for it would force her to sleep close beside Ragnar once again.

The bitter taste of shame lingered, for she'd made such a foolish mistake, thinking the kiss would pull him back from losing consciousness. She winced to remember it.

If it had been Styr, he would have kissed her back, taking command of the embrace. Ragnar's mouth had been cool, his lips firm. And though the kiss had meant nothing, her body had unknowingly responded to him. She took a slow, deep breath, ignoring the sensitivity of her breasts against the linen shift. Styr was the only man who had ever touched her. The only man who ever would.

But their lovemaking had grown stagnant, a duty they had both endured for the sake of conceiving a child. Sometimes her thoughts drifted away and she found herself going through the motions. Lying with Styr had been pleasurable and she hadn't minded it. But as of late, her thoughts had been so focused upon whether or not his seed would take root within her, she'd forgotten to enjoy it.

Finally, she'd asked him to stop trying. The bitter memory burned inside her, for she'd allowed her festering grief to transform into anger. She didn't want her husband to share her bed any more, for every time he lay with her, she was reminded of her failures as a wife.

Elena stopped sorting the wood, her eyes blurring with tears before she forced them back. She was stronger than this. She had to be. Sooner or later, they would find a way back to the ringfort and they would rescue Styr. Then she would do what she could to heal their shattered marriage.

It was best to ignore the kiss with Ragnar, as though it had never happened. It had been a foolish thing to do and his volatile reaction only reassured her that she had nothing to fear from sleeping close to him. Breathing a little easier, she walked back to the beach, her mind already envisioning the shelter. She would build a watertight lean-to that would keep out the rain and any harsh weather.

Along the way, she spied some wild strawberries and picked them, tying them into her apron. There were also some carrots, hardly bigger than her thumb, but they would still do well enough. Further inland, she spied the silvery surface of a pond.

Water. She breathed a sigh of relief, letting herself hope for the first time that they could survive here.

She wasted no time in getting a drink. Then she found a leaf larger than her hand and curled it into a cone, filling it with water for Ragnar. It wasn't much, but it was a start, until she could find another container. There was so much to do; her mind was reeling from all of it.

When she returned, she saw that he was leaning on his side, his eyes closed. Pain tightened over his face and blood darkened the bandage on his thigh.

Guilt flooded through her, for she shouldn't have left him this long. The cone of water fell from her hand and she ran to kneel beside him.

'Ragnar.' She tried to awaken him, shaking him slightly. He didn't respond and she loosened the torn fabric, peeling back the bandages. The skin was an angry red and at the sight of it, her spirits sank. He was beyond her healing abilities and she didn't know where she could go or what she could do.

'I'm not a healer,' she muttered, as she touched his cheek. 'But you can't give up. Not now.'

His wound was swollen and she racked her mind to think of any herbal knowledge she'd heard of. Ragnar remained unconscious and she didn't know what to do for him.

There were no people here. There was no one to help, no one to tell her the proper way to treat his wounds. He would die if she did nothing.

She had to reach inside and find a place of calm. Surely if she studied him more carefully, she would find the answers.

Elena took a deep breath, then another as she examined his leg. His skin was hot to the touch, so tight as if it were an animal skin bulging with water.

It needed to be drained, she decided. Some of the healers drew blood to bring out the evil spirits. Perhaps if she released some of the pressure, it would help.

She pulled her dagger from its sheath, starting to lose the edge of her courage. The idea of hurting him more, of causing him to bleed, made her wince. But neither could he tolerate this pain.

Beneath her breath, she murmured prayers to all the

gods as she cleaned the knife with a cloth and began probing his wound. His hands clenched at his sides, and his eyes flew open when she touched the raw flesh.

'Don't,' he gritted out.

'I'm going to ease the pain,' she said. 'The wound needs to be lanced.'

His eyes were wild, his mouth tight as she reopened the wound. The moment her blade touched the swollen area, it sliced through the poisoned flesh. Blood and pus mingled from the wound and she fought to hold back the wave of nausea. But as she bled him, the swelling did seem to recede. She couldn't tell how long she would have to let out the bad blood, but eventually, she held the edges of his flesh together and wrapped his leg tightly.

All she could do now was pray. She tried to make him as comfortable as possible, but inwardly she knew they needed a better shelter or they would both die. And that meant leaving his side to build it.

Only when she was certain he was asleep did Elena venture out again. Though it bothered her to leave him, their survival depended on it.

'Ragnar.'

Her voice awakened him from the harsh pain that flowed like a never-ending stream. It was twilight and the sunset haloed Elena's hair from behind.

By the gods, he'd never known anyone more beautiful. But he'd learned to mask any emotions, never to let her see what he felt. Even if he died here, he refused to surrender to the traitorous thoughts he felt towards her.

Her hand came to touch his cheek, and he didn't speak a word, taking comfort from the warmth of her palm.

'The rain will come soon,' she whispered. 'I've built us a small shelter for the night. Can you lean on me to walk?'

He almost laughed at that, but one glimpse of the sky made him realise that he could either struggle and walk with her or lie here on the sand while the rain poured down over them. The clouds were thick and a fog was rolling in off the shoreline.

She leaned down and put both arms around him, guiding him up to a seated position. At such a close distance, he saw the tints of red within her hair and her sea-green eyes held such fear, there were no words to allay it. Words would not stave off the hand of Death, if it came for him.

Ragnar bent his good leg and grimaced as she pulled him up to stand. The moment he did, white spots spun in his vision, threatening to pull him under. 'Elena, I don't know how far I can make it.'

'You're strong enough to get there,' she insisted. 'I've gathered some food and made a fire for us.' She continued talking, bearing the heavy weight of him as best she was able. The journey seemed endless. At one point, he asked, 'Why did you build it so far away?'

'I needed a tree to support the driftwood,' she explained. 'And we don't want our shelter caught in the tides.'

He hardly heard any more of what she said, for he was lost in his own sea of pain. But as they moved in closer, he thought he scented something cooking.

Surely he was imagining it. But the heady aroma of a roasting fowl made his mouth water.

'Did you catch something?' he asked, squinting at the glow of the fire ahead.

The chagrined smile on her face confirmed it. 'I set some snares, yes. And when we've both eaten, the night will be easier.'

He doubted if any food would settle the aching inside, but he would say nothing to cast a shadow over what she'd done to help them both. A ringing resounded within his ears and she caught him before he could fall, holding his waist.

'We're almost there.'

Thank the gods for that. It seemed to take an hour before he finally reached the tiny shelter she'd built of fallen limbs around a thick tree trunk. At first, it appeared crude, a mass of large branches and leaves. But as she eased him down, he realised it was wider than it appeared. The structure was circular, with stout branches as supports and smaller, more flexible limbs woven between them.

'How did you ever have time for this?' he questioned.

Her face flushed and she shrugged. 'I kept returning to check on you, but you were sleeping. It seemed like a better use of my time.'

The wind was increasing and he eased backwards until he was inside the shelter. Elena tended the fire and adjusted the roasting meat until the fowl was fully cooked.

He'd never smelled anything so good in his entire life. When she broke off a piece, she blew on it before bringing it to him. He tasted the meat and found it delicious.

'Styr is a fortunate man,' he remarked. Though he kept his tone even, it was far more than the food. It was the way she had laboured over the shelter, managing to build something of this complexity in a short amount of time. 'I don't think he realises half of what you do for him.'

The look in her eyes turned startled, as if she'd never expected him to say such a thing. Perhaps it was the belief that he might die that caused him to speak so freely.

'I am his wife. I want to make his home comfortable.' She ate but no longer looked at him.

Ragnar knew that in the past few months, Elena and Styr's marriage had suffered. Her barrenness had taken its toll upon her, and Styr had confided their troubles. It had put Ragnar in an awkward position. He'd urged Styr to talk to Elena, but he was torn between wanting them to reconcile…and wanting the marriage to end.

He was such a selfish bastard. What good would it do, if she and Styr parted ways? Elena would never turn to him. She knew his darkest secrets, of the vicious adolescence he'd endured…and the violence that still dwelled beneath his skin. He knew better than to think she would consider someone like him.

As the wind grew stronger, Elena moved deeper within the shelter and pulled out a panel he hadn't noticed. It had been disguised amid the other branches, but it formed a door. Almost within seconds, the rain began to pour down over the shelter.

But they didn't get wet. He stared up and realised

that she'd layered the leaves so thickly that they were fully protected from the storm.

'You did well, Elena,' he complimented. 'I suppose you're tired from the work.'

She nodded. 'A little. How is your leg?'

'It hurts. But it's not nearly as swollen as it was before.' The wound ached, but the pain was more bearable.

'I'll try to find some garlic bulbs or other herbs to draw out the poisoned blood,' she promised. 'When it stops raining.'

'In the morning will be soon enough.' He finished eating and an awkward silence descended between them. She wouldn't look at him and he realised that she was still embarrassed by what she'd done.

'I'm sorry for what I said before.' He leaned back against the structure, well aware of how close she was. 'I know you meant nothing by the kiss.'

She let out a heavy sigh. 'Thank you for that. I don't know why I did it. It was truly just to keep you conscious.'

He studied her. Though the rain had extinguished the fire outside their shelter, in the dim space, he caught a shadowed glimpse of her beautiful face. He wished he could admit the truth, that the softness of her kiss had caught him stronger than any blow might have. She tasted of innocence, and dreams that would never be.

'We will find a way to return,' he said to her. 'I'll bring you back to Styr, once my wounds heal.'

She nodded and as the rain poured faster, she moved across to him. 'I'm afraid for him. Even though we had our differences, I don't want him to die.'

When she leaned against him, he brought his arms around her. She was quiet, but he could feel the dampness of her cheeks as she silently wept.

'We'll find him,' he said to her. 'I promise you that.'

She sniffled again, and then admitted, 'There's another reason why I'm afraid. It—it's the moon.'

He didn't understand what she meant and waited for her to elaborate.

'When we left Norway, it was a full moon. It's gone through all of its phases and almost a second phase.'

She sat up, then, though he could not see her face as the night grew darker. 'I—I haven't had my woman's flow since we left Norway, Ragnar.' There was tremulous hope in her voice as she admitted, 'I think I may be pregnant at last.'

The night had been brutal. Visions and dark dreams haunted him, his body burning with fever. He was hardly aware of anything, except Elena offering him drinks of cool water.

He didn't want to admit the possibility of death, but he would not lie here and yield quietly. He'd vowed to bring Elena back to Styr.

'Elena,' he muttered, his voice sounding like a growl, 'we can't stay here.'

'We don't have a choice.' She moved beside him, as if to lend the physical comfort of her presence. 'You have to rest to heal.'

He sensed the fear in her voice, but he refused to dwell on the chance of death.

'To return to Styr, you must go southwest along the coast. Keep the morning sun to your left side and—'

'I'm not leaving you,' she interrupted.

'If I don't heal, you must go.' The last thing he wanted was for her to suffer beside him, starving in the middle of nowhere. Already, his stomach was roaring with hunger.

'You aren't going to die,' she insisted. 'Your wounds are much better. Though I imagine you're half starving, since you've been asleep for so long.' She drew back the door of the shelter she'd made. The sun blinded him, and he glanced down at his wound.

Although it was still painful, it wasn't nearly as swollen as he'd expected. Elena had made a poultice of garlic bulbs and he wondered how many times she'd changed it during the night. His entire body reeked of garlic. It was a wonder she could stand to be near him.

She brought him a bowl of stew and Ragnar questioned when she'd had time to make it. Within the hot liquid, he tasted rabbit and other vegetables. 'Has it only been one day since we arrived on this shore?' he asked.

Elena shook her head. 'We've been here for three days. Your fever was terrible and I didn't know if you'd awaken. I tried to feed you as best I could, but…it was difficult.'

Three days? It seemed impossible that the time had passed so swiftly. And yet he could not deny the truth of what he saw. The edges of the wound had begun to close and it wasn't nearly as hot to the touch.

'I was glad to find the garlic,' Elena continued. 'My mother told me it was good for healing wounds and she was right. I crushed up some of it.'

'I smell terrible,' he admitted wryly. But if it had

kept him alive, it was well worth it. The question now was whether he was capable of walking again.

Slowly, Ragnar eased himself out of their shelter and used her help to rise to his feet. With only a little weight on the wounded leg, it wasn't too bad.

Elena looked weary from the past few days but was no less beautiful. Her red-gold hair was braided back into a single tail and it brought into sharp relief her pale skin and heart-shaped face. Her green eyes studied him with relief.

'In another few days, you'll be fighting other battles,' she predicted. 'Though the scars will remain.'

'All warriors bear scars.' It was a physical reminder that they had conquered death, defeating their enemies. 'But I owe you thanks for my life.'

She shook her head. 'You saved mine on board the ship. You owe me nothing.'

'No. I swore a vow to Styr,' he reminded her. A vow he'd made to protect her. Although they were alive, he needed to bring her back to the ringfort settlement.

'I know you'll heal and we'll find him, as you said,' she promised.

His gaze moved down to her flat stomach, remembering what she'd told him about her pregnancy. Elena saw the direction of his attention and flushed slightly, moving her hand over her womb. 'I'm surprised I haven't felt sick so far.'

'Not every woman suffers during the early months,' he remarked. 'My sisters never did.'

Her mood lightened and he saw the hope in her eyes. She had wanted a child for so many years.

God help him, he was jealous of Styr. He wished

that Elena were *his* wife, that she were pregnant with *his* child. He wanted to awaken beside her, reaching over to feel the babe move within her skin.

He forced himself to walk, ignoring the dull pain in his thigh. The worst of the danger was over; he'd live. But with every day that passed, he wanted Elena more than ever. She was an obsession he couldn't abandon and all women paled beside her.

Why, by the gods, did she have to belong to his best friend? If she were with any other man, he'd damn the consequences, claiming her as his own. She was a desperate craving he needed to satisfy. When he glanced back, he saw the peaceful expression on her face, for she believed she would finally have the child she wanted.

An honourable man would be glad for her. She would return to Styr and this babe would heal the breach between them. No longer would she suffer in silence; she had achieved her greatest desire.

Ragnar stopped walking, staring down at the water below them. The grass was damp from earlier rainstorms, but now the sun warmed the earth. He didn't know how they were going to make it back, but likely their best course of action was to travel along the coast. If they happened to see ships, they could try to hire one to take them back.

'You shouldn't push yourself too hard,' Elena warned. 'You need to regain your strength.'

No, what he needed was space away from her. A chance to clear his head so he wouldn't give in to the instinctive urges taunting him.

Ragnar reached down for a fallen branch, using it to

help support his weight as he moved across the field. A faint noise caught his attention and he stopped, listening hard.

Elena frowned. 'Did you hear something?'

He nodded, pointing further inland. 'It was coming from over there.' Leaning against the staff, he continued his pace, moving towards the sound. It was as if a large group of people was approaching.

Her face broke into a smile. 'Thank the gods. They'll have food and supplies. I think we're saved.'

But as the sounds grew louder, he realised what he was hearing. These people were fleeing, not travelling. Dozens of men, women and children were running across the plains, while behind them, he spied men pursuing them on horseback.

Warriors with weapons drawn, ready to strike them down.

Chapter Five

Elena's heart was racing and Ragnar pushed her towards the fleeing women. 'Run!' he commanded.

She started to obey, but then saw that he was holding his ground, staring at the riders. Though he had only a sword, he held it steady, waiting for the men to approach.

The calm in his eyes belied the storm that was to come. She'd seen Ragnar fight before and he became a different man when the battle rage swept over him. His sword became part of him, cutting down any enemy who threatened those under his protection.

Few survived and he granted no mercy.

But this time, he stood as a wounded man. Upon his face she saw the grim determination of a man who would sacrifice himself before he'd allow any man to harm her. But even with his strength and fighting prowess, he could not hope to bring down all the men on horseback. He was outnumbered and likely he was shielding her, granting all of them time to get away.

She froze in place, stopping one of the Irishmen. 'He needs help,' she pleaded. 'He can't stop them alone.'

The man stared at her before she realised he could not understand her words. But he cast a glance at Ragnar, his expression holding surprise that a wounded man would stand against their enemy.

One of the riders lifted his sword, prepared to strike him down. Instead of raising his own weapon, Ragnar stood calmly, waiting for the killing blow.

Freya, protect him.

She knew what would happen—she'd witnessed it a thousand times. He would hold steady and the act of suicidal madness twisted his enemy into questioning their actions. No sensible man would stand and face charging horses.

Even as she trusted him, Elena couldn't bear to think of anything happening to Ragnar. He'd been her friend for so long, always there when she'd needed him. She bit her lip hard to prevent herself from interfering and when she stepped back, the rider's attention flickered for a moment.

It was enough for Ragnar to twist his sword, slicing the rider from his horse. The animal whinnied, rearing up, and Ragnar seized the reins, barely dodging another blow before he swung up on the left side, protecting his wounded leg.

It took all of Elena's courage to remain among the Irish instead of running towards him. She knew she was a distraction and a danger if she dared to intervene.

He guided the horse forwards, keeping his sword poised.

'You're Norse,' one of the riders said in their tongue.

'I am,' Ragnar countered. 'My name is Ragnar Olafsson from Hordafylke. We came to éire a few days ago.' He kept his voice calm, but Elena heard the trace of steel beneath it. He was not about to stand down and let these raiders continue their attack.

'I am Alfarr Gelinsson,' their leader replied. His gaze narrowed upon Ragnar. 'Why would you defend these men and women? They're not your people.'

'No, but we need supplies. They can offer that to us.'

'Join us,' Alfarr offered. 'We'll take from them and share what is left.'

From behind her, Elena sensed the Irish growing uncertain about the continuing conversation in a foreign tongue. She raised her hands in reassurance, hoping they would not interfere with the negotiation.

'Why do you not trade with them?' Ragnar asked calmly, drawing his horse closer until he was within reach of their leader.

Alfarr stared over at the Irish and then spit on the ground. 'They are weak. Taking their supplies would be an easy victory.'

'You look like a man who enjoys fighting,' Ragnar challenged. 'Would you rather make a wager?'

What was he doing? Elena took a step forwards, wondering what his intentions were. Ragnar wasn't strong enough to fight these men, not with his wound. She'd bandaged it heavily, but no doubt the other Norsemen were well aware of the injury. It would affect his speed, no matter how strong he was.

She wanted so badly to interrupt, but she held her tongue, afraid it would weaken his position before the men.

'I wouldn't mind a wager,' Alfarr agreed. His gaze passed over Elena with interest and she felt a prickle of uneasiness pass over her skin. 'Especially if a woman is involved.' Despite the short distance, she could feel his stare upon her and it made her skin crawl.

Ragnar didn't bother to look back. 'She is not a part of this.'

'When you're dead, she will be,' Alfarr answered.

'But if I win,' Ragnar warned softly, 'your man will be dead and you'll go raid another tribe. Not this one.'

'You're wounded, Ragnar Olafsson. You are no match for us.'

'Then I'll meet Odin in Valhalla, if my sword does not prevail,' he said.

So much rested upon this fight. Not only their fate, but the fate of the Irish as well. It angered Elena that the people kept a distance instead of joining him. Why had no one offered to help?

Fear quickened in her veins as the men faced off. Even if Ragnar prevailed, she suspected the men would not keep their word. Raiders who lived and died by their swords were not men of honour. The moment Ragnar's back was turned, they would cut him down.

She closed her eyes, trying to bring clarity to her clouded mind. If he were not wounded, she didn't doubt that he would strike down every last man.

But with only one good leg to stand on, he might not live through the rest of this day. She would become their prize of war unless she did something to stop them.

Elena turned back to the Irish, her mind spinning with ideas, most of which wouldn't work. But when she saw a woman carrying a basket of green apples, an idea began to take root. The apples were a symbol of the gods. Men like these might not honour the afterworld…but they would understand the effects of a curse. It was something to be feared.

There was one way to put an end to the fighting and drive the invaders away.

Freya, be with me, she prayed.

They chose their tallest man to fight him. The *hersir* weighed more than Ragnar, but Ragnar wasn't afraid to face the man. The larger the warrior, the slower he tended to move.

His thigh wound was aching, but Ragnar blotted all of the pain from his mind. If he failed in this fight, they would take Elena and use her. He had no doubt of it. In times like these, he had to use his wits, rather than his strength.

The man had chosen a battleaxe as his weapon and after dismounting from the horse, Ragnar took a round shield from the warrior he'd already killed.

Thor, guide my blade, he prayed. *Let me strike true.*

He waited for the man to make the first move, for in that motion he could determine his enemy's weaknesses.

'Your wound will slow you down, Olafsson,' the man remarked, eyeing the reddish stain on Ragnar's thigh. His enemy tossed his battleaxe and caught it again, the silvery gleam of steel revealing a sharp blade. The man was fair-haired with a reddish beard and wore a hauberk made of whalebone.

'Wounded or not, the gods favour me.' He nodded towards the sky, which was transforming from sunshine into a darker hue. Large clouds drifted into a grey mass, forming storms. 'In a little while, Thor will show his lightning and you will be in Valhalla to greet him.'

'Or you will,' the man countered.

Ragnar glanced back towards Elena, but was startled to see that she'd disappeared. It was for the best, he supposed. At least if she'd gone, he would not have to worry over her fate.

But he'd known her too long. She wasn't one to run from a fight. It was more likely she'd gone to fetch a weapon herself.

Better to end this quickly, then.

Instinct took over and he let the blood course through his heart, pushing back any trace of mercy. This man would die and soon.

Ragnar raised his shield to defect a blow from the battleaxe, biting back a gasp when the man kicked his thigh. Pain shot through him, but he slipped into the blur of fighting, no longer feeling anything. He was aware only of the weapon in his hands and the movement of his enemy. Blood seeped against his wound, but he dulled his mind against distractions.

'You're stronger than you look. But not for long,' the man said. He renewed his attack, using his own shield to press hard against Ragnar.

Ragnar's muscles tensed as he refused to surrender ground. He was a warrior, a man sworn to live and die by the sword. Wounds and pain were a part of the fighting and as he pivoted to dodge another blow, his father's words came back to taunt him.

You're weak and soft, boy.

He tasted blood in his mouth when his enemy's fist ploughed into his jaw, but he willed himself to feel nothing, just as he'd endured years of his father's beatings.

Pain was a part of him. He knew how to isolate himself from feeling anything at all, letting the hollowness claim his spirit.

You're worthless.

Every blow, every bruise brought out a ruthless side to him where there were no emotions to make him human again. He became predatory, slashing hard with his sword. He was blinded in this moment of battle, fully immersed in the kill. Anyone who dared to come near would suffer the consequences.

Metal bit through flesh and he was rewarded with his enemy's gasp.

They stood back, circling each other. Ragnar tasted blood and sweat, and he saw the moment of uncertainty in the Norseman's expression.

He gritted his teeth, feigning weakness. Waiting for the moment when his enemy would strike hard. Abruptly, the man shoved his shield against Ragnar's wound, lifting his axe high for a killing blow.

Ragnar threw himself to the ground, lifting up his sword at the last second. With all his strength, he forced the blade upwards, impaling his enemy.

Blood spilled from the man's lips as Ragnar's blade remained in his gut. It was not a clean death and he forced the man over, rising to his feet before he struck hard and ended the fight.

He kept his sword in hand, anticipating a second attack. The haze of fighting was still upon him, like a veil of red. Dimly, he grew aware that no one was going to approach him now.

'Take your men and go,' Ragnar ordered, his gaze fixed upon the leader.

'I never agreed to leave,' Alfarr countered. 'And now the rest of my men will fight. You cannot kill all of us—'

'No,' a woman's voice interrupted. 'But I can place a curse upon you, making you wish you were dead.'

The hair on the back of his neck seemed to stand on end, but Ragnar forced himself not to turn around. From the way the men were staring at Elena, something had caught their attention.

They'd gone white with fear.

'Leave us,' Ragnar ordered once again. Alfarr stared at him as if wanting to refuse, but he left the fallen body of his kinsman and drew his horse back.

'Honour your word,' Elena said. 'The gods command it of you.' Her voice held a low pitch and one of the men raised his hand as if to ward her off. Her command was underscored when lightning flashed in the sky, followed by a low rumble of thunder.

One by one, they turned to leave.

When Ragnar turned at last to see her, there was a black serpent coiled around Elena's throat. In each hand she held an apple. The creatures were symbols of the gods, in animal form, while the apples were sacred.

No wonder the men had fled. With her reddish-gold hair unbound, spilling over her shoulders, and the serpent twining upon her flesh, she looked otherworldly.

Slowly, she lifted the snake from her throat and set it upon the ground, watching as it slithered away. Only when it was gone did she begin to tremble. Her footsteps came closer until she threw herself into his arms and buried her face against his chest. She gripped him hard. 'Thank the gods, they're gone. We're safe.'

Instinct warned him to stand in place and do nothing. But he couldn't stop himself from holding her close, inhaling the scent of her skin. Her act of bravery had saved them, though he'd been ready to fight.

He wished that she belonged to him. If she had, he'd have tilted her head back, claiming her mouth in a kiss. Fighting always kindled another flare within him, the desire to take a woman.

And he'd wanted this one for years.

Ragnar held her in his arms, feeling the soft press of her breasts against him. His body ached from the fight and he was weary. But this moment was a reward of its own. He savoured the forbidden embrace, knowing it had to end.

The Irish were staring at them and finally, he broke away from Elena. She took his hand and one of the maidens approached. In broken Norse, she said, 'You… safe…saved us.'

Ragnar looked past her to the leader, who sent him an approving nod. Though he knew no Irish, he opened both of his hands to show that he meant no harm to them.

'You…eat now?' the maiden asked.

'I am hungry,' Elena admitted. 'I think we should join them.' Her gaze passed over him and she asked, 'What about you?'

Oh, he was hungry indeed. He wanted to take her back to their tiny shelter and claim her mouth, sating himself upon her sweet flesh. But he would never admit it; not in this lifetime.

'We should go with them, *ja*.' He limped slightly as she clasped his hand and moved forwards. The women smiled at Elena, as if they recognised what she'd done to save them.

'I hate snakes,' she admitted. 'I still feel as if my skin is crawling.'

'I don't know how you found one. I thought there were no serpents here.'

She squeezed his hand. 'I saw it after I voiced a prayer. I don't know how, but it was here when I needed it. Perhaps the gods *did* favour us.'

The sky was growing darker and rain was inevitable. The Irish had set up several fires, the women hurrying to cook a meal before the downpour. 'For you and your mate,' the Irish maiden said, offering Elena the choicest piece of venison. She didn't know where the roast had come from, but after an hour of warming themselves by the fire, the scent of meat was wonderful. She lacked the words to correct the woman, that Ragnar was not her husband, but what did it matter? In a few days, she'd never see these people again.

There was an air of rejoicing, in spite of the impending weather. While she and Ragnar ate, the children ran around with the dogs, laughing. One of the older men began to tell stories and though she could not understand him, Elena was caught by the deep tone of his voice. He used his hands to weave the tale and Ragnar's palm came over to her spine. The heat of his hand warmed her skin and he leaned in close. 'Could I ask you to tend my leg, if you've a moment?'

'Of course.' She swallowed the cup of ale the Irishmen had given her, rising to her feet. 'But I think they have a healer who may be able to help you more than I can. We'll go together and speak to her.'

With his hand in hers, she led him towards one of the older women. In her own language, she asked, 'Do you have a healer in your tribe?' Though the woman could not understand her, Elena pointed to Ragnar's wound and the meaning became clear.

The woman called out a command to someone else and an older matron approached, carrying a basket.

'Sit down,' Elena ordered Ragnar. He did and she began unwrapping the bandage she'd tied around him. The wound was slick with blood and the flesh would undoubtedly bruise from the blows he'd received. But all of them were alive and she gave thanks for that.

The healer dipped a cloth in cool water and washed away the blood. Then she muttered words beneath her breath, packing the wound with a poultice made of more herbs.

'I feel like a roast being seasoned,' he remarked drily, wincing as the woman wrapped the bandage tightly.

'But you'll heal,' Elena reassured him. She moved to sit by him and used a damp cloth to wipe the dust from his face. Though it was meant only to help him, his dark green eyes held her captive. She grew conscious of his sun-darkened skin and the firm line of his jaw. This man was a warrior, not an ordinary man.

When her attention rested upon his mouth, her skin tightened with heat. She'd kissed him, never imagining the feelings he would conjure.

There might be no harm in studying a handsome

man. But she was a married woman, one who might be pregnant. She had no right to let her imagination wander over a fair face.

When the healer had finished wrapping Ragnar's wound, she reached for Elena's hand and spoke words in Irish, joining her palm to Ragnar's.

'What do you think she said?' Elena asked him.

'Probably that you should take care of me and see to my every need.' His eyes flashed with a glint of humour. 'You should bring food and serve it to me.'

'Clearly, your enemy knocked your brains loose,' she retorted, but didn't hold back her smile. 'Or you're dreaming.'

His hand closed over hers, gripping her palm. 'Perhaps I am.' The heat of his skin against hers made her feel awkward and uncertain. But she didn't pull away.

The Irish seemed grateful to both of them and as they built fires and prepared food for a meal, many smiled at them. One young boy toddled over to her with his arms outstretched. Elena caught him before he could tumble and he laughed. She gave him back to his mother, smiling warmly at the woman.

Though she didn't know for certain if she would bear a child of her own, her heart wanted to believe. And now, instead of mourning her barrenness, she had a future to look forward to. She could only pray that Styr would be a part of it.

Like a physical blow, the memory of his capture slammed into her. She couldn't shut out the vision of him being struck down and later dragged away in chains. Was he alive? Would she ever see him again?

Her heart faltered, for although they'd had their marital troubles, she *did* care about him.

The weight of the past few days burdened her with so much fear. There were so many unanswered questions, but she could not indulge in cowardice. She had to stand strong and believe that they would find Styr. Once they did, she could rebuild their lives when she gave birth, come the early spring.

Her hand passed over her womb and she tried to imagine her body changing its shape while a precious baby grew within.

'Are you hungry?' Ragnar interrupted her thoughts, holding out a piece of the roasted venison. She took it, but although it was likely delicious, it tasted like dust in her mouth.

'You're troubled,' Ragnar predicted. 'Tell me.' He motioned for her to sit and he found a large rock to lean against. Though his tone was sympathetic, she was aware of how difficult this day had been for him. Behind his eyes, she sensed he was hiding the physical pain.

'It's been a hard day for both of us,' she admitted.

'But we're alive.' He motioned for her to come closer and when she stood before him, she felt as if he shared her burdens. His hand closed over hers and he squeezed it gently.

The comfort he gave nearly dissolved the tight control upon her emotions. She wanted to drop to her knees and sob out her frustration. But if she did, he would draw his arms around her, offering the comfort of his embrace.

She couldn't deny that the past week had altered their friendship. Ragnar had always been there, but being alone with him only forced her to compare him to her husband. Both were handsome and strong...but the touch of his hands upon her evoked a restless yearning she didn't want to face.

'We need to find Styr,' she insisted. 'We've been gone too long and I'm afraid for him.'

The mention of her husband drew a grim finality in Ragnar's eyes. He released her hand and she found herself turning away. 'They could be torturing him.' Or worse, he might be dead. She tried to imagine life without him and a cold dread sank into her.

'Do you want to travel with this tribe?' Ragnar asked. 'I don't think they would mind it.'

It was a reasonable suggestion, but something held her back. The people did not speak their language and, if they continued southeast, there was another threat.

'What if we encounter the Norse raiders again?' she asked Ragnar, shuddering at the thought. 'We might not defeat them a second time.' Although finding the snake had been a stroke of good fortune, her skin still crawled at the thought of its scaly warmth upon her throat. The Norsemen had believed her promise of a curse, for the gods often took the form of a serpent when they returned to earth. But it didn't mean she felt safe. They would as soon slaughter them in their sleep.

'My leg has almost healed,' Ragnar said. 'I won't let any harm come to you.'

She knew he meant it, but it didn't allay her fears. 'I need to think,' she told him. 'I don't know whether to stay here and let Styr find us...or whether we should go back.' They had no ship and it would take too long to travel on foot back to the settlement.

'If he's alive, Styr won't ever stop searching for you,' Ragnar said. Though his words were meant to reassure her, she sensed something more. Turning to face him, she caught a flash of longing on his face. Almost as if he never wanted Styr to find her. As if he wanted to take her husband's place.

An unbidden vision caught her, of Ragnar claiming her as his conquest. She sensed his unspoken words: *I would never stop searching for you.*

A moment later, he'd shielded all emotions, making her wonder if she'd imagined it.

'What if he can't look for me? We don't know what's happened.'

'No. We don't.' He ate his own food, staring off into the darkness. She was waiting for him to offer guidance, to tell her what they should do. But he was leaving the decision in her hands.

The healer beckoned to Elena to come with her, leaving Ragnar to rest. Though she didn't know what the woman wanted, she followed. 'I'll return soon,' she promised. Ragnar's expression was enigmatic, but he waved his hand as if he didn't care.

The Irish maiden who spoke a few words of her language came to bring her to their leader. She smiled, as if to put her at ease, and then nodded to the older man. 'Our chief ask...you...magic?'

Elena shook her head. 'I only let the raiders believe what they wanted to. I threatened to curse the men.'

The girl spoke rapidly to the chief, who inclined his head in approval. 'He say...give thanks. Gift to you.'

'What kind of a gift?' She wondered if they would offer gold or a horse. Instead, the girl pointed towards a folded hide. It was large and when she led Elena to touch it, she realised that it had been treated to make it repel water. It would keep them warm and dry inside their shelter.

'For your journey,' the girl promised.

Elena thanked them in her own language, even knowing they would not understand. She accepted the heavy cloth and started to return to Ragnar, but the wind began to blow hard, whipping at her hair.

'Tonight, you share our shelter,' the girl promised. 'Bad storm coming.'

The men and women began to set up an array of tents and Elena joined them, offering her help. The girl urged her to keep the heavy cloth and to use it on their travels later.

The Irish set up a tent and lined the interior with soft furs and hot stones from the fire. When it was ready, the girl invited her in. 'For you and your man to share.'

Ragnar had limped over to join her, leaning on a thick staff that someone had given him. 'You'd better go inside,' he told Elena, 'before the rain starts.'

'This will be more comfortable than our house of sticks,' she teased, holding the flap open for him. He entered and she closed it behind him, enveloping the room in darkness. The space was not large and if she stretched out her hands, she could touch him.

'I suppose so.' Ragnar's gaze settled upon the pile

of furs on one side. It was then that she realised they would sleep beside one another. Though it shouldn't have bothered her—after all, she'd already slept beside him when he was burning up with fever—somehow, this space seemed more intimate.

A flush of heat pressed through her and she imagined lying in this man's arms. Hard against soft...and the image was not unwelcome.

Elena knelt down on the furs, trying to push out the dishonourable thoughts. Ragnar was a friend, that was all.

He kept his distance and that was likely for the best. In the darkness, the hot stones warmed the air while outside the wind battered their shelter. Here, she was safe, protected from the elements. But there was nothing to protect her from the forbidden feelings rising inside.

To distract herself, she rested her hands upon her flat stomach. It seemed strange that she felt no different at all, even with a child growing within her. No illness... nothing except the absence of bleeding. Sometimes it seemed like a dream to imagine it.

Ragnar leaned upon the staff, limping towards her until he eased his way to the furs. Elena lay down on her side and heard the rustle of him doing the same. She froze when his leg bumped against hers. Though she knew it was accidental, it made her all too aware that she was sleeping beside a man who was not her husband. A man who tempted her to cast aside honour for a taste of the forbidden.

She curled up, but when she lay on the ground she

felt the icy wind slipping beneath the tent. Without meaning to, she shivered. When she adjusted her position again, she heard him let out a tense breath of air when her body bumped against his. Elena suspected that she'd somehow pressed against his wounded leg. 'I'm sorry, did I hurt you?'

'No.' He rolled on to his uninjured side, away from her. 'You surprised me, that's all.'

He kept far away from her, which was for the best. She huddled beneath the furs, trying to get comfortable. 'I'm glad you're here,' she said quietly.

And she was. In the midst of all the terrifying things that had happened, having Ragnar at her side had made it bearable. She believed that he would surrender his own life for hers without a second thought. He'd been her protector and a man she could rely on.

He said nothing in reply. Perhaps he had other matters on his mind. 'Are you in pain?' she asked. She waited, expecting him to answer yes or no. But again he held his silence. Which probably meant he was hurting, since no male she'd ever met would admit to feeling pain.

'Go to sleep, Elena.' His voice was gruff and she couldn't understand why he seemed reluctant to talk. In the past, he'd always been an amiable man, friendly and easy to be with.

Not tonight.

'What have I done wrong?' she asked.

His hand caught her wrist in the darkness. 'Do you know how much I envy your husband?'

The words held a dark edge and she could think of

nothing to say. Though his grip wasn't forceful, she sensed that he was on the brink of fury.

'He has a beautiful wife,' Ragnar said. 'Possibly a child on the way. A family.'

The envy in his voice revealed a lonely man. One who had never had any of those things. She swallowed hard, unable to find the right words for sympathy.

'You love him, don't you?' he said quietly.

'Yes,' she whispered. She would always be loyal to Styr. He was a strong man, a good provider. He'd done everything he could to make her happy. And now that they were going to have a child, it would all be better.

Wouldn't it?

In the darkness, Ragnar released her wrist and she huddled on her side. She remembered the last time her husband had joined with her. Styr had done everything he could to please her, touching her in a way he thought would give her a release. Instead, she'd been cold inside, unable to react. Thoughts of her childlessness had haunted her until it seemed as if a stranger were touching her. Her marriage had been breaking apart and she'd wept in her husband's arms. He was as frustrated as she was and both of them were ready to give up.

Freya, how she wished she could take back the words when she'd asked him not to touch her again. Though she'd meant only for a short time, Styr's expression had turned to frost. He'd done exactly as she'd asked and it was as if she'd thrown up a stone wall between them.

'I don't think Styr loves me any more,' she admitted. 'I was cruel to him when I didn't mean to be.'

'All marriages go through difficult times. He asked about you on the journey here,' he told her.

That only made her feel worse.

'And what if we don't find him?' she murmured.

Ragnar took her hand in his. 'I'll always take care of you, Elena. No matter what happens.'

She squeezed his hand tightly, grateful for him. 'We'll journey back to Gall Tír, starting tomorrow morning.'

Chapter Six

Ragnar was beginning to think that this was his punishment. The small tent was filled with her scent and it was a constant torment to be so close to Elena. Jealousy was eating away at his mood and he'd not slept at all.

Worse, the storm was growing more intense, the wind howling against the small tent. Despite the heated stones, the cold air slipped through the crevices, making it more uncomfortable.

Elena slept fitfully and once, she moved to snuggle against him. He tried to remain still, but when she pressed her bottom against him, it was nearly his undoing. Only a thin layer of cloth separated their bodies and his honour was worn down to a thread.

Not yours, his brain reminded him. Only a man without honour would touch her while she was unaware of it. She was his best friend's wife and he had to bury his desires and feelings. No matter how much he might want her.

But what if Styr is dead? The terrible thought twined around him until reason intervened. Even if that happened, she would never turn to a man like him. She knew of the countless men he'd slain and the violence he was capable of.

His father had taught him well.

When she tried to snuggle against him, he could not let her do it. 'Elena,' he said, pushing her from him. 'Wake up.'

She rolled over and ended up on top of him, which was far worse. Her breasts pressed against him while her face rested against his heart.

'Wh-what is it?' she whispered sleepily.

'You can't lie so close to me.'

Gently, he pushed her back and she sighed. 'I'm just cold, Ragnar. I didn't mean to bother you.'

You could warm her, his weak-willed body suggested. *Hold her in your arms for the night.* It was as close as he'd ever come to having her.

She was so close to him, he could feel her arm pressed near. Her skin tempted him, making him want to lie upon her and take the offering before him.

'Go back to sleep,' he commanded.

And stay far away from me. He didn't want her to know how she'd gotten under his skin. Better to let her think he was her husband's friend, someone who would never be a threat to her. She needed someone to trust.

She turned over and the wind tore at their tent once again, ripping open the flap. Ragnar rose from his sleeping place, limping towards the opening. He tied down the ropes, securing them to hold back the worst of the wind. Rain spattered down hard, making him glad of their shelter.

He tried to get back to sleep, ignoring the vicious pain that plagued him. But then Elena spoke softly, 'I meant what I said earlier. I *am* glad to be with you. All of this is more bearable with a friend.'

He couldn't answer, for she was far more than a friend to him. The innocent kiss she'd given him, days ago, was a memory burned into him. He'd never known what it was to kiss her and now it was all he thought of.

'I swore to Styr that nothing would happen to you.'

And it wouldn't. He'd throw himself upon an enemy blade for her.

'I'm so afraid for him,' she confessed, curling up with her back against his. 'And…even if we do find him, I don't want things to be the way they were. Especially now with the baby.'

She let out a heavy sigh and the weight of a marriage hung in her breath. 'Something's wrong with me, Ragnar. I don't enjoy sharing his bed and…that's my fault. He's tried so many things, but I just don't feel the way he wants me to.'

Ragnar didn't trust himself to speak a single word. This was a female question that was designed to ensnare a man, for there was no right answer. Anything he said would get him into trouble. Instead, he reached out and took her hand in his.

'He's never said it…but I'm cold to him. I don't know how to change that.' She rolled on to her side. 'I know you've been with women before. Should I—'

'This is not something I want to discuss.' He cut her off, not caring that his tone was harsh. 'Talk to Styr.'

'That's just it. I've never been able to talk to him the way I talk to you. He's so fierce and forbidding. It's like trying to talk to a mountain.'

Whereas Ragnar was her friend, someone who was hardly a threat at all. He wasn't certain whether to be complimented by that or offended.

'What should I do to make my marriage better?' she asked.

'Seduce your husband,' he said automatically.

'I couldn't!' Her words were shocked, as if he'd suggested that she slip a knife between Styr's ribs. 'He wouldn't like that at all.'

Ragnar forced himself to roll over and face her. 'If a woman as beautiful as you came to me one night, wanting me to lie with her, there's nothing on earth that would make me turn her away.' He tried to keep his words light, not letting her see the truth beneath them.

'I'm not a strong woman,' she argued. 'I'm too shy to do something like that.'

'You picked up a living snake and let it coil around your throat,' he pointed out. 'Most women would lack the courage to do that.'

'It was a matter of saving our lives.' She shuddered, adding, 'I hated every moment of it.'

'But you did what was necessary. And so you will, when it comes to your marriage. Especially for the sake of your child.'

'I suppose you're right.' Her fingers laced in his, reminding him of all the nights he wouldn't share with her. 'I've wanted this child for so long. I know it will make Styr happy after so many years.'

And if it doesn't? he wanted to ask. But he would never voice the question. For a woman like Elena would never belong to him.

Eight years earlier

'Ragnar,' came the voice of Elena. She stepped inside the home he shared with his father and her face dimmed at the sight.

'I'm here.' He stood up from his place by the hearth and felt ashamed of how dirty the house had become. Ever since his mother had been killed by raiders, his father, Olaf, had been lost in grief. He left every morning at dawn and didn't return until nightfall.

'I brought you some food,' she said, holding out a basket to him.

He stared at her for a long time, not knowing what to say other than to utter words of thanks. She nodded and when she glanced around again, asked, 'It's very dark in here. Can I open the door wider?'

He nodded and blinked when the sunlight illuminated the interior. Elena peered inside and offered him a tentative smile. 'That's a little better. At least now I can see you.'

Her gaze was strained as she saw the condition of his home. Ragnar felt his cheeks warm, but he made no excuses. The last time he'd tried to put away a few things, his father had beaten him.

'Never, ever touch her things!' Olaf had roared. Then his anger had crumbled into grief and he'd wept. Since that day, Ragnar had done nothing at all, for fear of destroying his father's carefully erected shrine to the memory of his wife. He was grateful that his older sisters were married, with their own households, so they did not have to see their father in this state.

Elena opened up the basket and handed him some bread. 'Your father is gone a lot, isn't he?'

Ragnar wasn't aware that anyone had noticed, but nodded. 'He is.' When he took the bread, he resisted the urge to tear it apart and cram it in his mouth. Despite the fact that he went out fishing most days, it had been weeks since he'd had real food.

Elena poured him a cup of ale and when he took it from her, his fingers brushed against hers. Though he was five and ten while she was two years younger, her face held the promise of beauty. Red-gold hair was braided into a single tail down her back and her sea-green eyes held him captive.

A flush came over his cheeks and he looked away.

'When will your father be back?'

He shrugged. 'Sunset, maybe. Sometimes he's gone all night.' When she looked appalled at that, he added, 'But I'm not afraid to be alone.'

He was used to it now. Sometimes he wondered if there would come a night when his father never returned. But he was old enough to care for himself. Olaf might have forgotten he had a son, but Ragnar wasn't going to bother him. He wasn't a child any more.

Elena sent him a slight smile as if she were trying to reassure him. 'If you want to join my family for our evening meal, my mother won't mind.'

Her father was high ranked within his tribe and Elena was his second-eldest daughter, out of ten children. Ragnar suspected that the man would hardly welcome someone like him at their table.

'I should stay here,' he answered.

'They won't notice either of us,' Elena remarked

with a wry smile. And perhaps it was true, but the idea of visiting her household without his father seemed wrong.

He offered her a piece of the bread, but she refused it. Ragnar finished eating and in the meantime, Elena walked across the room and grasped a wooden bucket. Without asking, she began picking up the fallen bones and the remnants of the fish he'd burned the night before when he'd tried to cook it.

'You shouldn't,' he started to protest.

But as soon as he spoke the words, she answered, 'Do you really like living in this way?'

No, he didn't. And though his father might beat him for it again, he supposed there was no sense in keeping the refuse.

Yet he was embarrassed that she would begin working like this. Ragnar reached out to take the bucket from her. 'You shouldn't trouble yourself.'

'I don't mind.' Elena let him take the bucket and reached for a broom. 'It's a way I can be useful.' She began sweeping out the old rushes and he helped her put the house back in order. When it was done, she washed the wooden cups and put them away.

'There, now. That's much better, isn't it?'

It was, even if he was certain his father would beat him for it. No one was supposed to touch the house or *her* things, like the broom. Seeing the clean interior made him remember the way his mother used to scrub the table and put out bundles of fragrant herbs upon his pillow at night. Ragnar's eyes stung, but he bit back the pain of loss.

'Will you come and walk with me?' Elena asked,

holding out her hand. 'You shouldn't stay inside on a day like this.'

Her gesture was innocent, as though it were nothing to hold his hand. But when he moved in closer, he felt his throat closing up with no words to say. Her hair smelled like the herbs his mother had used—sage and rosemary—and the idea of holding her hand was too awkward to consider.

Instead, he walked beside her, pretending as if he hadn't seen the gesture. Outside, the sun was bright and he shielded his eyes. It was midsummer and the days were still long.

'Where are we going?' he asked.

'To my parents' house,' she explained. Before he could repeat his protest, she put up a hand. 'You've gotten too thin since your mother died and it's not right.'

'Elena, I can't go. Not like this.' He'd been living in dirt for weeks and the idea of entering her father's house was impossible. Even if Ragnar scrubbed himself clean, her suggestion made him uncomfortable. Although his father was a freeman, Olaf had been little more than a farmer.

'Are we friends or not?' she demanded. 'Because I always thought that friends should look after each other.'

He didn't know how to argue with that, without offending her. Friends should, *ja*, but this was more than that.

'I want you to follow me,' she insisted. 'There's someone else who will come with us.'

She smiled at him and the warmth in her eyes caught him like a physical blow. Girls hardly ever paid him any attention at all. This was the first time one had sin-gled him out, sympathising with his plight. He fumbled through the words caught in his throat, wanting to say something. Anything.

Instead, he took her hand in his for the first time. The touch of her soft palm made his heartbeat quicken. Her hand squeezed his and when her smile didn't fade, he dared to hope.

Elena had come to him, offering him food. She wanted to bring *him* to her father's table. Did that mean that she didn't consider him beneath her? He straight-ened, wondering if this meant more than he thought. Was there another reason why she wanted him to dine with her family? He squeezed her hand in return, wish-ing he dared to do more than that.

He'd never kissed a maiden and of all the girls he'd seen, Elena was the one who entranced him. Her mouth had a full upper lip that sometimes tightened when she was thinking.

Before she could lead him further, he stopped walk-ing. 'Why do you want me to go to your parents' house, Elena?'

She shrugged. 'I thought you might want to share a meal with us, that's all.'

He studied her, still suspicious that there was an-other reason. Elena took a deep breath and eyed him, adjusting her braid over one shoulder and pushing back a few stray hairs behind her ears. 'Do I look all right?'

'You always do,' he said, then immediately wanted to take back the words. He should have told her she was beautiful. The prettiest girl he'd ever seen. Anything but the awkward words that had spilled out.

She didn't appear to notice, but said, 'Good. Wait here.'

Mystified, he obeyed, until he saw her walk over to Styr's house. She knocked upon the door, shifting her weight from one foot to the other. Then she nervously touched her hair again.

When his best friend came to the door, he saw the flush come over her face. Her smile was bright, as if wishing Styr would notice her.

The truth of her emotions deflated his earlier thoughts. Her feelings were that of friendship, nothing more. He should have known better.

Soon enough, Styr came out to join them. 'How are you?' he asked Ragnar, oblivious to Elena's interest.

He shrugged, for there was little to say. 'I suppose I should return to training. I need someone to spar with.' His hand moved to the short sword he carried at his side.

'You've gone weak, have you?' Styr teased.

'I can still best you,' he shot back.

His friend flexed a muscle. 'You can try, Olafsson.'

Elena cleared her throat to get their attention again. 'I thought we could go to my father's house and join them for a meal.'

Styr reached out and tugged her braid lightly. 'That's kind of you.' But his gesture was that of a teasing brother and he seemed not to notice Elena's disappointment.

The three of them continued to walk and Ragnar realised that Styr was effectively shutting Elena out of the conversation by discussing weaponry and fighting. She looked as if she wanted to speak again but kept silent. When they reached her father's house, she excused herself to go and speak to her mother, leaving the pair of them alone.

'Why would you talk about sharpening battleaxes around her?' Ragnar said. 'Are you blind to the way she looks at you?' Though it bothered him to speak of it, he wanted to know if his friend held a prior claim.

Styr sobered. 'She's just a girl.'

'She's also the daughter of a powerful warrior,' Ragnar pointed out. 'She'd make a good match with you.'

His friend let out a sigh. 'I know it. My father and her father have already discussed a betrothal. I suppose it will happen when she comes of age.' He didn't sound at all enthused about the idea.

'But you don't want her?' A flare of hope kindled inside Ragnar, although he knew it was unlikely the outcome would change.

Styr's expression remained neutral. 'There's nothing wrong with her. And there are years yet, before I'll wed.'

Before he could speak again, Elena returned. Her face was flushed and she appeared upset. 'Styr, my father wants you to come and dine with him.' She nodded towards the open door and his friend waited a moment.

'We'll walk together, then.'

'Go on without me,' Elena asked. 'I need to speak to Ragnar for a moment.'

After he'd gone, Elena's face revealed her disappointment. 'I—I was wrong. I wanted you to come with us, but—'

'Your father refused, didn't he?' Ragnar kept his expression shielded, making it seem as if it didn't matter.

'He said I could bring you food. Outside,' she said quietly. Shaking her head, she added, 'This isn't right. You should be a welcomed guest, the same as any other man.'

'It doesn't matter.' He knew his place, even if she'd wanted him to rise above it. 'Go and join Styr. I'll return home.'

He started to walk back, but Elena hurried forwards and blocked his path. 'No. It *does* matter.' Her green eyes held anger and she put her hands up to stop him. 'You're going to be a strong fighter one day. One of the best men we have.' Her hand reached up to touch his arm and the touch of her fingers was a gentle warmth. 'My father will welcome you at his table, soon enough.'

Her faith in him strengthened his resolve to make it so. He wasn't the man her father would ever choose. But perhaps, if he fought hard and made himself into a man of worth, he could change the opinion of others.

'I'll come to his table, one day,' Ragnar promised. 'But only if you're there.' He reached out and squeezed her hand, before turning away. The startled look in her eyes turned to embarrassment.

One day, he swore, everything would change.

Chapter Seven

Present day

Elena walked down to the shoreline, her mind feeling uneasy. Despite the terrible storm, the sun glittered upon the sea.

She shielded her eyes, watching from her place on the sand, when she caught sight of a ship in the distance. It was a small fishing vessel, carrying only a few people. Her heart pounded at the sight of it, though she could not say why. It was not Styr's ship—the Danes had taken command of that.

But there were few ships in this region. In the four days since she'd arrived, she hadn't seen any.

Until now.

She strained her eyes, trying to see who it was, but the sunlight blinded her. One of the men was wearing chainmail and his hair was the same colour as Styr's.

Was it her husband? Had he come in search of her? Her heart was pounding and she grasped her skirts, running towards the shore.

The winds had picked up, and before she could get

a closer look, they had sailed past the small green island where she'd first landed with Ragnar. It was too late to signal to them.

She should have called out to them. Though it might not have been Styr, she'd done nothing except run.

Perhaps you don't want him to find you, came an insidious voice inside her. *Perhaps you'd rather leave him.*

No. Not now, when she was finally going to have a child. *His* child. She owed it to Styr, to tell him. It would change everything.

And what if it doesn't? the voice asked. *What if he still finds you cold?*

She didn't mean to be. Truly, she wanted to be an affectionate wife, one who brought him comfort. But Styr hadn't wanted to wed her. He'd obeyed his father and agreed to the arrangement. And in spite of the years between them, he'd never claimed to love her. No matter how she tried to keep his home clean or prepare his favourite foods, it wasn't enough.

A splinter of anger irritated her mood. She'd tried to change herself, to be the woman she thought Styr wanted. The thought made her weary, for she didn't want to go back to being that wife.

When she glanced behind, she saw Ragnar leaning against a large boulder, his leg wrapped in bandages. His expression was unreadable, but she grew aware of the way his muscles tightened against the tunic he wore. He'd always been a strong warrior, stronger even than Styr. Though he lacked highborn blood, he'd been one of the greatest fighters in their tribe.

A cold chill caught her as she remembered the terrible price he'd paid for that honour.

'What is it, *søtnos*?' Ragnar asked. 'You look as if you've seen an evil spirit.'

Elena pushed away the memories, blurting out, 'I saw a ship just now.' She pointed out towards the waves, and even as she stared out at the grey water, she questioned what she'd seen. Yet, after all these years, she knew her husband's profile. There was a strong chance that it had been him.

'Was it our ship?' Ragnar asked. He leaned in, his interest suddenly piqued. 'Did our men escape from the Danes?'

She shook her head. 'It was a fishing boat.' Taking a deep breath, she added, 'But one of the men looked like Styr.'

Ragnar started to rise to his feet, but she shook her head. 'It's too late. They've already sailed east.'

'Do you want to search for him?'

'No.' She closed her eyes and went to sit beside him on the rock. 'I should have shouted. I should have run into the water and made noise to get their attention. But instead, I just watched them leave. I don't know why.'

That wasn't the truth. She knew why she'd stood there—because she'd been too startled to respond in time. It had seemed impossible that it could be her husband…and yet, she couldn't let go of the thought. Styr wasn't the sort of man who would turn his back on her. He would find her, no matter how long it took.

What she didn't understand was the sense of foreboding that had caught her. Dread mingled with anticipation, and those were the wrong things she should be feeling. If it *had* been her husband, shouldn't she be overjoyed?

Her hand moved down to her middle and the old fears rose up to taunt her. 'Do you think I'm a cold woman? The way Styr does?'

'He doesn't think you're cold,' Ragnar responded. 'He knew you were upset about not having children and he didn't know how to make you feel better.'

She took a deep breath, willing back the feelings of insecurity and doubt. 'I want to believe that this child will improve our marriage.'

Ragnar eased himself to stand, putting little weight upon his leg. 'It's a lot to ask of an infant.'

'Maybe. But if it doesn't help...' She rubbed her arms, so afraid of the alternative. For so long, she'd rested her hopes upon a baby. And now that it had come to pass, she ought to feel happier than she did.

Sometimes it didn't feel real. It was as if she'd only imagined the pregnancy, but she couldn't deny that she'd missed her monthly and would likely miss it again in another fortnight.

Ragnar's gaze passed over her body once more, but she couldn't read the thoughts within him. It was as if he knew something she didn't.

'Let's go back and eat,' he suggested. 'You can think about what you want to do.'

But she had already made her decision. 'We won't leave yet. Not until you've healed.' The Irish had no horses to make the journey easier and it was unfair to ask him to walk such a distance.

'The wound will be fine in a few days,' he told her. 'It's already closing up, if you want to see it.' A hint of amusement crossed over him. 'And the healer took out all the garlic, so it isn't so bad any more.'

She started towards him, but then a sudden shyness overtook her at being so close. *You're being foolish*, she told herself. *It's a wound, nothing more.*

But when she knelt down before him, she was intensely aware of Ragnar's body. His muscles were visible beneath the tunic he wore and his thigh was strong and powerful. A few days ago, she'd cut away his leggings near the wound. And when she touched his thigh, Ragnar gave a slight intake of breath. Though her hand was not upon his bare skin, her imagination suddenly conjured the image of touching him. And the forbidden nature of her thoughts sent a sudden tingle of arousal through her.

Her breasts rose up against her gown and between her legs, she began to ache. As she began to unwrap the bandage, she was deeply aware of his masculine scent. It was leather mingled with salt and a hint of pine. It made her want to rest her cheek against his heart, burrowing against him.

Stop this, her mind commanded her. But her breathing was unsteady, in spite of her willpower.

As she pulled back the bandage, she saw that Ragnar was right. His skin had grown together and, despite it being raw, she imagined within a few more days he would be able to put his full weight upon it.

'It is better,' she admitted. 'And if we wait here a little longer, you'll be able to walk on it.'

'Do you think that's wise?' he said, his eyes narrowing upon her. Her face burned as she wondered if he'd read her thoughts. No, it wasn't wise to be alone with him for that long. Not even if he'd once been her best friend. She could sense things shifting between them, the barrier weakening.

'The Irish would be able to guide us back to the settlement,' he continued.

Oh. Her embarrassment deepened at the realisation that he wasn't at all speaking about the wisdom of being alone together.

Elena took a breath. 'I believe it was Styr sailing past us. And it's possible that he'll start searching along the coast. It will make it easier for him to find us if we remain in one place.'

'And what if he doesn't return?'

She shook her head, lifting her shoulders in a shrug. 'We can decide what to do later. But if we stay, you'll heal. And then we'll know.'

She drew his arm around her shoulders, helping him to stand up as they returned to the others. But even as Ragnar leaned against her, she felt sensitive to his touch. His arm around her was only for balance, but her mind was conjuring more vivid details. Worse, she remembered lying with him this morning. He'd been aroused by her and, though she knew it was a reaction any man might have in the morning, it made her uneasy.

Because of the way she'd responded: in kind. She'd softened against him, aching for a man's touch.

His touch.

She told herself that it was only a natural reaction, that if it had been Styr, he'd have turned her on to her back and made love to her. Perhaps, now that she'd had so many weeks of distance from her husband, she was beginning to crave a joining. She'd been so caught up in her desire to have a child, it had taken away the pleasure of being with a man. That was what she needed—her husband to fulfil her needs.

But Ragnar wasn't her husband. And she would have to spend a few more days alone with him. She would have to find a way to occupy herself, to drag her mind away from the forbidden thoughts.

When they reached the others, Ragnar stopped walking but didn't take his hand from her shoulders. His dark green eyes moved over her as if he were drinking in the sight. Elena grew flustered, wondering if it was just her imagination.

'The Irish have given us some of their supplies,' he said. 'Including one of their tents to take with us. We should be comfortable enough.'

Though he spoke in a nonchalant air, the idea of sleeping beside him another night was intimidating. She couldn't say why, but perhaps it was because she'd slept in his arms last night. Her mind was conjuring up all sorts of strange imaginings.

Even though there was nothing wrong with sharing a tent with this man, she began to think that it wasn't wise at all. He was a temptation and the thoughts within her were a betrayal of her husband.

'I'm going to get the tent and work on our shelter again,' she told him. 'Why don't you rest here?' She needed to take her mind off the stormy thoughts brewing. Hard work was what she needed to stop thinking of this man.

Something had made her nervous. Ragnar couldn't say what it was, but from the moment the Irish departed, Elena had begun finding ways to stay away from him. She'd gathered enough wood to build twelve bonfires, sticks of varying sizes, along with larger logs.

'How many fires do you think we'll need?' he asked, when she returned with her sixth load of firewood.

'This isn't for a fire,' she said. 'It's to improve our shelter.'

She set the load down and began sorting the wood according to size and length. Her hair had spilled free of the tight braids she usually wore and several locks hung against her face. Irritated, she shoved them out of the way, struggling to lift the heavier logs.

'We're only staying here a few days longer,' Ragnar reminded her. 'We'll watch for Styr's ship and if we see it, we'll signal them.' But she was behaving as if they were going to live here permanently.

She was focused upon measuring the wood and he saw her unwrap a small axe. Soon, she began the work of chopping notches from the larger logs. 'I'd rather not sleep in the rain again,' was all she told him. 'The ground is still wet after the storm.'

But there was an undercurrent of tension within her. She was filling her hours with this task, behaving as if she was desperate for a distraction.

'Where did you get the axe?' he asked her.

'It was a gift from the Irish, after I helped you get rid of the other Norsemen.' She set it down a moment and regarded him. 'You don't think the invaders will come back, do you?'

'No. You had them convinced that they would be cursed if they did.' But it might be wise to investigate

the surrounding area. Ragnar rose to his feet and hob-
bled towards Elena.

'I don't need your help,' she protested, but that
wasn't why he was there. He reached down for two
long poles and took them from her pile, then chose
some smaller pieces that he could use to form crutches.
Once she realised what he was doing, Elena gave him
the use of her tools and said, 'Wait here. I have something that will help.'

Ragnar began shaping the crutches, using notches
to fit the top piece into the bottom poles. He tied them
together with some strips of leather. After a short time,
Elena returned with more leather and the leftover fur
of a rabbit she'd skinned a day ago. 'You can use this
for padding,' she offered, arranging the fur and leather
on top of the crutches.

While she helped him, he ventured, 'How are you
feeling? Any sickness?'

She finished tying down the fur and shrugged. 'The
same, really. Sometimes I forget about the baby, because it's still too early to feel movement.' Her hand
moved down to her womb and her face grew wistful.
'I can't wait to hold him for the first time in my arms.
Or her.'

The joy on Elena's face took away all of the tension
in her and she smiled openly. By the blood of Freya,
she stole his breath. Her sea-green eyes held him spell-
bound, while her fiery golden hair tangled around her
face. He wished again that it was *his* unborn child,
and not Styr's, growing within her. But the child was a
fervent reminder that she did not, and would not, ever
belong to him.

Still, he thought it strange that she'd experienced so few symptoms. His sisters had shared with him their own woes, often in more detail than he wanted. Sometimes, he wondered if it was true at all that Elena was pregnant.

She believed it, and he would say nothing to diminish her joy. But it was so early…women often miscarried or discovered their mistake.

His conscience berated him for even thinking such a thing. Elena and Styr had waited a long time for a child. She wanted it desperately and regardless of the jealousy within him, he hoped all would go well. 'I'm going to go look around the shore to see if there are any ships,' he told her. He needed a few moments to clear his head and remind himself that he had to forget about this woman.

'All right.' But after he took the crutches, Elena turned back to her work as if it were the most fascinating task imaginable.

Though she behaved as if there was nothing wrong, he saw the dark flush against her cheeks. There was a barely discernible change in Elena, as if she, too, sensed that the next few days were going to test their honour.

Chapter Eight

She dreamed of him that night.

In her vision, the fires of a battlefield raged, while the scent of death hovered around them. Bodies littered the ground and the carrion birds swooped overhead. The Viking warrior rode towards her, searching. His helm covered his face and his armour was stained with the blood of his enemies.

He was like a god of war, coming to claim her.

The warrior's eyes locked upon her as he rode through the carnage. He reached down and Elena went willingly, knowing that she was his prize of war.

Her heart pounded when he drew her up in front of him on the horse. From behind her, she could feel the iron muscles of his chest, the powerful thighs surrounding her legs. His body held the caged restlessness of a predator, and he rode hard across the field, taking her miles away from the battle.

Until they were alone.

The small thatched hut was hardly any shelter at all, but when she went inside, hot coals glowed in the hearth. The air was warm with anticipation, and his cold eyes stared at her with unfettered lust.

'Remove your clothing.'

Fear balled in her throat, along with the need to refuse. But before she could speak, he turned his back and removed the iron helm, then his chainmail corselet and gloves.

Her pulse quickened at the sight of his bared skin, for she knew why she was here. What he wanted from her.

Elena turned towards the fire, her skin pebbled with gooseflesh.

'Obey me,' came his husky voice.

In this place, she belonged to him. She was his to command and she revelled in the desire to be conquered, like a slave for his taking. Elena reached to her shoulders and unfastened the heavy golden brooches, setting them aside. She took off the long apron and then loosened the ties of her gown. Beneath it, she wore nothing at all.

His hands came up from behind her, helping her until the gown hung upon her slender frame. Her body was burning with need, for she knew this man well. She ached for him, wanting to be touched. Knowing the dark pleasure he would give.

Her gown pooled to the dirt floor, baring her flesh to him. He didn't speak, but she felt the warm caress of his kiss upon her shoulder while his hands glided over her delicate skin.

She closed her eyes, welcoming the sensation. The heat and aching lust were burning within her skin, making her wet for him.

He cupped her breasts and against her bottom, she

felt his erection pressing. He was still wearing his leggings and she dared to speak. 'Take them off.'

In response, he gripped her breasts tighter, flicking his thumbs over the hardened nipples. 'You don't command me, *søtnos*.'

His strong arm held her in place, his right hand stroking and tormenting the nipple until she was heavily aroused. His left hand moved down, over her stomach, down between her legs. 'You don't ever tell me what to do.'

He was punishing her, she realised, when his hand slipped between her legs. With his fingers, he found the wetness, sinking two fingers inside her while he used the heel of his hand in a rhythmic pressure.

She was dying against him, her body yielding and craving him. He pinched a nipple, driving her higher with excitement until she was so desperately close to the edge.

Abruptly, he drew away, leaving her starving for his touch.

'What do you say to me?' he demanded.

'I— Forgive me,' she begged. She needed his hands upon her and his mouth. Her body was quaking for him, wanting to be filled by this warrior. She craved his hot shaft piercing her with a relentless penetration.

But he gave her nothing at all.

And when she turned to see his face, Ragnar's eyes glared down at her.

'Elena.' Ragnar heard her cry out in her sleep and she was trembling violently. 'Wake up.'

He couldn't tell if it was a nightmare or something with the baby, but he moved beside her, reaching out.

But the moment he touched her shoulder, she let out a moan. 'Please.' Her breathing hitched and he was taken aback when she gripped his hand and pulled it around to her breast.

She was still dreaming, but the moment she felt his hand upon her, she let out another cry and shuddered like a woman finding her release.

And just like that, he grew hard. He didn't know what she was dreaming of, but hearing her climax was enough to bring his own arousal.

In his mind, he let out a curse, knowing it was wrong. But for a stolen moment, he drew his hand over her swollen breast, seizing a fleeting touch he never should have had.

He wanted her so badly, it was all he could do not to pull her to her back and lift her skirts. From the deep scent of her skin, she was ready for him. He would sink into her wet depths and bring her to another release.

Ragnar jerked his hand away as if it were on fire. He didn't know if she was awake or not, but he prayed she wasn't. What in the name of Thor was he doing? She was likely dreaming of her husband, missing Styr when she'd reached for him instead.

Careful not to wake her, he left their shelter, seeking the frigid darkness to cool his ardour. He drew his hand down to his wound, resting it against the bandage to provoke pain. Anything to fight against the lust she'd conjured.

Staying with her had been a mistake. He couldn't lie anywhere near her without wanting more. She was, and always had been, the woman he'd dreamed of. He limped forwards, resting his hand against a nearby tree. With slow, deep breaths, he calmed his heartbeat.

No more.

He would not betray his best friend, nor would he give rein to his desires. Elena was not a woman he could ever have. She had joined with another man and was likely pregnant with an unborn son.

And like a fool, he'd kept pining for her. Hoping for what? That she would divorce her husband and seek him instead? It would never happen. Though he'd watched their marriage falter as her barrenness took away her spirit, Styr wanted to make his wife happy. He'd shown Ragnar the ivory comb he'd bought for Elena as a gift, though he'd not had time to give it to her. He'd planned to offer it when they had finished building their new home together.

Ragnar rested his forehead against the rough bark, knowing that it was time to turn from Elena. She had been sent by the goddess Freya to test his limits, to prove his honour.

It was better to stay far, far away from her. And find another woman to love.

Elena avoided Ragnar over the next two days. He didn't speak to her at all about the night he'd touched her and it was better to pretend it hadn't happened. Every time she remembered the dream, she felt her cheeks burn with embarrassment.

For she remembered the way she'd shamelessly taken his hand to her breast. In the darkness, she'd feigned sleep, though she'd known perfectly well what she was doing. The intensity of her own needs had broken through like a raging fire and she'd said nothing of that night. But her body knew that the dream was only a prophesy of what might happen between them if she allowed it.

She didn't know what was wrong with her. If anything, she should have dreamed of Styr, not this man. Her hand moved down to her unborn child and she walked along the shore, searching for ships. There had been none since the day she'd spied the fishing boat. Elena was beginning to wonder if she'd imagined it.

Her leather shoes sank into the sand while the cool morning wind buffeted her hair. The sun was bright and she shielded her eyes against it, eyeing the grey water for a glimpse of hope.

In one hand, she carried the axe in the hopes that she might find more fallen limbs or driftwood. Although she'd rebuilt a solid shelter for herself and Ragnar, the time stretched on until she realised she needed more tasks to satisfy her. She'd set some snares for hunting, but an even greater challenge was keeping her distance from the man who attracted her.

It wasn't right and she locked away the feelings, hoping he would never guess them. Once she was reunited with Styr, her sinful thoughts would vanish.

When it was clear there were no more ships, she climbed the hillside back to the clearing. A sound caught her attention, and she turned towards the west. Listening hard, she tried to detect what it was, but now there was only silence. Still, she kept her grip firmly on the axe as she approached their shelter. Ragnar had been sleeping when she'd left at dawn, but from the nearby coals of a fire it appeared that he, too, was awake.

When she reached the trees where she'd build the small lean-to, there came the sound of men's voices, speaking the Norse language.

Her heart thundered inside her and she *knew*. The raiders had come back for her, as she'd feared. And this time, a trick would not deter them. If she wasn't careful, both of them would die. She wanted to call out to Ragnar, but was afraid her voice would alert the men. Then, too, they were outnumbered.

Elena remained frozen in place, trying to calm the rush of fear roaring in her veins. Instinct demanded that she run, but that would only draw them to her. Her eyes scanned the surroundings, searching for a means of escape. Hiding was her best option.

But before she could take a single step, a man's voice called out from behind her. 'I've found her!'

Terror iced within her body, numbing her to this fate. They would try to rape her, beating her until at last they killed her. She had no doubt of it.

She couldn't stand here and let it happen. There was no way to know where Ragnar was, but she had a weapon in her hands.

And only one chance.

Before the man could make his first move, she spun, swinging the axe. The blade bit into flesh and his battle cry cut off as his life's blood spilled upon the grass. Elena tore the weapon free, inwardly shaking. She'd never killed a man before, had never had to.

Don't look, her mind warned, but her stomach

swirled with nausea. The other men emerged from behind her shelter, and when they saw the fallen body of their kinsman, they began to run. All were armed and it was only a matter of seconds before they cut her down; she knew it.

She turned to run, though it was futile. Her lungs burned as she grasped her skirts in one hand, holding the axe in the other. Where was Ragnar? Had they already killed him?

The dull ache within her, the terror at being left alone, was preying upon her courage. She heard the sickening sound of a man's scream and the thunder of a horse's hooves.

She reached the edge of the grass where it shifted into open sand. Her footing slipped and she barely corrected her balance before she continued running. Risking a quick glance behind, she saw one of the Norsemen running towards her. In his hand, he carried a long sword and his hands were stained with blood.

Elena's sides were aching and she couldn't breathe, but still she ran. The sand slowed her footing, yet she had no choice but to keep going.

Her attacker was going to catch up to her soon. And then he would kill her and her unborn child.

It was the thought of her baby that stopped her from running. She'd waited so long for this child, praying nightly to the gods. If she continued to flee, there was no hope at all. Slowly, she stopped and, gripping the bloodstained axe, turned to face the man. He was catching up to her, despite the weight of his heavy armour. Elena stood her ground, while a cold chill spread through her spine.

She had to fight for her life and that of her child. No one could save her now. Though she suspected Ragnar had begun attacking the men from the other side, she'd seen no sign of him. With both hands, she held the axe steady, waiting for the moment to strike.

The Norseman stopped his running and began to walk, his dark eyes upon her. 'Did you think you could run, little witch?'

'Did you think my curse would not follow you?' she countered as he strode across the sand. 'Your men are already dead.'

She would have only one chance to kill this man and she could not hesitate. He wore chainmail armour, unlike the others. The axe would not penetrate the chain links.

Her panic began to rise up again, gathering in her stomach, until she felt as if she would be physically ill. She swallowed hard and he took a few swings with his sword.

'Shall I behead you, witch? Or would that be too quick?'

She kept her eyes locked upon him, though she grew aware of a motion from behind. He lifted his blade, adding, 'If you run, it will be a slow death. I'll gut you and leave you to bleed on the sand.'

Elena took a deep breath and waited while he drew back the blade. A split second later, she threw herself to the sand, slicing at his upper thighs with the axe. He made not a sound.

Only then did she see the spear embedded in his back that had pierced his heart. Before he could fall upon her, she scrambled away. Atop the hill stood Ragnar, with another spear in his hand.

Her knees buckled and a rushing noise filled her ears. She couldn't move, couldn't breathe. Upon the sand, she half choked, trying to inhale a deep breath. In a moment he was beside her, pulling her into his arms. 'They're dead. No one will harm you.'

'Th-there were so many,' she stammered.

'I killed four. You took the fifth.' He gripped her hard against him, stroking her hair. She couldn't even take comfort from the embrace, for she'd truly believed she was about to die. Though her axe might have made the Norseman bleed out, it was Ragnar's spear that had ended it.

'We're all right,' he said, helping her to stand. 'Are you hurt?'

Her legs were still shaking and she leaned against him. 'N-no.' She kept her arms around his waist and then remembered his injury. 'What about you? Don't you need your crutches?'

'It hurts, but I can manage without them,' he said. Whistling to the horse, the animal trotted towards them. 'We're going to spend the night here, one last time. And then, in the morning, we're leaving this place.'

She nodded slowly. Styr wasn't going to come back this way. Either she'd been mistaken in what she'd seen, or he'd gone to Dubh Linn. 'All right.'

Ragnar kept his hand around her, but she was so caught up in the residual fear that she couldn't seem to get warm. Never before had she been so close to her own death. It frightened her past all reason and she couldn't stop shaking.

When they reached their shelter, Ragnar helped her down from the horse. He built up the fire until it was burning hot and she sat as close as she dared. He moved to sit beside her, and Elena closed her eyes, needing the comfort of human touch.

'Thank you,' she managed at last. 'I've never been so afraid. I thought they'd killed you.'

His hand moved over her hair, quietly stroking it back. With his fingers, he unravelled the braids until the long wavy strands fell over her shoulder. 'I wouldn't have let anything happen to you, Elena. Not ever.'

His hands were soothing her in a way that pushed back the fear. The warmth of the fire was starting to calm her and she leaned her head against his shoulder. 'I'm sorry I was avoiding you these past few days,' she admitted.

'Why did you?' He kept his gaze fixed upon the flames as if he didn't know the answer.

Her pulse quickened, but she wanted to remain honest. 'Because I was…afraid of being too close to you.'

Ever since she'd dreamed of lying with him, she no longer trusted herself. She didn't know the woman she was becoming, one ruled by desire instead of honour. But she needed him to know the truth, for that would keep him at a distance.

Her face flamed with embarrassment. 'You made me feel things I haven't felt in a long time.'

Ragnar let out a slow breath. 'You wouldn't have

betrayed Styr. Nor would I.' He tossed a stick on to the fire and admitted, 'I wanted to marry you, years ago. But I never dared to ask, after the arrangement your parents made.'

His confession startled her, for she'd not expected this. She drew her knees up and looked at him. In his eyes, the stark longing set all her defences on edge.

'I'm not telling you this to make you uncomfortable. Nor would I do anything to take you away from Styr. He's a good man and you deserve to be together.'

But she understood why he was speaking now. Both of them could have died this day.

'I was dreaming of you,' she confessed. 'That night in the tent when I made you touch me. It shouldn't have happened and I'm sorry for what I did.'

His dark green eyes fixed upon her, as if he couldn't believe what he was hearing. She half expected him to move away from her in disgust. Instead, he took her face between his hands, remaining silent. And she knew, without him speaking a single word, that he'd desired her, too.

Elena covered his hands with her own, drinking in the touch of his palms. The heat of this moment sank beneath her skin, conjuring up the lost feelings she'd put aside. She remembered how his lips had felt beneath hers and a sudden longing flushed through her skin.

It was as if a part of her had been brought back to life, resurrected in this man's touch. She wasn't used to feeling so strongly or yearning for something she couldn't have.

Finally, he took his hands away and regarded her. 'I

believe that Styr is alive and that you'll go back with him. I kept my word to protect you, and I promise to keep you safe until the day I have to let you go.'

The words were a stark reminder that nothing would happen between them. No matter how much she might want to take comfort from his touch.

But though his hands were no longer upon her, he was still staring at her with unbridled longing. 'If you were my wife at this moment, I'd kiss you now,' he said. 'I'd taste your sweetness and run my tongue over your lower lip.'

The words flowed through her, pushing the forbidden feelings to the surface.

She closed her eyes, trying not to envision it.

'I'd use my mouth all over your skin,' he continued. 'Your neck…your bare breasts, and then I'd go lower,' he said huskily. 'Until you're craving me inside you.'

Just like the night she'd dreamed of him, her body went soft, imagining him. He shouldn't be speaking such words, tempting her in such a way. She could hardly bear it and her face was flushed.

It didn't matter what had happened these past few days. No matter that she'd grown so close to him. She was a woman of honour and would never be disloyal to her husband. 'I can't be yours, Ragnar,' she whispered. 'I belong to him.'

The tension in his hands was palpable as he drew them back. 'Don't fear, Elena. I'll never touch you again. Whatever I might desire, I'll never do anything to act upon it. He won't know.'

'He can't,' she whispered. 'I won't be disloyal to him.'

'Neither will I.' He stood up, opening the wooden door to their shelter. 'When you're warm, go and sleep. I'll keep watch for the night.' Reaching out, he dropped a kiss upon her forehead, the way a brother might.

Yet all she could think was that Styr had never affected her in that way. And Ragnar hadn't laid a hand upon her.

Chapter Nine

The ship came at night.

Ragnar had left Elena sleeping back within the shelter while he'd spent time alone, walking along the beach. He'd never expected to see anything among the waves, but when he heard voices, he stared out at the water, wondering who was there. In the distance, he spied the flare of torches, revealing a vessel that paused momentarily near the outcropping of stone before it continued to the shore.

He remained hidden, a weapon in each hand. Although they had survived the first attack and he'd burned the bodies of the raiders, there could be more invaders. And yet he wanted to wait before alerting Elena.

The ship anchored further out and soon enough, Ragnar realised it was *their* ship. The brass weather-vane proclaimed it as the one that had brought them from Norway. At long last, he spied the face of his best friend, Styr.

The sight of the man should have filled him with an

immense relief. He should have run to Elena and awakened her, telling her that her husband had come at last.

But Styr was carrying a woman in his arms. And from the look on his face, he had strong feelings for her. He was not only holding her to keep her from the cold water—it was more than that. Styr was drinking in the sight of the dark-haired beauty as if she were his beloved. And when he lowered her to the sand, his arms lingered around her.

The bastard.

Ragnar's anger blasted through him at the sight of them together. How could his friend do this to Elena? The young woman had fought for her life, time and again. She'd been willing to travel across éire in search of her husband. And in repayment for her loyalty, her husband had found someone else—his captor.

Ragnar didn't move from his place, even when his friend and kinsmen made camp and built a fire. He spied the faces of Onund and a few other men who had been taken captive that night. They set up tents and Ragnar waited to see if Styr would take the woman within his shelter.

He could hardly bring himself to watch them, when he knew Styr was about to break Elena's heart. He didn't want to be right. Not in this, not when she was expecting a child. When Styr found out, would he turn away from her? Or would he stay?

The woman went inside a tent far away from the others and Ragnar breathed a little easier. And yet he couldn't forget what he'd seen.

He moved away from his hiding spot and returned to the shelter. This was his last night with Elena and he suspected that the morning would bring nothing but despair. But he was here for her now and he would not leave. Even if her husband abandoned her.

Inside the space, Ragnar could hear the rhythm of Elena's breathing. She was curled up on her side and he moved in close. She didn't awaken, but nestled against him while he drew his arms around her.

He'd vowed not to touch her, but Styr's actions had shattered those vows. If his friend had found someone else to love, Elena deserved more.

The scent of her skin and the warmth of her body allured him and it was a physical pain to be so near. He didn't care any more. Tonight he would lie with the woman he loved in his arms and damn the consequences.

At dawn, she awakened to feel Ragnar's body pressed close. Elena blinked, knowing she should get up…and yet wanting to remain where she was. His strong arms were wrapped around her, while her head rested beneath his chin. The heat of his skin permeated her and she felt a peacefulness in his embrace.

He must have returned late last night, for she'd not heard him. She didn't know why he'd slept beside her. Perhaps he'd moved during his sleep and hadn't been aware he was so close.

'Ragnar,' she whispered.

'*Ja?*'

Elena hadn't known he was awake. She waited for him to pull his arms away, to retreat towards his side of the shelter. Instead, he tightened his grasp around her. 'There's something you need to know.'

Something in the timbre of his voice held foreboding. That, and the way he was holding her now.

'What is it?' She tried to extricate herself, rolling over to face him, but he kept her imprisoned in his arms. In the dim light of morning, it brought her body flush to his and she sensed that whatever he had to say was not good news.

'Styr's ship landed here last night.'

It was the last thing she'd expected him to say. Her husband had returned? A rush of relief filled her and she couldn't stop her smile. 'He's alive. Thank the gods.'

'And he—' Ragnar's words broke off, as if he'd suddenly caught himself.

'And he what?' She sat up and this time, he released her. When she turned to him, there was a fierce cast to his face, the harbinger of bad news. 'Is he wounded?'

Ragnar shook his head. He eyed her for a moment and said, 'I suppose if it's of any importance, he'll tell you himself.' He rose from his place and moved to leave the shelter. 'I'll build a fire and we'll wait for him.'

'Is he down by the shore?'

'He and our kinsmen, yes.'

'Then we should go to them now,' Elena insisted. 'You should have woken me last night.' It made little sense why Ragnar would let Styr and the others make camp along the shore when they could have been together.

'We'll wait for them here,' Ragnar said. 'Let them awaken on their own. They must have travelled for hours and likely need the sleep.'

His answer made no sense at all. She'd been apart

from her husband for a week, and Ragnar was concerned about them sleeping enough? It was evident that he wasn't telling her something. From the shielded expression on his face, it had something to do with Styr. Elena didn't press him, however. Whatever it was, she'd learn the truth sooner or later.

She joined him outside by the fire, but when there were no signs of anyone approaching from the shore, she returned inside the shelter to get food. She had a bit of meat left over from last night. It wasn't enough to feed all of their kinsmen, but it was something.

Then, when she emerged from the enclosure, she caught her first glimpse of Styr approaching in the distance. Her husband didn't look at all pleased to see them and his arms were crossed.

Was he angry with Ragnar? For what reason?

She studied her husband, so relieved that he was unharmed. His dark gold hair was tied back and he still wore chainmail armour. It didn't appear that he had any outer wounds and for that she was grateful.

Elena approached him, wondering if he was going to welcome her into his arms. But instead of embracing her, Styr held back. Upon his face, she saw regret. Why? Wasn't he glad to see her again?

The shaky feeling of uneasiness sharpened at his reluctance to greet her.

She decided if he wasn't going to speak, then she would. 'I'm glad you're all right. When they took you prisoner…I wasn't certain you would live.' She offered a tentative smile to him, hoping it would break the invisible distance between them.

'I see that Ragnar protected you,' Styr answered. His

voice remained neutral, offering no words like: *Thank the gods you're alive* or *I'm so glad to see you again.*

His behaviour was wrong, in so many ways. She forced herself to nod, but when she risked a glance back at Ragnar, she saw fury in his eyes. Whatever was wrong, he knew about it and had since last night.

Say something, she wanted to beg Styr. *Tell me that you still love me. That everything will be all right now.*

Instead, he held his silence, looking for all the world like he didn't want to be here. She struggled to think of what to say, but there was one piece of news she felt certain would bring him joy. Slowly, she moved her hands down to her womb and said, 'We're going to have our first child, Styr. I learned of it only a few days ago.'

The expression on his face paled, as if she'd taken an axe to his stomach. There was no joy at all. No happiness at her revelation. His lack of response made her feel as if someone had knocked the wind from her.

'Aren't you—happy?' she asked at last. 'It's what we wanted for so long.' But he didn't speak or move. The fear inside her froze up, flooding through her body with a coldness she couldn't dispel.

Something was very wrong with her marriage and she couldn't guess what could possibly have gone so wrong in the past week. Ragnar came up behind her, as if to offer his support.

'That's good,' Styr said at last. Only then did he come closer and embrace her. But his arms did not hold her tight, nor did he seem at all pleased by the news. Elena blinked hard to hold back the tears, feeling as if something terrible had happened and she couldn't name what it was.

Her husband seemed like a stranger now, a man who no longer loved her. The foundation of her marriage was shaped around this unborn child. She'd believed that the baby would bring them back together. But he didn't look pleased. Instead, he looked dismayed by the news.

She bit her lips so hard she nearly drew blood, but by the gods, she would not cry. Whatever had come between them, they would work through it.

A noise from behind caught her attention and Styr turned as well. There were two people in the distance watching them, and one of them was a woman with dark hair. The pieces of memory reshaped together, and Elena realised who the woman was. It was the one who'd struck Styr down, taking him as her prisoner.

She cast a glance at Ragnar, but his face was stony, unmoving.

'I'll return in a moment,' Styr said. 'Wait here.' He started to hurry towards them, as they returned to the shoreline.

'Don't,' Ragnar warned, catching Elena's wrist when she was about to follow.

But she had to know. Her heart was freezing over with fear and pain, and she felt as if she'd already lost her husband.

'That's what you saw last night, wasn't it?' Her voice was the barest whisper, the pain breaking down her courage. 'You saw the woman.'

'Yes. I saw her,' Ragnar admitted.

'What were they doing together?' The idea of her husband being with someone else, even as a captive, filled her with a sudden resentment.

'Talking.' But there was more hidden within the words he hadn't said.

'I don't believe you.' Styr had lived with the woman over the past week. And if he'd brought her all this way, there had to be something between them. Elena had no doubt of it, especially after her husband had pursued the woman just now.

A hot rage filled up within her, seething. 'He doesn't want the baby,' she said to Ragnar, feeling the edges of her courage crack apart. *Or me.*

He came up behind her, wrapping her in his arms. 'There's more to this than we know. Give him a chance to tell you what happened.'

Though his words were reasonable, the edge in his voice held an anger that matched her own. Elena stepped out of his arms. 'I have to know the truth about them. Let me go, Ragnar.'

He did, raising his hands as he stepped back. 'I'll be here, if you've need of me.'

She nodded, steeling herself as she strode towards the shore. In the distance, she saw a fishing boat approaching, with a few men rowing closer. Elena raised a hand to block the sunlight as she stared down at her husband and the woman.

It should have made her uncomfortable to spy on them, but anger made it impossible to turn away. He'd betrayed her and she needed to know the truth of his feelings for this woman.

Styr had come up behind the Irishwoman, resting his hands on her shoulders. The gentleness of the gesture and his caring posture were a dull blade twisted into her heart. Elena could see their profiles and while the woman's face held misery, her husband's held longing.

He was in love with this woman. She could see it in his bearing, in the way he turned her to face him and embraced her hard. They were holding one another as if no one else existed.

She sagged to her knees, feeling like she was intruding upon a private moment. But Styr was *her* husband, not this woman's. They had given promises to one another and had been together for years.

Years should have mattered more than days.

Yet she'd never seen her husband look at *her* in this way. He was tormented inside and bitterness took root in Elena's stomach.

Why couldn't he love her like that? Was she not woman enough for him? Had her past failings as a wife made him so eager to turn to another?

The woman was crying and Elena watched while her husband wiped away her tears and embraced her hard again.

And when she walked to the water's edge, waiting for the fishing boat to approach, Elena realised that the woman wasn't going to stay. She was sailing away, while Styr had chosen to remain with her.

But never before had she seen such desolation on her husband's face.

Ragnar hadn't wanted to see them together. Not after all this. He'd walked a long distance, needing the space away from everyone. He walked nearly a mile away from the shelter before he realised that Styr had followed him. They stood near a small copse of trees, beside a large clearing.

'Abandoning her again, are you?' Ragnar stopped walking and turned to face the man who had once been his friend.

'I was a captive,' Styr countered. 'I was only freed a few days ago.'

'By her,' Ragnar said. 'The woman you brought with you.'

Styr gave no answer, but his expression tensed. 'I wanted to thank you for looking after Elena.'

'While you were betraying her with that Irish whore?'

The words provoked the response he'd wanted. Styr's temper erupted and his tone was rigid. 'Don't call her that.'

'You're a bastard who doesn't deserve Elena.' Ragnar gripped Styr's tunic with both hands, slamming the man up against a tree. After seeing her weep over him, after the way she'd fought for their lives, she deserved far more than Styr.

'She's my wife. I know my obligations.' Styr wrenched himself free, sending Ragnar off balance. They circled one another, each looking for an opening to throw a punch.

'She deserves better than you,' Ragnar countered. 'You took a mistress and only stayed because of the baby. If Elena weren't pregnant, you wouldn't be here now.'

When he didn't deny it, fury boiled within him. Ragnar threw himself at Styr, knocking the man to the ground. 'Did you think of her even once while she was fighting to live? When she threw herself off a ship to escape slavery and nearly drowned? Or when she was nearly killed yesterday by Norsemen?'

He knocked Styr's head against the ground, driven by the need to avenge Elena. She'd wept over this man, trying to find out what she'd done wrong in their marriage.

Styr's fist caught him across the jaw and Ragnar rolled away before the man could strike again.

'I'm staying with her, damn you.' Styr's breathing was heavy, and he got to his feet, wiping at a bloody lip. 'I never lay with Caragh.'

'But you're in love with her.' It was obvious, from the way Ragnar had seen them together last night. Styr had carried her across the water, holding her as if he'd never wanted to let go.

Styr's silence was the answer he'd dreaded. 'I won't divorce Elena. Not now, not when she's wanted this baby so much.'

Ragnar let out a breath he hadn't known he was holding. 'Don't hurt her, Styr. You don't know what she's been through these past few days. If you turn from her now—'

'I won't.' Styr crossed his arms and levelled a glare at him. 'Whatever was between Caragh and me is over. I'm taking Elena back to Dubh Linn, and we'll settle there, among our people.' A heaviness crossed over his expression and he added, 'We'll be all right.'

Ragnar eyed the man, seeing a reflection of himself in the man's restless demeanour. 'Don't make her unhappy,' he warned.

Or I'll steal her away from you.

* * *

At nightfall, Elena walked alongside the shoreline with Styr's hand in hers. When he'd returned from talking with Ragnar, both men had bruises and cuts from fighting. She didn't know what they'd said to one another, but neither did she ask. Her suspicions centred on the young woman who had left.

Although Styr had let her go, Elena wanted to know how strong his feelings were. She wanted so much to believe that they were acquaintances and that her suspicions were unfounded. But she feared what she'd observed between them.

'I've seen the woman before,' she began, trying to keep her voice calm as if his answer didn't matter.

'Caragh Ó Brannon,' he admitted. 'Brendan was her younger brother.'

Elena remembered the adolescent who had led the raid, taking her and the others captive. His move had been foolhardy and dangerous, but she guessed why he'd done it. Whether or not it was his intention, by seizing her he'd effectively drawn the Norsemen away from the settlement and protected his sister.

But what Elena didn't understand was what had happened to her husband after the ship had sailed. 'She took you as her captive, didn't she?'

Styr nodded. To her surprise, he showed no anger at being the prisoner of a woman. A thousand questions surged within her, to know what had happened. Whether he'd been hurt...or why he had been taken.

Instead, she caught a flash of guilt upon his face.

No. She didn't want to think that he'd found someone else to love. Not in this short of a time. But her mind couldn't conjure up a good reason why he would embrace the woman.

He stayed for you, her brain reminded her. *He let her go.*

Was it enough? She didn't doubt that he'd stayed because of the baby. But if there hadn't been a child, would he have divorced her? The icy hollowness spread within her, the fear growing.

She'd left her home in Norway, travelling where Styr had wanted to go. He'd always dreamed of roaming the world, while she'd wanted to remain home and start a family. Their differences had strained the marriage, but surely he wouldn't abandon her now. Not in this unfamiliar land.

'Do you…have feelings for her?' She was trying not to sound accusatory, but Styr wouldn't look at her. That, in itself, told her a great deal.

'Why would you ask me something like that? I only knew her for a few days.'

Again, he was behaving as if it meant nothing. 'I have eyes, Styr. I saw you with her.'

I saw you holding her as if you didn't want to let go, her heart raged.

'She left with her brothers. I told her farewell.' He shrugged it off as if it didn't matter.

Her anger began to take hold, for she knew he wasn't telling her the whole truth. How could he act as if nothing had happened? 'You were embracing her.'

He spun and for the first time, his dark eyes met hers. 'Nothing happened between us.'

The flash of his temper only ignited her frustration. 'Then why are you so angry?' she shot back. She wasn't a blind fool who couldn't see what was before her. 'If she were nothing to you, you wouldn't be acting this way.'

It took an effort, but she pulled back her rage and forced herself to remain calm. Inside, she was hurting from the unanswered questions and the invisible wounds to her faith in him. She was finding it difficult to trust anything he said.

He let out a breath and changed the subject. 'I heard from Onund that you jumped from the ship.' She recognised the tactic, understanding that he didn't want to fight about this. And neither did she.

Elena nodded. 'We were attacked by the Danes and there was only one chance to escape. Ragnar helped me to reach the shore.' He'd saved her from drowning, even though he'd been wounded himself. His courage had kept her from breaking apart, giving her strength to endure the past few days.

'Both of you could have died,' Styr said.

It was true and she fought back the tears, just remembering it. Not only because of what might have happened to Ragnar and her...but also to her baby.

'I wasn't about to let myself be sold into slavery,' she told him. 'This might be the only baby I'll ever have.'

Styr's expression fell and he let out a sigh. He said nothing for a time, but his attention shifted to the boat disappearing in the mist.

There was nothing worse than knowing that someone no longer loved you. If he ever had.

Finally, he spoke. 'Do you know how long I searched for you? I thought you had died.'

The worry in his voice granted her a measure of

comfort and she came to stand behind him. Her heart was heavy as she spoke. 'I didn't think they would let you live, either. But I'm glad you returned.'

She recognised that he was trying to make peace between them, putting aside the past. If she kept pushing him for answers, it would only damage the fragile reunion between them. Slowly, she walked to stand at his side, trying to lay her apprehensions to rest.

The fragile truce made it hard to converse and Styr finally led her to walk along the beach, while she followed.

'How long have you been here?' he asked.

'Nearly a week. The Danes wounded Ragnar, but he kept me safe.' Her cheeks flushed at the memory of his arms around her only this morning.

The knowledge unravelled part of her anger, for she was not blameless herself. Although she hadn't betrayed Styr with her feelings, she *had* kissed Ragnar and craved his touch in a sinful way.

It unsettled her, for she was trying to lay all the accusations at his feet, when she had made mistakes of her own. The past few days had brought her closer to Ragnar. She'd relied upon him to survive and he'd supported her through the darker days.

'We found food and built this shelter,' she finished.

For a moment, Elena looked at the water, wondering if he could see the blush of her own guilt. Out of the corner of her eye, she saw Styr's arm coming towards her and without thinking, she took a step backwards. 'What are you—?'

Oh. He'd been trying to embrace her in welcome. She couldn't believe she'd misread his actions that badly. 'You caught me unawares.' She leaned in, putting her arms around him in a light embrace. But he didn't hold her tight, the way a husband missing his wife would.

To emphasise her welcome, she stood on tiptoe and kissed his cheek. Again, he didn't return the gesture, which made her feel uncertain about this.

Styr pulled back and asked, 'How are you feeling?'

'The same,' she admitted. 'I wouldn't have known about the baby, if it weren't for the fact that I haven't bled in two moons.' She reached down to touch her stomach, wondering when she would begin to feel movement. 'It seems so strange to think of a child growing inside me. I haven't been sick at all.'

His face had gone distant again, staring out at the water, and she began to talk faster. 'I think the child will be born in early spring next year, if I've counted right.'

He gave no answer and she suspected he wasn't listening to her. His mind was focused upon the horizon and the woman who'd left. 'We're going to be all right, aren't we, Styr?' Her voice was barely a whisper, all of her hopes bound up in that sentence.

But when he gave no answer at all, she feared the worst.

Chapter Ten

Dubh Linn—three weeks later

Ragnar tried to stay away from her, but despite Elena's valiant attempts to restore her marriage with Styr, he could see the sadness beneath her forced smile. She was hurting and it killed him to stand by and do nothing.

He'd helped Styr build a small house and he'd poured his efforts into constructing another dwelling for himself and his kinsmen. Thankfully, none of them were slaves now. Styr had sailed to Dubh Linn in search of Elena and had found the men. During a fierce battle against the Danes, the men had fought bravely and earned their freedom.

Elena had asked to help today and he'd been amused as, once again, she began comparing the lengths and widths of the various logs.

'This needs to be carved smoother,' she said, pointing to a raised edge. 'It will fit more tightly together and keep the wind out.'

'Go ahead, then.' Ragnar pointed to the hand-held draw knife that they'd used to smooth out the wood.

Elena eyed him as if he'd lost his mind. 'I haven't the strength to carve the wood and you know this.'

'It's not hard. Come and try.' He wanted to take her mind off her troubles and he hoped that the distraction of work would be welcome. Her hair was unbound, except for a section she'd pulled back from the crown and tied off with a bit of thread.

'There are things I need to do at home,' she argued. 'I haven't swept the floor or cleaned or—'

'You did those things yesterday. And the day before. You can spare one hour.'

He gestured for her to come and sit astride the log and handed her the draw knife. 'You'll pull this back across the surface of the wood and smooth out the space you want to flatten.'

She tried it, but when she pushed it forwards, the angle was wrong and the blade caught in the wood. 'This isn't right.'

'It's not a downward motion. Pull it towards you.' He motioned for her to get up and demonstrated until curls of wood fell to the ground. 'Like this.'

A smile played at her mouth. 'Keep going, Ragnar. You're doing well.' Her sea-green eyes were bright with amusement and, despite her initial protest, she appeared interested in learning how to use the draw knife.

He stopped using the tool and propped his hand upon the log. 'You think I'll do all the work for you?'

A laugh broke from her. 'Isn't that what you're doing?'

He held out the draw knife to her. 'You were the one who thought it needed to be smoother.'

'You like it rough, don't you?' she challenged. But

from the words, his mind abruptly conjured a different meaning. One she'd never intended.

He imagined making love to her against the wall, her legs wrapped around his waist while he conquered her. He remembered the way she'd grasped his hand that night in the tent, arching in release when he'd touched her breast.

Rough, yes. He wouldn't mind that at all.

'Will you show me how to use the draw knife?' she asked softly.

Ragnar hesitated, for it would mean having her sit between his legs in front of him. Being so close to her would be a mistake, especially when she was trying to reconcile with Styr. He didn't want her pressed against his arousal, breathing in the scent of her skin. It would only deepen the temptation.

'No,' he told her, standing from his place. He walked over to her and stood facing her, so that no one else could hear his words. 'I don't want you that close to me.'

She gave a nod, but her eyes remained clouded. 'Nothing would happen, Ragnar.'

Did she believe that? After all the time they'd spent together, she thought he had that much restraint? He'd been going out of his mind over the past few weeks, dreaming of her. When he went to bed at night, he imagined her making love with Styr and jealousy boiled within his veins.

The only reason Ragnar had stayed in Dubh Linn was because he suspected Elena would soon learn that she wasn't pregnant after all.

He had sisters and all of them had borne children.

Most had been sick in the mornings, but all had fallen asleep in the middle of the day. His sister Jorga had complained of her growing midsection and she'd burst into tears over something as ridiculous as another woman holding a newborn. He was well accustomed to being around pregnant women and Elena had experienced none of their symptoms.

Her stomach had remained flat and he suspected the worst.

Even more than that, his friend Styr was treating her as if she were a ghost. He hardly spoke to his wife and, no matter how Elena tried to please him, it was clear the man had no interest in her.

'Go home to your husband, Elena,' he advised. 'We'll finish building on our own.'

Elena stared at the wall while Styr sat at the table for the meal she'd prepared for him. It was midday and her mind was filled up with uncertainty. Styr had been distracted all these weeks and he'd shown little joy in the prospect of a child.

No longer did he sleep close to her at night. He slept far away from her and not once had he touched her since they'd left Norway. He didn't love her any more, and he didn't want their baby.

He wanted the other woman, Caragh Ó Brannon.

The knowledge burned through her with a blend of anger and pain. For no matter what she did or said, her husband had fallen in love with someone else.

She took a bite of her own stew, but although the flavour was good, her stomach twisted at the idea of eating. Perhaps it was the child growing within her… or perhaps it was her own anxiety.

The truth shadowed her heart, filling her with unrest. The marriage with Styr had been arranged, yes. They had tried to be happy together. But he'd never loved her, no matter how she tried to change herself.

'Don't you like the food?' she ventured.

'It's good.' He tried to smile, but she suspected he would have said the same thing had she served him sawdust.

'Is there anything I can get for you?' she ventured. 'I cleaned your armour earlier today.' She didn't like how desperate she sounded, but she wanted conversation from him in some way.

'No, there's nothing.' He started to clear away the food, but she took it from him.

'I'll take care of it.' But at the grim look in his eyes, Elena set down the cup she'd taken. She needed to know if the growing distance between them could be healed at all. Was there any chance to bring back the husband who had been her friend? Or was he lost to her, now that he loved another?

He started towards the door, but she asked, 'Wait. Before you go…'

He paused to look at her and she steeled her courage. If he would not make the first move to ease the tension, *she* could.

Elena moved forwards to embrace him, hoping he would accept the affection. There had been a time when he'd hugged her often, stroking at her braid.

But though he accepted her arms around him, his

returning squeeze was hardly there at all. It was as if he were embracing a child, not his wife.

'I'll see you later,' was all he said when he departed. There was no kiss, no offer for more. He'd become a living, breathing stone with no life in him at all.

Elena stared at the remaining food and his cup. It was hard to catch the breath in her lungs, she was so angry at both of them. When had she become such a meek shadow of a woman? Why was she twisting her life around his, doing everything to please him when he couldn't even be bothered to speak to her?

He doesn't love you, her mind insisted. *He never did.*

Then why stay? Why keep trying to heal a marriage that held so many scars, it bled from the wounds they'd inflicted on each other?

The tears blinded her and she shoved the food and cup to the ground, overturning the table in her fury. She wanted to shatter something, to relieve the dark anger inside. But destroying their home wouldn't accomplish anything. Although the instinct was strong to put everything back in order, she forced herself to walk away.

Outside, the afternoon sun was high, casting brilliant rays over the settlement. Their home was built among the others, and all around were the sounds of conversation, weapons striking shields as men trained, and children running around. She stopped to watch them and at the sight of their young faces, the familiar heartache slid back.

This was why she stayed with a man who didn't love her. To give her unborn child a father. The idea of raising a baby alone, in a country filled with strangers, terrified her. Were it not for this child, she would divorce Styr.

It was simple enough to do—she merely had to announce her intentions in front of witnesses. She wrapped her hands around her slender midsection, wondering when she would feel the swell of new life. And whether it would change both of them.

It's a lot to ask of an infant, Ragnar had said. But what other choice was there? To bring this new life into the world without a father? She didn't want to look into her son or daughter's eyes and admit that their father had left them.

Though it destroyed her pride to remain married to a man who didn't want her, she would do what was necessary for this unborn miracle. She had no idea how to win back Styr's heart, but she would try. It was all she had left.

Her mind returned to thoughts of Ragnar. He might know what else she could do, since he was friends with Styr. But unbidden came the memory of sleeping with his arms around her. He had been such a comfort to her, she was grateful to him for his protection and companionship.

But there was more between them, much as she might try to push away the forbidden thoughts. She hadn't forgotten the warmth of his mouth or the stolen touch of his hand against her breasts. She closed her eyes, aware of how wrong it was. And yet…her own husband had turned to another.

Elena forced herself to walk back to the dwelling Ragnar was building with their kinsmen. She needed to see him again, to gain his advice.

If there was any hope of saving her marriage, he might know what to do. Or he could find out.

You just want to see him again, her mind taunted.

No. He was only a friend. But even as she continued towards the longhouse, she sensed that she would not like the answers he would give.

Ragnar had spent all afternoon with the hammer, pounding at the beams as the shelter took form. He was grateful for the physical activity, hoping it would exhaust him until he didn't dream of Elena any more. But she returned to the dwelling a few hours later and he couldn't guess why.

'May I join you?' she asked, coming to sit near him.

He didn't answer, but kept pounding the hammer. His mood was growing even darker and he knew the reason. The woman he loved was married to a man who didn't want her any more. Styr was only staying for the sake of the baby that Ragnar was more and more convinced didn't exist.

'Do you want a drink of water?' She poured some into a cup, moving closer. He didn't know what her reason was for coming here, but the last thing he wanted was for her to start taking care of him.

When he ignored her, she came closer with the drink, waiting. But when she lifted it towards him, he tossed the hammer aside and pushed the drink away. 'Stay away from me, Elena.'

Go back to Styr. Go back to your husband and leave me alone.

Her face went white, and she looked so stricken. He realised she had no idea why he was angry. She honestly didn't know the way she tempted him and got under his skin.

'I'm sorry. I'm in no mood to see anyone just now.' He calmed his anger and tried to push away the frustration.

'I came to ask for your help,' she said quietly. 'But if it's not a good time, I'll go.'

He doubted if it would ever be a good time. The longer he stayed near her, the more he wanted her. Ragnar rested his palms upon the wall for a moment, taking the time to regain control of his anger. She wanted his help, did she?

He turned to face her, walking closer while he waited for her to speak.

'What is it?'

'It's Styr,' she admitted. 'Ever since he came back, I don't know what I can do to please him.'

The flush on her face spoke of sharing a bed with her husband. Was she truly asking him what would please a man? No. He couldn't even begin to talk about that. 'We are *not* having this conversation.'

Her face turned scarlet. 'No, I didn't mean…that. We haven't—not since the baby.'

Relief crashed through him, though he knew it was wrong. Ever since he'd had his own moments with Elena, the idea of Styr touching her was enough to provoke him into violence. He was jealous in a way he couldn't name and believing that Styr had claimed her body was a torment in itself.

'He won't even talk to me,' Elena continued. 'He's so distant, I don't know what to do.'

'Why do you stay married to him?' Ragnar demanded. 'If you have no feelings for one another and you don't talk, what reason is there?'

'He's been good to me,' she said. 'And there's the baby.'

'You're not pregnant, Elena.' He couldn't stop himself from saying the words he believed. It had been too long and it was the only strand holding Styr and her together.

Elena's hands moved to her womb and she stood up. 'Yes, I am. It's been months now. I must be.'

The worry in her voice held enough fear that he wished he didn't have to say this to her. 'I've had sisters who have had children. If you were truly with child, you would be much bigger by now.' He returned to his hammer, adding, 'Go and speak with the midwife. She'll tell you.'

It was a cruel thing to cut down her dreams and he knew it. But if he was right, better for her to learn it now, rather than later.

When he turned back to Elena, her eyes filled up with tears. The visible heartbreak made him feel as if he'd just cut her off at the knees. But he wouldn't take back the words.

She hugged her waist, meeting his gaze. 'If there's no baby—'

'Then you have no reason to remain wed to him. Let him go, Elena. You'll be happier for it.' She looked as if he'd just knocked her down with the words and he hated seeing the pain on her face.

But Styr was in love with someone else, enough that he was grieving for the loss. Elena had no hope of winning him back. Not now.

'Come here,' Ragnar commanded, drawing her into an embrace. He pulled her close, not even caring who saw them.

She started crying and admitted, 'I've already lost him, haven't I?'

'You haven't lost me,' he said. Nor would she, even after all this. He refused to feel guilty about offering her comfort. Her tears dampened his tunic, but he didn't care at all.

When she finally left, he suspected that she would indeed seek out the midwife. And regardless of the answer, it wouldn't change the fact that she was still in love with Styr.

She hadn't gone to see the midwife. There had been no need.

After she'd begun bleeding that afternoon, Elena knew that Ragnar was right. There was no child and never had been. The realisation had drowned her in sorrow and she'd remained in bed the rest of the day, staring at the wall. Styr found her there and the interior of their house was dark, the fire burned down to only coals.

Though she'd cleaned up her earlier mess, she hadn't bothered to prepare anything for an evening meal. When Styr walked inside, he paused a moment and stared at her, seeming to sense that something was terribly wrong.

'What is it?' he asked.

Elena shook her head, pulling back the coverlet upon their bed. 'The baby.'

The baby that had never existed. Even speaking the

words made her grieve. It had broken away a piece of her heart to think that her greatest dream had never come to pass. She was still barren and might always be.

Styr was staring at her with such fear, she forced herself to tell him all of it. 'I was wrong,' she admitted. 'There never was a baby. I began bleeding today.'

The raw pain wrenched a sob from her and she couldn't stop herself from weeping. 'Sometimes a woman doesn't have her moon time…if she faces peril or times of fear.'

And certainly she'd endured that. Still, she'd never before missed her menses and she'd had every reason to believe she was with child. It made her question if she'd offended the gods or done something to deserve this barrenness.

Styr's arms came around her and she gripped him hard, still crying as she said, 'I wanted this so much.'

'I know.' His voice was heavy and she knew that he truly was sorry for her. He might not love her, but he did care. She clung to him and in that moment regretted the times when she'd pushed him away. Especially the times when he'd wanted to share her bed and she'd refused him.

It was just that she'd been so caught up in the desire for a child, after a time there was no joy in being together. That was her fault, not his.

'And I haven't been a good wife to you. Not the way I should have.' Not only because of the moments she'd spent with Ragnar, but…everything.

'I tried to keep everything orderly,' she continued. 'But it wasn't enough.' She now understood that he didn't care at all about whether their home was clean and organised. He'd never understood that it was her way of taking command of one aspect of her life, since she couldn't control her ability to bear children. It had annoyed him, though he'd never said it.

Elena stared at her husband, at his dark blond hair and the sadness in his eyes. Styr was a good man who deserved to be happy. She'd seen the way he'd looked at the Irishwoman—it was as if he'd lost the best part of himself. It had hurt, knowing that he had never loved her like that, not once in all five years.

'I never cared about the house.' He rubbed her back and the gesture of comfort somehow made everything worse. She didn't want his kindness now. Anger and frustration she could bear...but not the man who had once been gentle and tender.

'You wanted to travel across the seas,' she said. 'And I never let you go.' When there was dissent over who would become the next leader of their tribe, he'd taken her away from home rather than fight against his older brother to become *jarl*.

She'd been afraid to travel, for she hated sailing. But she'd gone with him to éire in a last effort to make him happy. Perhaps if she'd let him follow his own dreams, to sail across the seas to distant lands, he might not have resented staying at home.

'I knew you didn't want to travel with me,' he said. 'And if I was away, you couldn't conceive a child.' He raised his shoulders in a shrug as though it meant nothing that she'd held him back.

'That was your dream, not mine,' she said. 'I should have given you my blessing, but I was too afraid to be alone.'

A sliver of fear reached down her spine, making her question her courage now. She didn't want this life any more. She didn't want to live in the shadows as the wife he'd kept for reasons of honour, not love.

She wanted a man to look at her the way he had looked at Caragh.

For a moment, she pulled back to look into her husband's eyes. This man had remained at her side for so long, allying their families together. But he didn't love her. He never had.

It hurt more deeply than any pain she'd known, but the truth was there, before her eyes. He hadn't wanted to return to her. He'd been happy with the Irishwoman in a way he'd never been with her.

She needed to let him go.

Elena reached up to touch his cheek and admitted, 'I still love you, Styr.' Her heart remained heavy, wishing there was a way to mend the broken years between them.

Her husband didn't answer at first, but Elena didn't want lies or words of reassurance. 'Don't say it. I've known you too long and that isn't what you feel for me. Not any more.' She couldn't stop the tears that ran down her cheeks, knowing how much she was about to lose. Five years had been so long.

Her words hadn't been a lie. She *did* love him enough to do what was necessary now. And that meant making the decision to end this marriage and set him free. A tremor resonated in her heart, for he would be so angry with her. But it was the only chance they had at happiness.

'We had some good years together,' she whispered, through a smile she didn't feel.

'We did.' His hand came to stroke her hair and there was a thickness to his voice. 'And we'll have more.'

No. No, it was too late for that. He was grieving, not only for the loss of a child they'd never conceived, but for Caragh—the woman who had utterly captured his heart.

Her courage faltered a moment, but Elena knew this had to be done now, before she could change her mind. It was the best course of action for both of them.

'Will you walk with me?' she asked, hoping he would not guess what she was about to do. Her nerves were unsteady, but he nodded, holding her hand.

Elena led him towards Ragnar's house, knowing that this was where they both needed to be. Here, among friends, they would make a new beginning. She could only pray that Styr wouldn't despise her when it was over.

Glancing at the structure of the longhouse, she could smell the fresh thatch and wood shavings. She ran her hands over the surface of the logs, knowing that Ragnar had laboured for many hours.

'He'll finish it in another few days,' Styr said.

Elena didn't answer, but opened the door, her heart pounding wildly. Inside, Ragnar was seated with their friends at a long table. He was dressed in a leather tunic and leggings, his rough-cut brown hair framing a strong jaw and dark green eyes.

Those same eyes fixed upon her and in them, she saw a hunger. She froze a moment, caught up by the intensity. Then a moment later, he responded to something his kinsman said and Elena was left to wonder if she'd imagined it all.

Roasted pheasant and boar were on large platters, along with pitchers of ale. The men had been telling stories and laughing, but some of their discussion died down when they saw Styr and her.

Her heartbeat was pounding so fast, her ears were ringing. She knew her husband was curious as to why she'd brought them here. He might believe it was to spend time with their friends, but she had a different purpose in mind.

You must do this, her conscience insisted.

'There is something I would ask of you,' she said quietly to their friends. She had their full attention now and Styr's as well. He gave a slight nod and her heartbeat pounded faster. A roaring sensation filled her ears, but she continued. 'I ask you to bear as witnesses.'

Though she didn't want to look into her husband's eyes and see the anger, Elena forced herself to meet him squarely. She raised her voice so that everyone could hear her, but her gaze remained fixed upon him. 'I have been wedded to Styr for five years now. In that time, I have been barren and it is unfair of me to bind him in this marriage.'

She released his hand, her heart crying out as she said clearly, 'I divorce you, Styr Hardrata. In the presence of these witnesses.'

Thrice she spoke the words, until it was done.

Chapter Eleven

Styr appeared stunned at her proclamation and no one spoke in the house. When Elena caught a glimpse of Ragnar's reaction, his expression, too, was unreadable. Whether or not he cared, she could not say.

Better to leave now and let them believe what they would. She walked outside, returning to the house she'd shared with Styr. A lightheaded sensation rippled through her. It was done now.

He would not have admitted defeat, but she loved him enough to let him go. There was no sense in holding on to something that was never meant to be.

She heard his long strides approaching from behind her. 'You think to divorce me? Just like that, with no word of explanation?'

He gave her no opportunity to answer before he lashed out again. 'Why? I thought you wanted to try again!'

But there was no sense in trying, when his heart belonged to another. Whether or not he would admit it to himself, she could see it.

'We don't belong together, Styr. We never did and the gods refused to give us children.'

It was a possible reason, though she didn't truly believe that. In her heart, she suspected the fault had always been with her.

'Did I make you that miserable?' he demanded.

'Yes! And don't tell me I didn't do the same to you.' She stood, facing him with anger of her own. Whether he'd meant to or not, he'd made her unhappy every time he'd looked at her with disappointment. Every time he'd held his silence, while she'd done her best to make him love her.

In the end, she couldn't force him to have feelings for her. And she was weary of trying to shape herself into the woman he wanted instead of the woman she was.

Elena gripped her hands together to stop them from shaking. 'You tried. Both of us tried, but you were never happy. It doesn't have to be this way.'

At least, not for him. He had a woman who adored him. A woman whom he wanted…and she would never forget the sight of them embracing.

'I saw the way you looked at her, Styr. I saw the way she held you. She loves you. And you love her, the way you never loved me.'

She wanted to cry again, but instead it was a resonant pain that squeezed her heart. When he came up behind her and held her, it was not the embrace of a man who regretted what she'd done. There was thankfulness in it.

He never would have divorced her. He would have lived out the rest of his life, dreaming of someone else he could never have. And for that reason, she'd made the right choice. At least one of them could be happy now.

'I want you to go to her,' Elena said softly. 'Marry her, if she's the one you want. And perhaps you'll have the sons I could never give you.'

'What about you?' He spoke quietly, but there was compassion in his tone.

'I'll stay here for now. I don't know where I'll go after that.'

He dried her tears and took her hand in his, leading her to sit down. Instead of choosing the bed, she sank down to the floor, leaning against the raised pallet. Styr sat beside her.

'I'm sorry I wasn't the husband you needed.'

It was strange that he should be the one to apologise. Both of them had made mistakes, but she'd never expected him to say so.

'It wasn't terrible,' she assured him. 'There were some good moments.'

The early years had been awkward, but sweet. He'd tried to be a good husband, bringing her gifts and building her their own house. It had been a comfortable life, even if he hadn't loved her.

'Is this truly what you want?' he asked. 'A divorce?'

Asking her this now was hardly worthwhile. 'I've already done it, Styr.' She forced a smile past the tears. 'I don't need your permission to declare it before witnesses.'

Even so, she softened the words when she leaned her head against his shoulders. Silence fell between them, but it was no longer a silence filled with anger or regret. It was a wistful moment, of a marriage that had ended.

Styr stood after a time and went over to his belongings. He searched through them, before he retrieved something small, hiding it in his palm. 'I bought this for you, before we left Hordafylke.'

He revealed a small ivory comb with the goddess of Freya carved upon it. She took it, recognising it as a token of forgiveness between them. She combed her hair with it, then held it in her hands. 'It's beautiful.'

It was such an unexpected gift and she knew it would be the last. As she studied the ivory, she decided to share the memories of their marriage. For there had been good moments between them.

'I was so afraid on the morning of our wedding. So many women warned me that I wouldn't like our first time together. I thought you would be rough with me.' She managed a furtive smile. 'I should have known you'd never do anything to hurt a woman.'

'No. And I still never wanted to hurt you,' he admitted. 'Even when I met Caragh, I remained faithful.'

'But she makes you happy, the way I never did.' She reached out to touch his heart, knowing it was the truth. It embarrassed her to say it, but she wanted him to leave this night with no guilt. It had to be a new beginning for both of them.

'You made me happy, too. In a different way.' He held her close, stroking her hair. 'I want you to wed again. Not an arranged match, like ours was. But to a man of your choosing.'

Likely, he thought that would make her feel better. She had no doubt that he would find Caragh Ó Brannon and wed her, as soon as he could. But she had to decide what to do with her own life.

She didn't want to return to Hordafylke. There, she would have to explain to the others that she'd divorced Styr and why. Despite the fact that it was her decision, she didn't want to see their looks of pity.

Styr began talking about memories of their marriage that he'd enjoyed. Moments when they'd been younger, still learning about what it was to be man and wife. But she recognised it for what it was—sympathy. He was trying to make her feel better, to ease the blow to her pride.

She let him talk, even offering her own thoughts from time to time. But inside, the restless feeling grew. Her pride was shredded and she felt the impulse to do something rash. The urge was kindled even higher, with the reckless need to feel as if someone wanted her.

She couldn't remain here with a man who didn't want her, reliving the memories of a failed marriage. If she stayed, she would succumb to the tears of humiliation. She needed to leave right now. Though she could not wander the streets of Dubh Linn, she knew exactly where to go. Ragnar would never turn her away.

A sudden tension took hold in her stomach as she remembered the forbidden touch she'd shared with him. The caress that never should have happened. And yet it had left her reeling with desire.

Styr was starting to fall asleep and she urged him to lie down. He did and Elena remained seated on the floor. Once he was asleep, she stepped outside their home. It was long past midnight, but she wasn't tired at all. The restlessness had evolved into a yearning.

Though she didn't know what she would say to Ragnar when she got there, she wanted him to kiss her again. She wanted him to make her feel as if *someone* wanted her, even if her husband no longer did.

He was a good friend, a man she trusted.

She only hoped he wouldn't turn her away.

Ragnar jerked awake as a woman's mouth touched his. It was Elena who had slipped beside him. He knew it from her scent and the shyness of her kiss.

'What you are doing here?' he demanded in a whisper. It was only hours before dawn and several of his friends and kinsmen were sleeping around them.

She said nothing at first, though her body was pressed beside his. Her hands came up to his face. 'Don't send me away. I can't sleep in my own house this night.'

He was surprised she hadn't sent Styr away. After she had announced the divorce, Ragnar had expected his friend to return. The longer the hours had crept on, the more he'd wondered if perhaps Styr had argued with her to change her mind.

'He's going back to the Irishwoman,' Elena said softly. 'With my blessing.'

Pain laced her words and when she burrowed her face against his chest, Ragnar knew he could not force her to go. She needed a sanctuary and he could give that to her now.

'I'll find a bed for you,' he whispered, starting to sit up.

'No.' She pulled him back down and lay face to face with him. 'I want to be with you this night.'

Her meaning became clear when she pulled him back for another kiss. This time, a very different emotion cracked through him. She was tentative, trying to coax a response.

Her warm mouth moved against his, her tongue touching the seam at his lips. The raw desire to claim her, to conquer the lips that had tormented him over the years, was stronger than he'd ever known.

But he knew why she was here. And it wasn't because she wanted him. The dark truth was undeniable—she was using him to forget about her husband. She'd come to him, wanting an escape. And although his body was rejoicing in it, his brain was raging.

Ragnar kissed her back, but not as a gentle lover would. No, he became the aggressor, ravaging her mouth. She mistakenly believed that he would give her what she wanted. But he refused to be a substitute for the man she desired in her bed.

He fully intended to frighten her away, but instead she let out a shuddering breath, meeting his tongue with her own. She was aroused by this. He could sense it in the way her skin warmed beneath his hands and the way her back arched.

Her fingers pushed through his hair and his body hardened as she thrust her tongue against his. He could take her here, without anyone knowing of it. It was a matter of lifting her skirts and sliding between her legs. She would allow it, for that was why she'd come. He could silence her moans. The idea of joining with the woman he'd loved for so long was a dark temptation.

But she doesn't want you, the voice of reason reminded him. *She's using you to forget her pain.*

The more Ragnar thought of it, the angrier it made him. He didn't want to be her escape. If she had come to him because she'd genuinely cared, that might have changed his mind. Instead, he broke away.

'You don't want this, Elena.'

Her breathing had quickened and she traced her fingers over his cheek. 'Yes, I do,' she whispered. 'This has been the worst night I've ever endured and you were the only one I wanted to be with.'

God help him, but he wanted to believe it. In the shadowed darkness, he took her hand and led her to sit up. 'Come with me.'

Ragnar didn't want her here, not surrounded by so many kinsmen. He led her back outside, to the small lean-to where he'd stored grain and hay for the animals. The space was dark and enclosed, with no one to see them.

When he pulled the door closed, her hands came around his neck, pulling him near. 'Make me forget all of this,' she pleaded.

He tasted the desperation in her lips, mingled with the yearning of a lonely woman. If he were a cruel man, he'd take her offering. Tonight he would finally taste her skin and know the pleasure of loving her.

But he wasn't that man. And he didn't want his first moment with Elena to be like this.

'No.' He stepped back, and the cold night air spiralled between them. 'You're not thinking clearly right now.'

'I don't want to think at all.'

'I won't let you compare us,' he said harshly. He didn't care how stark the words were. 'I don't want to be the man you use, for the sake of forgetting your troubles. You're better than that, Elena.'

She let out a heavy sigh and reached for his hands. 'Ragnar, I didn't mean it in that way.'

'You did and you know this.' He pressed her back against the wooden wall, letting her feel his arousal pressed against her. 'If you want me, it won't be because you want to drown out the memories of another man. Especially when that man is my friend.'

'I'm sorry,' she whispered. She leaned her cheek against him, and added, 'It's just that...he never really wanted me. It was duty and a means of conceiving a child. Never out of joy.' She lowered her head. 'I always thought there was something wrong with me.'

The scent of her skin and the temptation of her flesh were starting to unbind his good intentions. 'Look at me,' he commanded. 'There's nothing wrong with you. You were two good people who weren't meant to be together.'

'Then who am I meant to be with?' she asked. 'I can't feel things the way a normal woman would. I didn't enjoy my marriage and there weren't any children to bring joy to it.'

He reached a hand up to her face and felt the presence of tears again. Freya forgive him, but he hated to see her cry. 'Don't, *kjære*. Not with me.'

He leaned in to kiss her, wanting only to reassure her. But her hands slipped beneath his tunic to touch his bare skin. She stroked his lower back and the touch tore apart his sense of responsibility.

She helped him remove the tunic and her hands moved over his skin, learning him. 'Why did you never marry, Ragnar? Any woman would be glad to call you her husband.'

Because he couldn't have *her*. Elena was the one woman he'd ached to possess. Though his body wanted to claim her now, he knew it would damage what there was between them.

'Do you want me to take you back?' he asked, ignoring her question. He wasn't going to bare his thoughts before her, not so soon.

'Not yet.' Her hands moved away from him and she stepped back. There was a rustle of fabric and then she admitted, 'I wasn't intending to use you tonight, Ragnar.'

'If you had, you'd regret it, come the dawn,' he said.

'Perhaps. But I wanted you to know…when you kiss me, I feel beloved.' She leaned in to embrace him and he inhaled sharply when her bare breasts touched his chest. Gods above, she'd let her gown fall to her waist. He could feel the taut buds of her nipples and at that moment, he lost sight of every shred of honour.

She had come to seduce him—that much was clear. But tonight he refused to let her direct him.

'This is your last chance to leave,' he said quietly, drawing his hands over her bare back. 'If you stay, you'll do as I command. And I'll claim your body, whether you will it or not.'

Thank the gods. The storm of tremulous feelings was flooding through her in a way she craved. She knew what there was between a man and a woman and didn't fear it. Styr had never hurt her and there were times when the sensations had pleased her.

But in the past two years, she'd been so consumed with thoughts of having a child, she could no longer take pleasure in the act.

Tonight would be different. Just the touch of Ragnar's hard body against her softness had evoked an aching desire she could not deny. He kissed her hard, plundering her mouth as he demanded her surrender.

She didn't yield to him the way he wanted her to. Instead, she kissed him back, trying to make him understand why she was here. She was tired of being a shadow, ignored and overlooked.

His mouth trailed down her collarbone, closer to her breasts. She wanted to feel the warmth of his kiss upon her nipples, to feel the pull of dark desire.

Instead, he circled ever closer, without giving her what she wanted. The proximity of his mouth was torture and between her legs, she grew wet with need. Elena stripped away the rest of her gown, stepping out of it until she was naked before him. She wanted to be consumed by Ragnar, to lose herself in this.

'Slow down,' he ordered. 'We have time.'

She didn't want him to take his time. She wanted a quick coupling, to release the tension and frustration inside. Just as she was about to speak, his tongue flicked against one nipple.

It was like the crack of a whip lashing over her body and she shuddered at the sensation. By the gods, she'd never known such a fevered reaction.

He echoed it with the other breast, his heated breath tormenting her. His hands moved over her hips to her bottom and he guided her legs apart.

'I want you crying out for me, before I fill you,' he

murmured against her ear. 'I want you so ready, you're shaking.'

His words deepened her arousal and when he bent to take her nipple in his mouth, she felt the sudden intrusion of his fingers sinking inside her. The shock made her knees buckle and her fingernails dug into his shoulders.

'Not enough,' he said, penetrating her with his hand and withdrawing. 'You came to me, wanting this. But it will be on my terms, not yours.'

She reached for the ties of his hose, wanting to feel his body against her. He was hard and powerful, and the excitement of his touch was already causing her to tremble.

Anticipation filled her imagination and as he kissed a path lower, his hands moved again. He filled her with two fingers while his thumb teased the hooded flesh of her womanhood.

It was dizzying, the feelings crashing over her. Though she shouldn't be here with him, not like this, it felt incredibly sinful to take pleasure from his forbidden touch. She was leaning in to him, opening her legs wider in preparation for more.

Her breathing was uneven as he continued to touch and tease. Her hand slipped beneath the waist of his hose and she was rewarded by the velvet softness of his length in her hand. When she tried to remove his clothing, he stopped her.

'Sit down,' he ordered, moving her towards a sack of grain. 'I've not finished with you yet.'

Elena obeyed and when he stopped touching her, she felt the coolness of the night air against her skin. Her

mind began to think more clearly and she suddenly realised that she'd divorced her husband and was about
to give herself to his best friend.

What did that make her? Was this the woman she'd
become? The rise of understanding made her feel awkward, uneasy about this choice.

But then his mouth closed over her breast, suckling
hard while his hand abruptly filled her. He blew against
the sensitive nipple, nipping at her flesh while he in-
vaded again and again.

Elena was in shock, unable to grasp the wild frenzy
of need that possessed her. He was in command of her
body, evoking a reaction she'd never felt before.

'Ragnar, I can't breathe.' She shuddered against him,
leaning back as her hands clutched his head. He slowed
the pace of his finger thrusts and she prayed he would
soon end this.

'I want you inside me,' she begged.

'You won't have me,' he countered, nudging his
thumb against the nub that was now a delicious torture.
'Not in that way. At least, not yet.' His breath moved
over her stomach, down to the hollows of her hips, and
she felt his mouth rest upon her mons.

His fingers remained sheathed within her and her
imagination bolted with a burst of heat as his mouth
moved closer. And when his tongue touched her intimate flesh, she came apart, writhing as the climax
ripped through her. She clenched against his fingers,
pulling his mouth back to hers. When she kissed him,
she pleaded, 'Now, Ragnar.'

Instead, he broke the kiss, his eyes narrowed. 'No.'

She didn't understand him, but when he adjusted the

ties of his clothing, she realised that he wasn't going to make love to her. He'd given her a searing taste of what it would be like to share his bed, but that was all.

He pulled her gown over her head, helping her to dress. As he did, his hands slid over her breasts, rekindling the need.

Confusion swelled up inside her, for he'd given her a sharp release, taking nothing for himself. And when he'd finished tying the laces of her gown, he leaned in to her ear.

'I won't let myself be used by any woman, *søtnos*. Not even you.'

Chapter Twelve

Ragnar continued building his house over the next few days, needing the distraction from Elena. Guilt weighed upon him from the night he'd touched her, despite the fact that she'd ended her marriage. He should have turned her away from the moment she'd come to him.

And yet it was impossible to release the years of longing. He'd been unable to refuse her, knowing that she'd needed someone to comfort her...but he never should have let things go that far. More than that, Elena had begun avoiding him, as if she regretted what they'd both done. Neither of them had been thinking clearly and he questioned what to do now.

For the past few years, he'd dreamed of the day when he was free to love her openly...and yet the invisible barriers had not lifted. He didn't delude himself into thinking she was over the loss of her husband.

It would take time to let go of five years. And even though she'd turned to him that night, he knew better than to think she'd wanted him.

Five years earlier

She was standing before the edge of the fjord, staring into the silvery water. Ragnar watched over Elena, just as the tall hills shadowed the water running between them.

Her hair was braided back from her temples, the long waving strands falling to her waist. The green apron she wore accentuated her slender waist and golden brooches fastened it near her shoulders.

'Come and stand with me,' she offered, turning to face him. Though she attempted a smile, he saw the rise of anxiety on her face.

Within another day, she would be married to Styr. The thought of it was like a fist squeezing the life from his throat.

'I'm nervous about what will happen on the morrow,' she admitted. 'I know that's foolish, since I've known Styr for so many years.' She crossed her arms, rubbing at her shoulders.

'He will make a good husband for you,' Ragnar agreed. His friend was the second-born son of their *jarl* and more likely to be the next leader. 'You've nothing to fear.'

She reached for his hand, guiding him along the edge of the lake. Though it was only a gesture of friendship, inviting him to walk with her, the simple touch of her palm upon his was a jolt of fire from their joined hands all the way to his heart.

'I know I should be happy about this marriage,' she said. 'He's handsome, and I do think I love him. But it's just—' Her words broke off and she shrugged. 'He intimidates me.'

Whereas she'd never held any such reservations with him. A rise of frustration came forth, for he was a warrior, the same as Styr. He was a stronger fighter now and he could defeat any enemy with his sword.

'And I don't intimidate you?' he teased, his voice holding a darker edge.

There was a sudden flush on her cheeks and she averted her gaze. For a brief moment she hesitated, before saying, 'Of course not. We're friends and you would never harm me.'

He drew her to stand before him, his height making it easy to stare down on her. 'I can be very intimidating,' he said, leaning even closer.

When Elena had to tilt her head back, she returned an honest smile. 'To some.' She rested her palms on his chest and gripped his tunic as she tilted so far back, he had to hold her to keep her from falling.

A slight laugh escaped her before he set her back on her feet. 'Styr will take good care of you. Or I'll kill him.'

They continued walking along the edge, until they reached a cluster of large stones surrounding a pool.

'I'll tell him that,' she teased in return. But there was still a flustered air about her. When she leaned back against one of the stones, she appeared uneasy.

Ragnar came to lean beside her and he stared up at the sky. 'There's something else bothering you.'

She wouldn't look at him, but agreed, 'Yes.'

'Go on, then.' He waited for her to talk to him,

though he wasn't certain he wanted to hear her confession.

She let out a sigh and at last turned to him. 'I'm worried I won't please him. I know he doesn't feel the same way about me.' Her face turned red and she shook her head. 'It's nothing you can help with.'

'You don't have to marry him,' he said suddenly. *You could marry me.* The words were on the edge of his mouth and he bit them back before he could say anything more.

'My father would be furious with me if I didn't. It's a strong alliance.'

'And one that doesn't have to be made through your marriage. Another of your sisters could marry him.'

But Elena shook her head. 'No, all the arrangements have been made. My father has spent a great deal of silver on the feast and the celebration. It will happen, whether I'm ready for it or not.'

He reached out to take her hand. *Tell her*, his conscience urged. *Give her the choice instead of remaining silent.*

But instead of words, he laced his fingers with hers and moved in front of her. His time was running out. If he said nothing, she would marry his best friend the next day. He was torn between his own desires and what was best for her. She deserved a man of high wealth and social standing. Not someone like him, only good for wielding a sword.

'You always have a choice, Elena.' He released her hands, watching her sea-green eyes. He wanted her to know that he would always be there for her.

The colour stole away from her face, but she didn't

take her eyes from his. Her lips parted and he wondered if she would allow him to kiss her. To show her the words he'd buried away behind years of frustration.

Ragnar rested his palms on either side of the stone, giving her every chance to pull away. His heart was quickening within his chest and her own breathing had grown shorter, as if she were afraid of what there could be between them.

Neither spoke and he sensed that if he made a single move, the moment would shatter.

'Ragnar,' she whispered, reaching up to touch his cheek. The warmth of her fingers pooled inside him, awakening a hunger he'd held back for years. He wanted this woman with every breath that was in him.

'Elena!' came another voice.

The spell was broken immediately and she pushed him back, moving away from the shelter of the rocks. Ragnar closed his eyes, damning himself for not speaking. The chance was gone now.

He followed her and saw her father, Karl, approaching with Styr. 'There you are,' the older man said. 'Before you are wedded, I thought you and your betrothed should spend one last day together. I've made arrangements for the both of you.' The shielded glare he sent towards Ragnar spoke volumes.

Styr, on the other hand, greeted him warmly. 'Tonight, our kinsmen are having a celebration to mark the last day I am unwed. You'll come, won't you?'

Ragnar nodded. The idea of getting drunk to the point of oblivion was a welcome one.

'Go on, then,' Karl said. 'I want to speak with Ragnar a moment about the preparations.'

The older man waited until they were out of earshot and he sent Ragnar a dark look. 'Stay away from my daughter. Or I'll see to it that you're whipped within an inch of your life.'

'You can do nothing to me.' Ragnar drew himself up to his full height, resting his hand upon his sword hilt. If Karl so much as dared to threaten him, he wouldn't hesitate to defend himself.

A slow smile curved across the man's face. 'Whose word will they believe? I am a respected leader and a friend to Styr's father. The *jarl* won't allow anyone to interfere with this marriage. I could claim that you've stolen silver from me. Or perhaps you've dishonoured another of my daughters. My words hold more power than you'll ever have.'

Karl spat upon the ground. 'That's as much as your life is worth, Ragnar Olafsson. You'll never come near any of my daughters.'

A black rage swirled inside of Ragnar, and he longed to crack his fist across the man's jaw for the insult.

But it was her father. He couldn't lay a hand on the man or risk Elena's hatred. His hands were clenched at his sides and he struggled to contain his fury. The need to release the violence was rising hotter and once the man was gone, he ran along the edge of the lake. He drove his pace harder, running past the quadrants of houses until he reached his father's house on the furthest side.

But even the exertion did nothing to diminish the vicious hatred. He was sick to death of being treated like an outcast. He'd trained hard, learning to wield every weapon until he'd mastered them.

He saw an axe lying near the woodpile and reached for it. As he split the wood chunks, the rhythmic motion of the work did nothing to calm the storm brewing inside him.

Not good enough, the wood sang as the metal bit through the log. He hacked at the pine, letting the rage pour through him. Sweat dripped from his brow and his muscles strained as he worked.

The door to their house opened and he saw his father stagger outside, a wooden cup in his hand.

'I saw you go off with Elena,' came his father's voice from behind him. 'But she's promised to Styr. She would never leave him for a man like you.'

Ragnar let the axe sink into the wood before he spun to face Olaf. 'We're only friends.'

'Are you?' Olaf met his gaze with hardened eyes of his own. 'Or did you want to steal her away because you think you're in love with her?'

Ragnar could smell the mead upon his father's breath. But this time, when the man's fist came towards his jaw, he blocked the blow with his forearm and retaliated with a fist to his father's head.

Olaf exploded with anger, but Ragnar welcomed the fight. For so many years, he'd been too young to defend himself. Too weak to shield himself from the blows that had cracked his ribs and broken his nose.

This time, he returned blow for blow, releasing the years of anger. Fighting back for the sake of the young boy who had suffered in silence, knowing there was no one who cared to stop the man.

His father's blood was upon his hands, but the bleakness of his past drowned out all else. He heard nothing, saw nothing except the man who had taunted him. There was only the mindless blur of exchanging blows.

'Ragnar!' Elena was hurrying towards him, but even she could not stop him from the destruction that had been unleashed.

He didn't care what happened to him any more. His own father hated him and now Ragnar would have his own vengeance. His fist crunched against bone and he was dimly aware that his father was on the ground, unmoving.

Styr dragged him back and Ragnar fought to free himself. 'Don't,' his friend warned. 'He's nearly dead as it is.'

Dead. The word sank into him like talons. The haze of anger lifted and he saw Elena staring at him as if he were a monster. His father's face was covered in blood and Ragnar stared at his own hands in disbelief.

By the gods, what had come over him? He hardly knew himself and he took a step back when Elena came near.

'Are you all right?' she whispered.

'Stay back.' He didn't trust himself. Never before had such an uncontrollable rage come over him. His hands were shaking and he realised an undeniable truth. He'd become just the man his father had been.

Violent. Filled with unstoppable rage.

'Send for a healer,' Styr ordered Elena, and she hurried off. Ragnar couldn't move and when his friend guided him away, he barely heard the man's words.

'I'll swear to any witness that he raised a hand to you first. He deserves this after the way you were beaten all your life.'

But Ragnar could only shake his head. *He* had fought, out of rage and frustration. This was his fault and he dreaded the thought of looking into the *jarl's* eyes, admitting his deed.

'I'll go,' he said. But his friends had refused to allow it.

Olaf had died a few days later. Whether it was from the wounds or from the illness of drinking too much, it didn't matter. From that moment on, Ragnar had known that a darkness lurked within him, a violent temper beyond his control.

It was for that reason that he could not be with Elena. Though he wanted to start over, to try to be the right man for her, he feared the violence that lay buried inside.

Elena didn't know the man he was. She believed he was a good man, a close friend whom she could turn to, now that her life had fallen apart.

He wasn't a good man. A good man would never have touched her so intimately, taking advantage of her wild grief that night.

Ragnar was grateful when Styr left with a few men to return to Gall Tír. At least now he wouldn't have to face his friend, after what he'd done to Elena.

Elena walked through the marketplace, her thoughts in turmoil. In her mind, she'd replayed every moment of the night she'd tried to seduce Ragnar. Never in her wildest imaginings had she guessed that there could be such fire between them.

He'd brought her to fulfilment, taking nothing for himself. And she had to admit to herself that not once in her marriage to Styr had she felt such a connection. She'd revelled in Ragnar's touch, wanting so much more from him. Confusion spun within her mind, for she'd never guessed that it could be like this with any man. Especially her closest friend.

Or was he a friend any more? By the grace of Freya, he'd made her feel desirable. He'd awakened her to sensations she'd never dreamed of and she no longer knew what to believe. She'd been blinded, never seeing the man who was beside her all along. Although she didn't know what was happening between them, the line of friendship had been breached.

Shame darkened her cheeks, for she'd wanted him to lie with her, to make her feel desirable, when that wasn't fair to him. He'd all but shoved her away that night, claiming he would not allow her to use him.

And now he was avoiding her.

Elena knew why. Yet she didn't want to turn away, behaving as if nothing had happened. She wanted to spend time with Ragnar, trying to make sense of the muddled thoughts in her mind. They had grown so close when they'd been stranded together and she'd come to rely upon him. Now that she was alone again, she didn't want their friendship to end because of her foolish impulse.

She finished making her purchases in the marketplace, while her kinsman Hring shadowed her. Though she would have preferred to go with Ragnar, she'd hardly seen him these past few days.

The sound of merchants arguing with one another blended with the noise of animals being herded through the streets. Elena spied two children chasing one another and it evoked the ache of envy within her. The dream of bearing a child hadn't faded, despite the years. She still wanted to cradle an infant in her arms, no matter how long she had to wait.

Her gaze shifted to the crowds of people and in the shadows, she saw many children with lean faces, their eyes revealing hunger. Some were born of slaves and had almost nothing to call their own. Others had lost their parents in raids.

She walked deeper into the city and in one section the scent of smoke lingered. Several fires had been set by the Danes a few weeks ago, after she'd returned with Styr. At the sight of the skeletal houses, Elena was glad she'd been gone during the attack. She couldn't imagine what horrors that night must have wrought.

She frowned, suddenly realising that many children might have been orphaned that night if their fathers or mothers had fought for them. They might need someone to take care of them, if they had no living relatives.

The idea took root within her, circling with possibility.

'Where is Ragnar?' she asked Hring suddenly. She wondered what he would think if she fostered some of the orphans. It would give her a sense of purpose, a way of filling up the endless hours of the day.

'He's been spending his time sparring against some of the Irish. They wager on whether or not he'll win. It's a good way to earn silver.'

Elena frowned, not wanting to think of it. Although Ragnar was undeniably a strong fighter, if he defeated many men, it would also give him more enemies—

enemies who wouldn't hesitate to hunt him down and take back their silver.

'Will you take me to him?' she asked quietly.

Hring obeyed and they crossed through the crowd of people gathering to watch the fighters. Elena pushed her way to the front and saw Ragnar standing off to the side, bare from the waist up. His skin was oiled and it was clear from the blood on his lip that he'd already fought.

She met his gaze and saw not a trace of remorse in him. He'd come here wanting to fight and judging from the pouch at his waist, it seemed that he'd won a few matches.

Elena ignored the people around her and strode forwards to speak with him. Had he forgotten the arrow wound in his leg so soon? Why would he do this? Though she was angry, she forced herself to hold her tongue.

When she stood before him, she suddenly felt small, in contrast to his strength. His biceps were so thick, she couldn't span them with both palms. The gleam of his skin caught her attention and her mouth went dry. Although she knew the oil made it more difficult for an enemy to seize him, she could not help but wonder if a woman had helped to rub it into his skin.

A jolt of resentment caught her and once again, she felt uncertain about her feelings for this man. There was no reason to be jealous.

Yet she could not deny the invisible ties between them, especially after the night he'd touched her.

'I would like to speak with you, if you've finished here,' she said in a low voice.

'And if I haven't?' He crossed his arms and again she saw the corded muscles flex across his broad chest.

Her pulse tightened with frustration, but she reached out to rest her hand upon his heart. Slowly, she drew her palm over his oiled skin. 'Please.'

A low hiss sounded from him and his dark green eyes flared. There was the sound of men laughing and a few ribald jokes. Ragnar silenced them without a word and his hand came to rest upon the back of her neck. When he guided her away, his hand wasn't at all gentle.

Hring was following them, but once they were away from the others, Ragnar ordered the man to return home alone.

'Do you want to put on your tunic?' Elena asked, feeling suddenly awkward that he was still half-clothed.

'What I want is to know why you interrupted.' His anger made it clear that he didn't appreciate her interference. She was taken aback by it and her first instinct was to retreat and apologise.

But then, that was what she would have done with Styr. She'd allowed herself to fall away into the background, never once voicing her own opinions.

That woman was gone. Now, she would speak her mind and, if Ragnar did not care for it, what did it matter?

'You shouldn't fight among the men,' she said. 'It's dangerous and I don't want you to be hurt.'

'It's nothing I'm not used to, Elena,' he responded, starting to escort her back.

But she refused to be mollified. 'You could die.'

'Not always. Sometimes when blood is drawn, a victor is chosen.'

He made it sound as if there was nothing to fear. But she'd seen fights before and didn't delude herself into thinking that a man could walk away from every battle. 'It isn't worth the broken ribs or the risk of dying,' she told him.

'It's a way for me to earn a living. Unless you'd rather I went raiding with the others and left you here.' His palm touched her spine as he guided her through the people.

'I don't want you to leave, no. But neither do I think you should wager your fighting against theirs.'

He didn't answer her at first. When they reached her house, Elena stopped. 'Why are you doing this?'

'Because I need the distraction.' His face turned fierce and she felt her body responding to his words, knowing exactly why he was distracted. Although he could fight to release the restless energy in him, she could not do the same. And with each day that passed, she found herself searching for a way to fill the hours.

'Fighting is my skill, Elena. I'm not a merchant or a sailor. It's not who I am.'

She knew that and was well aware that he kept up his daily training to maintain strength and agility. In his eyes, she saw the stony pride. It wasn't doubt in his abilities. But this was about a risk she didn't want him to take.

'Why don't you build houses?' she suggested. 'You're strong and you have a good eye for it.'

'No, you're the one with the eye for it,' he countered. 'It's not what I want, Elena.'

She knew that, but it was the only thing she could

think of. 'I worry about you. I don't want you to be hurt.'

'Is that the only reason?' he demanded. His voice deepened and she was caught up in the spell of his green eyes.

'No,' she whispered.

Ragnar reached for her hand and she threaded her fingers with his. The warmth of his palm was a touch that pulled her deeper into an awareness of him.

'I would never want anything to happen to you,' she said quietly. 'And I want things to be as they once were between us.'

He pulled her closer, leaning in against her ear. 'You already crossed the line, *søtnos*. It won't ever be the same.'

Her face coloured and she bit her lower lip. There was a new tension between them, now that Styr was gone. And it was entirely her fault, for seeking him out that night. No longer was there the easy sense of camaraderie between them. It felt as if she'd not only lost her husband, but she'd also lost her best friend.

'Don't waste your pity on me, *kjære*. I'll do what I must to earn my way.'

'It's not pity,' she insisted. And although he likely wanted to turn from her now, she wanted to confront him, to make him see the truth.

Elena opened the door and waited for him to follow. He hesitated, crossing his arms as if he had no desire to enter. But a moment later, he did.

The air within her home was cool, for the fire had died down. Yet the anger emanating from Ragnar was a fire in itself. He didn't want to be here; that much was clear.

Elena set down her basket and added a few bricks of peat to the hearth. The space had grown tighter somehow and she felt her skin rise with gooseflesh in memory of the other night. His silent stare was unnerving her right now.

'I don't like fighting with you,' she said at last. 'I used to be able to talk with you about anything. After all that's happened, I don't want to lose that.' She reached out to take his hand and his rough palm was warm against hers.

His expression remained dark and stoic. 'You don't want a man like me, Elena.'

From deep inside, she found a courage she'd never expected. 'But you want a woman like me. Don't you.' It wasn't a question. She kept her eyes locked upon him, daring him to walk away.

Ragnar stepped forwards, backing her against the wall. Instead of feeling cornered, she felt as if she'd fallen under his possession.

She didn't understand the power Ragnar held over her, but she couldn't tear her gaze away from him. Once again, the sudden ripple of awareness slid over her body, making her wonder what was happening between them.

'I've always wanted a woman like you,' he murmured. 'But you deserve better.'

'I think you're afraid of me.' Another breathless flood of warmth passed over her. She didn't understand the stormy feelings, but she didn't want him to walk away now.

'You don't owe me anything, Elena.'

She stared at him, realising that he was trying to push her away. He didn't want or need her opinions.

But this time, his words fired up more anger. She *did* care about what happened to him, whether he believed it or not. 'I owe you my life,' she said. 'You guarded me when we were both stranded and you saved me from the men who tried to attack me.'

She took a step forwards, adding, 'Fighting to save lives is one matter. Fighting for profit is too grave a risk.' She softened her tone, trying to make him see. 'I don't want anything to happen to you, Ragnar. You're—' She struggled to find the right words. 'You're important to me.'

'No.' He pulled her hands away from him, holding them fast. 'You're only hurting after losing your husband. You want someone to take his place.'

Did he truly believe that? Elena frowned, because she didn't want another husband. She simply wanted Ragnar to be safe after all that they'd endured together. 'That's not true.'

'What about the other night when you came to me?' His gaze locked upon hers. 'Did you think I wouldn't guess why you were there?'

His fury was seething and she'd had enough of his suspicions. 'I came to you for comfort.' She stood up to him, adding, 'I thought we were friends.'

'I'm not your friend, Elena.' His voice cracked against the silence like a roll of thunder.

'No,' she whispered. *You're more than that.*

Anticipation heightened within her, the memories

of his touch compelling her. He said nothing and she leaned back to look into his dark green eyes.

'I feel as if I don't even know you,' she admitted. 'Not the way I thought I did.'

'You know exactly who I am.' His body tightened with tension. 'And you know what I've done in the past.'

'What happened to your father wasn't your fault.' Elena reached up to frame his face in her hands. 'I don't blame you for it.'

Ragnar strode away from her, as if he didn't want her touch. He tossed his weapons, one by one on the table before he crossed over to her. 'Don't make the mistake of believing I'm safe, Elena. When Styr was between us, honour kept my hands off you.' Slowly, he took her hand in his, leading her towards the bed. He pressed her back on the mattress, trapping her wrists with his hands until she lay beneath him. 'I can't make that promise now.'

Her heartbeat slammed within her chest as she felt the evidence of his arousal pressed close. Her body responded instantly, flaring with needs she couldn't name. 'You're trying to frighten me.' When he held her imprisoned in this way, she felt like a conquest of battle, about to be taken. But she was not afraid. Not of the man whom she knew would die before harming her.

Ragnar's eyes were like stone, his mouth a firm slash. He moved in lower until she felt the weight of his body against her.

She knew he was waiting for her to push him away. He was trying to provoke her into hatred and she could not name the reason. But she saw through his actions to the man who believed that he was worth nothing.

'Tell me to leave you alone,' he demanded, while his mouth descended to the softness of her throat. A thousand shivers broke forth. Though she knew she should speak, no man save Ragnar had ever made her feel this way.

He was reaching past the years of hurt, pushing back the boundaries until she was made new again. She was weary of being made to feel that her body was only meant for childbearing and that she was a failure. She closed her eyes, savouring the sensation of his mouth.

'It's too soon for this,' he said against her skin. He moved his hand up the hem of her skirt until his palm touched her bare skin. 'If you let me touch you, you'll hate me for it.'

In spite of his dark anger, the merest pressure of his fingers sent her body into shock. He drew his hand between her thighs, his knuckles brushing against her intimate opening.

She was wet already, almost ashamed at how fast he'd made her respond. His expression was unyielding and she forced herself not to move. Ragnar fumbled with the ties of his leggings and, a moment later, she felt his arousal pressed against her.

'Is this what you want from me?' he demanded. 'To forget about Styr by using me?'

'No,' she breathed. But his actions were so unexpected, she couldn't stop the thrill of desire that pushed through her. Needs pounded within her veins and she wanted him closer still, hoping he would slide inside.

Elena revelled in the turbulent desire that he'd kindled. It had been such a long time since she'd been with a man. And this forbidden lover brought out a side to her that she'd never known was there.

He was swollen and hard. A moment later, he lifted her to straddle him. His hands dug into the mattress, his eyes flaring. 'I swear, I won't touch you. If this is what you want from me, you'll have to take it yourself.'

His fury held a violent edge that frightened her. He was trying to prove a point and though she ought to be ashamed, she'd never imagined it would go this far. She sat upon his lap, her skirts tangled in her knees. Likely he expected her to balk and refuse him.

He would never expect her to take the offering.

Elena reached for his erection. He was large and firm, his skin like heated silk. The moment she took his shaft in one hand, he nearly sat up, giving a sharp intake of breath.

Without speaking, she held him, fisting his length while she adjusted her skirts. He was trying to intimidate her, and it had nearly worked...except that she'd never felt such arousal before.

She wanted him inside her, despite the cold rage. He would hate her for this and she didn't care.

Gently, she pushed the rounded head of him into her moist entrance, a cry escaping her at the delicious friction. Ragnar sat up, his hands clenching her hips. There was a blend of lust and hatred in his eyes, as if he'd never expected her to obey him.

She began to move up and down against him and the act took on a more primal note. With both of them clothed, she could only lose herself in sensation, for she could not see his body entering hers. She could only feel.

It was like a steel dagger sheathed within her as she continued to move against him, thrusting gently.

'You didn't think I would, did you?' she accused. She lifted his hands to the thin linen covering her breasts, needing his touch to push her harder.

But he let them fall back to his sides. 'No. And I'll not help you in this, either.'

His words struck her cold and she understood, then, that he truly believed this was about using him. Her conscience cried out at how wrong it was, while her body continued to squeeze him, thrusting and withdrawing.

There was perspiration on his brow and a tightness on his features. He was trying not to take pleasure and the more he fought her, the more she decided that she *would* enjoy this.

She unfastened the brooches that held her apron against her gown, then loosened the laces until her bodice fell lower. With her own hands, she reached for her breasts, letting him see them as she rode him at her own pace.

The sight of her bare flesh *did* evoke a reaction, for she sensed him pressing back. With her hands, she caressed her own nipples, letting him look his fill. No longer did she care that he wasn't going to touch her. The heady sensation of being in command was something she'd never before experienced.

Always she'd been beneath her husband, accepting him into her body. Never had she taken him. Her breathing went unsteady and she bounced harder, pinching her own nipples as she rode him. Ragnar's eyes were closed, his face taut as he struggled against her.

He was an iron shaft within her, so rigid—she had never felt so filled. *She* had done this to him. And by the gods, she would bring him to such a release, he would regret what he'd said to her.

With one hand on her breast, she moved the other down her body to the place where they were joined. Her finger and thumb surrounded him as she sank upon his erection.

More. She wanted him writhing beneath her and she increased the pace. He closed his eyes, his face strained as she continued to thrust against him. The pressure against her sensitive nub was enough to make her come apart, shuddering as the pleasure crested within.

He was fighting to breathe and she squeezed him hard, demanding, 'Did you feel the way you pleasured me, Ragnar?' She never ceased her motions and she saw how close he was to the edge. 'It felt so good.'

Her words were what changed him. His hands came against her hips, jacking against her with violent thrusts as he filled her. A groan tore from him as he emptied himself, taking the release he needed.

Elena lay atop him, her heart thundering inside. She rested her cheek against him, her body still filled with his heat. Her thighs were slick with his essence and it suddenly occurred to her that this joining might result in a child. She'd not considered it before, but what if it was Styr who could not sire children? What if Ragnar could give her the gift that she wanted most?

He didn't embrace her or whisper words of love. Instead, he gently extricated himself from her body and adjusted his clothing, rising from the bed. Without a word, he left her there.

Leaving her to wonder what she'd just done.

Chapter Thirteen

Ragnar didn't see her for a full day. He avoided Elena, furious with himself for what he'd allowed to happen.

Last night had been his mistake, for thinking boldness would push her away. Never in his life had he imagined Elena would take him. The memory of her haunted him, of her pliant flesh and the way she'd taken her release from him.

He'd let her use him. His body had savoured the night of joining with her, feeling her body sheathing him. And yet, there had been no love in it. The act was empty, a means of easing physical desire, but nothing more.

It burned him that he'd sunk to those depths. And although he loved her still, the need to create distance was strong. He needed to separate from her, to start over.

He walked through the city, his hand resting upon his sword hilt as he wandered. He hardly knew where he was going, nor did he care. But no matter how he might try, he couldn't escape the guilt and frustration inside him.

He hungered for Elena in a way that bordered on

madness. It strongly tempted him to take her, to claim her like a prize of war. But he knew better than to believe that she might care for him.

He walked towards the centre of the city, but before he made it there, he was stopped by his kinsman Hring. 'Elena sent me to find you. She asked if you would escort her while she's searching the city.'

Ragnar frowned. What would she be searching for? 'Why wouldn't she ask you?'

His friend shrugged. 'I offered, but she said she wanted to speak with you. She told me if you wouldn't come, she would go alone.'

Ragnar had little desire to talk, but neither did he want Elena exploring dangerous parts of the city. As he walked back with his kinsman, he questioned whether she had told Hring the truth—or whether it was merely an excuse to see him.

His instincts warned him to stay away, but then, he knew how stubborn Elena could be. If she'd made up her mind to go into the city, then she would do it, with or without him.

He found her inside her home, scrubbing the interior from top to bottom. There was no speck of dirt, save on the hard earthen floor. The coverlet on her bed gave no evidence of the night they'd shared. When he closed the door behind him, she looked up from her work and nearly toppled the bucket of water.

'You startled me.' She set down the cloth she'd been using and dried her hands on her apron. 'But I am glad you're here. I wanted to ask for your help.'

He remained beside the door, waiting for her to

speak. She seemed preoccupied, keeping her face turned away from him. No doubt she was having regrets about what had happened last night.

'I started thinking about the Irish children,' she said, her gaze fixed upon the ground. 'I know the Danes raided the city several weeks ago. Many people died in the fires, and I—I wondered about those who were orphaned.'

Already Ragnar could guess what she was proposing. He waited for her to continue and at last she met his gaze.

'Not everyone has family,' she continued. 'I saw a few who appeared half starving. Someone should take care of them.'

'And you want my help in searching for any abandoned children,' he predicted.

'Yes.' She faced him and in her eyes he saw the concern. 'I have nothing to do right now. No one to take care of. No child of my own.'

'Not yet,' he said quietly. Although it wasn't likely that she would bear a child after last night, the possibility was there.

Elena let out a slow breath, colour rising in her cheeks. 'No. Not yet.' She rubbed her arms, as if she felt a sudden chill. 'Are you angry about…what I did?'

Ragnar leaned against the wall and regarded her. 'It won't happen again.' Although the night had brought him unspeakable pleasure, if they became lovers, it would only bring them closer. He didn't want her trying to replace Styr with him.

Then, too, around Elena, he could hardly control himself. The moment he'd been sheathed inside her, he'd lost sight of all else. The walls could have caught on fire, and he'd have been completely unaware of it. The physical release had been so powerful, he'd been lost in sensations that drowned out his sense of reason.

'I wasn't using you,' she whispered. 'And I spoke the truth when I said I care about what happens to you. We've endured too much.'

He didn't want her spinning off dreams of the two of them together. 'I'm not the man you need, Elena.'

She studied him a moment. 'I don't think you know what you need, Ragnar.'

'And you do?' he prompted.

She reached for a basket, filling it with food and drink, before she hung it over one arm. With a shrug, she said, 'I think you're trying to punish yourself. As though you don't believe you deserve to be happy.'

He ignored her words, but stood in her path, blocking her way to the door. 'I'll guard you while you search, Elena. But nothing more.'

She held motionless for a long moment, searching his gaze. Then she took his hand in hers and raised up on tiptoe. 'For now.'

The light kiss she pressed to his cheek was like a physical brand and he realised that she'd cast down a challenge of her own.

A challenge to resist her.

Elena watched Ragnar from the corner of her eye. He remained at her side and whenever they passed another Norseman, his hand came to rest upon her spine. He wore a chainmail corselet with a sword at his waist and another dagger in a hidden fold of his cloak.

'Are you expecting to be attacked?' she asked, uncertain why he was so tense. The dark expression on his face held a hidden threat to others. Though she spoke in a lighter tone, she knew that he'd made enemies here.

'Have you forgotten the Danes who tried to make us into slaves?' he said.

'No.' But even so, one look at Ragnar would terrify any would-be assailant.

His grip tightened upon her palm as he guided her towards the outskirts of Dubh Linn. 'It's been only one moon since the Danes attacked the city. I wouldn't put it past them to try again,' he told her.

They walked for a mile and his mood didn't lighten. He seemed to study every face, searching for the subtle signs of a person concealing a weapon they were about to wield.

Beneath the harsh scents lay the charred memory of the night the Danes had attacked. The remnants of ash and burned longhouses stood all around them. Several men were attempting to repair the damage, lifting logs into place, while others wielded an axe to notch the wood.

As they walked further, she leaned in closer to Ragnar. Though it was meant to seek his protection, he stiffened at her proximity.

She tried not to let it bother her, but it reminded her of the way Styr had not desired her. Of how she'd felt like a cold, unfeeling wife, never able to enjoy marital pleasures. At least, not until she'd shared a forbidden night with Ragnar.

Her mind was tangled up in confusion, not knowing what to think of him. He'd been there for her always, a friend she'd come to rely on. But now he was avoiding her and she didn't know how to mend the breach between them. It was as if he wanted nothing to do with her.

Words wouldn't mean anything to him. Ragnar was a man of action.

His eyes missed nothing, as they moved into the shadowed parts of the city. He kept his expression rigid, letting other men see that he would murder them where they stood if they dared to threaten her.

When they reached the outskirts of the market, they passed by the *thralls* who were being auctioned. There was a woman being led up to the block, her hands bound before her. She wore a shapeless dress and her eyes remained fixed upon the ground.

Elena winced at the sight and she could almost imagine herself in the woman's place. 'Thank you for saving me from that fate.'

'I would never have let them take you, that night on the ship.' Ragnar gripped her hand to emphasise his words. 'Our men may have survived it…but it's harder for a woman.'

His words were underscored when the slavers stripped away the gown, baring the woman's naked body to those about to bid upon her. *May the gods have mercy*, she prayed. The female slave was heavily pregnant.

'It's not right,' Elena argued. '*Thrall* or not, a newborn babe should not be born into a life of slavery.'

His grip upon her hand gentled and he inclined his head. 'But we can't save her,' he said. 'We haven't the silver for it. Perhaps one day her master will free her and her child.'

Elena couldn't stop staring at the woman's swollen womb. This woman would suffer, as well as her child. Her childbearing would be fraught with hardship.

Sadness weighed upon her as she turned away, reminded of her purpose. There were many children and she moved towards them to pass out the food she'd brought. One boy hung back from the others. He was tracing his hands along one of the walls and when she called out to him, he never looked back. His clothing hung upon him and he appeared frailer than the others.

Elena reached out to touch his shoulder. The moment her hand made contact, he jerked away and began to run. She stared at the street for a moment, wondering about him. When she handed another girl a piece of bread, she pointed in the direction the child had fled. 'Who was that boy?'

'Matheus,' the girl answered. She pulled the centre of the bread out, eating it first.

'And does he have a family to take care of him?' Elena prompted.

She expected the girl to answer no, but she shrugged. 'He lives with his parents.' When she said nothing else, Elena turned back to Ragnar. He beckoned for her to return with him, now that the food was gone.

'We should go,' he told her. 'I'll have our kinsmen ask if there are any others who need help.'

It seemed that his earlier anger had diminished and she was glad of it. 'Thank you.'

But instead of leading her back the way they had

come, Ragnar took her in a different direction, towards the water's edge.

'There's something I want to show you.' He led her past all of the boats to a small outbuilding where several men were bringing long planks. Curious, she followed him, wondering why he had brought her here.

'I spoke to a shipbuilder a few days ago,' he said. 'After I win a few more fights, I'll have enough for a boat.'

She tried to keep the reaction from her face, but all she could think was: *He's leaving.*

Though Ragnar was free to come and go as he pleased, the thought of not seeing him again brought an empty ache to her stomach.

Two *thralls* were spreading pine tar upon the new wood of a ship they were building for their master. Another mixed yellow ochre with boiled linseed oil to form paint. Elena feigned interest, but she kept wondering why he had brought her here.

They hung back to observe and Ragnar motioned for them to continue their work. 'It's fascinating to watch them,' she marvelled, pointing to the wood that had been steamed to reshape it. 'And the colours are so bright.' Inwardly, she was uneasy not only about why he wanted a ship, but also the means to gain the silver. The more he fought, the greater the risk.

She turned to him and asked, 'Why do you want a ship?'

Ragnar leaned in. 'I thought you might want to go back to Hordafylke and your family. I could take you there.'

'I've no wish to set foot on a ship again,' she admitted. And returning home was the last place she wanted to go. She had no desire to see the pitying looks on the women's faces when they learned of her divorce. No doubt they would believe Styr had cast her aside for her barrenness.

'Where were you planning to go?' she asked.

'Wherever the wind carries me.' He guided her away from the *thralls* and they walked along the water's edge, continuing until they were past most of the ships.

The hollowness in the pit of her stomach ached, though she tried to ignore it. What did it matter if Ragnar sailed to the other side of the world? He was free to make his own choices. And though he'd sworn to guard her, she was beginning to think that he no longer wanted her at all. They had shared a stolen night and the memory of it warmed her body from deep inside.

Yet now he couldn't get away from her fast enough.

Just like it was with Styr. She hadn't known what to do to kindle her husband's desire and while she'd been obedient, lying beneath him, she'd always felt awkward.

Perhaps she'd been wrong about seducing Ragnar. He'd wanted her before, when she'd been forbidden to him. But now that she'd shared his bed, he no longer desired her.

All along the walk home, she berated herself for succumbing to her own urges. Ragnar had claimed it would never happen again and it humiliated her to think that she'd destroyed their friendship on the night they'd shared together.

He led her back home again and she murmured her

thanks that he'd escorted her. Before he left, she ventured, 'Are you going back to fight again?'

His hardened gaze fixed upon her. 'I am.'

'I wish you wouldn't,' she confessed.

Dark green eyes fastened upon her with the iron resolution of a man who would not be swayed. Of a man who hardly cared about the risk to his own life.

'Your life is worth more to me than a pouch of silver,' she said, reaching out to touch his heart.

He gripped her fingers for a moment, squeezing her palm before he released her hand. 'It isn't to me.'

Ragnar lunged against his opponent, his sword cutting into the man's shield. He struck over and over, circling the enemy while all around him voices shouted for blood.

Your life is worth more to me than a pouch of silver.

He tasted the bitterness of regret as he avoided a blow, Elena's words ringing in his mind. He wanted to believe them. But he was torn by physical frustration and honour. The joining with Elena haunted him, as he remembered her pliant flesh and the way she'd taken her release from him.

He'd let her use him. He had savoured the night with her, feeling her body sheathing him.

But she didn't love him. The act was a means of easing physical desire, but nothing more. It burned him that he'd sunk to those depths. And though he wanted her still, it felt like a betrayal of his friendship with Styr.

He continued fighting, meeting his opponent blow for blow. Metal clanged as their weapons struck hard—

he used the fight as a means of releasing the sexual frustration.

Elena didn't know the man he was. He'd been careful to shield his darker side, never wanting her to know this part of him. Blinding rage tore through him as he continued the fight. He struck out at the memory of the adolescent who hadn't been good enough for Elena or her father. His forearms strained while he ruthlessly slashed down the memories of his father's temper. As a boy, he'd been unable to fight back against the man who had sired him.

But he could fight now.

He lost himself in a haze of violence, his muscles straining, sweat rolling down his cheeks.

Not good enough, the blade seemed to chant.

Not good enough.

A battle cry tore from his lips, and he was dimly aware that the crowds were roaring their approval.

Until his blade sliced through flesh and bone.

Thor's blood, he'd never meant the fight to go this far. His opponent was on the ground, writhing in pain, trying to stanch the blood with his hand.

Ragnar took the silver, but the weight of it seemed to burden his soul. He'd cut down another man for this—a man who'd done nothing except challenge him to a fight.

Elena believed he was worth more, but that wasn't true. He was a man of violence, one who could never give her the life she deserved. He couldn't allow himself to believe for a moment that she actually cared about him. He might as well bare his beating heart to her.

Then he would become the warrior who let down his guard for a single moment, only to have his life-blood spill out.

Elena didn't see Ragnar at all that night or most of the next morning. Though she suspected he was still fighting for silver, the last thing she wanted was to watch him risk his life. It angered her that he would not relent—that he believed she valued wealth over his safety.

The resentment was growing stronger and she decided a distraction was best. She wanted to find out more about the starving boy Matheus, who had run from her. Her friend, Agata Mánisdotter, might know. Agata was acquainted with most of the Norse who lived in Dubh Linn, and it was possible that she knew where the boy lived. Perhaps the child's parents were unwell. Or he could be suffering from neglect at their hands.

Ragnar had endured the same as a boy. Despite her attempts to help him leave his father, he'd refused. Nothing Elena said or did had changed his mind and it had bothered her to see a close friend suffer at the hands of a man who should have taken care of his son.

Now that it was unlikely she could bear children of her own, it infuriated her all the more to see boys like Matheus suffer from a lack of food or shelter. Something had to be done.

Her footsteps carried her down the pathway leading to Agata's house and when she saw the tall blond-haired woman holding a bucket of water, her friend sent her a knowing look. 'It's been too long since I've seen you, Elena,' Agata remarked. 'Come inside and tell me everything.' She opened the door and Elena stepped inside gratefully.

The interior of the house was a wonderful mess of unwashed dishes, scattered clothing and children. Without asking, Elena scooped up Agata's youngest son, who was barely six moons of age. The baby gurgled and grasped a handful of her hair, babbling nonsense words.

The thought of spilling out all of her troubles was a welcome relief and Elena sat down while Agata ordered the rest of the children to go out and play.

'I heard about what happened between you and Styr,' her friend said. 'I'm sorry for it.'

Elena ignored the tightness in her stomach at the thought of her failed marriage and nodded. 'It was the right thing to do. Styr loved someone else in a way he never loved me.'

She rubbed the baby's soft back and Agata brought her a cup of mead. 'And I suppose now you're wishing you could kill the woman for stealing your man.'

'No, I wouldn't want that, but—' She stopped short, realising that her friend was right. The muddled feelings inside her were more than just sadness. There was anger and frustration, too. She'd been married for five years, only to have her husband fall in love with someone else.

Then she'd turned to Ragnar for comfort, only to be pushed away from him. He'd offered to send her back to Norway, as if that would make her feel better.

Anger such as she'd never known was starting to take hold, like a flame coursing through oil. 'Or maybe you're right. I would like to knock Styr in the head for the way he made me feel.' And Ragnar as well, she thought. He'd claimed to want her, only to distance himself after she'd given herself to him.

Elena glanced down at the baby, whose blue eyes were staring at her. 'I suppose that's awful of me to think such a thing.'

Agata raised her own cup in a mock toast. 'You could dig his heart out with a sharp stick. That's what I'd do if my husband dared to look at another woman. I'd end *him* before I'd let him end our marriage.'

Elena only smiled. The baby was starting to fall asleep and she went to put him down. 'Agata, what's wrong with me? I keep asking myself what I could have done to make Styr love me.'

Her hand started to shake and she forced herself to take a deep sip of the mead. 'I did everything I could to be a good wife to him. I shared his bed, I kept his house clean—'

'It's unnatural, the way you clean,' Agata interrupted. 'But even so, I'll agree with you. You were right to divorce him and let him go off to that *skjøge*.'

'He claims he never touched her.' Elena sighed. 'I imagine she's a good woman. Even if she did take him captive.'

Agata's eyes gleamed. 'She did what?'

Elena shrugged. 'I believe Styr was chained up for a few days in her house.'

Her friend started to laugh. 'By the goddess, I believe I would have paid gold to see that. Can you imagine how furious he must have been?'

'He wants to wed her!' Elena blurted out. 'After all that she did to him, he's in love with her. I gave him everything and he fell in love with a woman who locked him up!' Her rage flooded through her until she clenched her fists.

A snort escaped Agata. 'Perhaps the Irishwoman had a good idea with that one.'

Elena didn't know whether to laugh or cry, but when her friend began to smirk she buried her face in her hands. 'And then I seduced Ragnar.'

Her friend let out a snort of laughter. 'That's the first sensible thing you've done, then. Ragnar is a wickedly handsome man and he would do anything you asked.'

Elena didn't doubt it, but that was one thing she wished she'd never asked of him. 'Now *he* wants nothing to do with me,' she said, her gaze passing over the sleeping infant. 'Perhaps I'm behaving like a *skjøge*.' She winced at the thought.

'I don't think so.' Agata patted her shoulder. She tilted her head to one side, studying Elena. 'After your husband did that to you, it's only natural that you'd want a man to feel better about yourself.'

'It was a stupid impulse and it will never happen again,' Elena said. She should never have let her body's needs outweigh common sense. 'I don't even know why I seduced him.'

Agata glanced down at her sleeping baby and sent her a rueful smile. 'Because it was fun?'

Elena's face turned crimson, not wanting to answer that. 'He's been avoiding me ever since. I shouldn't have done it.'

'He's guilty,' Agata predicted. 'There's not a man alive who doesn't enjoy a woman who seduces him. And if you've the desire to take him to your bed, that's your choice.'

'I don't know what I want,' she admitted. For so long, all the decisions in her life had been made for her. Her father had arranged the marriage to Styr when she was hardly more than seven and ten. She'd never questioned it. And then her former husband had made the decision to come here.

'You have time enough,' Agata reassured her. 'And you are fortunate to have no one to answer to but yourself. There are days when I would love to walk through that door and never come back, especially when the children are whining and crying.'

'Even if I never wed again, I *do* want to be surrounded by children,' Elena said. It reminded her of her purpose in coming here and she told Agata what she had seen that morning. After describing Matheus to the woman, she added, 'He looks half starved. I want to find his home and see if anyone is taking care of him.'

Agata eyed her for a moment. 'He's not like other boys, Elena. They call him simple-minded.'

She had guessed as much, when he'd been tracing his hand along the walls. Which meant he needed help even more than the others.

'I want to see where he lives,' she insisted.

Agata shrugged. 'I'll show you, then.'

When they stepped outside, Agata called her oldest daughter to come and watch the baby. Then she took Elena's arm in hers, and they began walking towards another part of the city.

She followed Agata through the quadrants of longhouses, past the Irish dwellings on the other side. They passed the wealthier homes and moved into the shadowed part of the city where Ragnar had taken her the other morning.

The houses were closer together and the scent of earth and human waste mingled in an unpleasant way. Elena moved her hand to the small knife she carried with her and she glanced back at her friend. 'I don't think we should be here without an escort.'

Agata shrugged. 'It isn't far. But you did say you wanted to know where he lived. It's just over there.' She pointed to a small dwelling on the far side. The roof thatch appeared to be rotting and Elena didn't like the look of the place.

'He doesn't speak,' Agata continued. 'He never has, from what I've heard.'

Elena's hands tightened at her sides and she suspected she would not like what she discovered when she reached the boy's home. 'Is he Irish?'

Her friend shook her head. 'He's Norse, like us. But they built their home further away from the others.'

When they reached the door, a sudden rise of nerves took hold in Elena's stomach. 'How old is he?'

'Six or seven, as far as I can tell.' Agata led her to a rectangular dwelling that was shadowed. Her friend stopped outside the door, looking upset. 'When I came this far the last time, they were beating him. I wanted to stop it from happening, but I was alone.' Her face reddened, as if she were embarrassed that she had done nothing.

Elena knocked lightly on the door, but no one answered. Inside the house, she overheard the sound of water splashing. At first, she thought it might be someone washing, but a choking noise caught her attention.

An uneasy feeling settled in her stomach when there was another loud splash. Something was very wrong.

Instinct made Elena throw the door open, only to see a woman holding Matheus's head under the water. She was trying to drown him.

Elena didn't stop to think—she threw herself at the woman and pulled her off the boy, dragging him out of the water. He was choking and coughing, his face nearly blue from lack of air.

'What are you doing?' she demanded, though she already knew the answer.

The woman glared at her. 'He's cursed by the gods. Nothing but an empty-headed fool who can't do anything. He should have died when he was born.'

'And now you're trying to kill him?' Elena was aghast at the thought. 'He's just a boy.' She went over to Matheus, who was on his hands and knees, water dripping down his matted hair. He wouldn't look at her, nor did he speak.

'He won't obey and I've had my fill of it. No one will foster one such as him.'

Elena touched the boy's shoulder, but he wouldn't look at her. He sat upon the dirt floor and had wrapped his arms around his knees. He was trembling hard. In the corner, an older dog whimpered, his tail thumping the ground.

His mother opened the door wider. 'If you're wanting to take him, do it now before my husband returns.'

The boy appeared in a state of shock and he seemed younger than the age of seven. His arms were thin and bony. Bruises covered his small frame and a few cuts had scabbed over on his legs. She couldn't even tell the colour of his eyes.

'I will take him,' Elena heard herself saying. 'But he won't come back to you when he's grown. Not after you tried to drown him.'

'I don't care what happens to him.' The woman spat on the ground. 'If you want a boy who's naught but trouble, I won't be sorry. He's just a mouth to feed. He'll never be of any use to anyone.'

Elena glanced back at Agata, who was still waiting outside. Her friend peered inside and asked, 'Do you need my help?'

She wasn't certain. Though she hoped the boy would come of his own accord, he might cry or scream if she tried to touch him. Gently, as if approaching a wounded animal, Elena said, 'I'm going to pick you up and you'll come with us now. We won't harm you, I promise.'

He didn't protest when she lifted him up and he was so light, she could hardly believe he'd been fed at all. Possibly he hadn't.

Agata held the door for her, not speaking a word. Elena's heart was heavy as she turned her back on the boy's mother, but there was a renewed sense of purpose. She would take the boy home and look after him, teaching him that cruelty did not have to be a part of his life.

'My name is Elena Karlsdotter,' she told him.

Throughout the walk home, she continued to tell him about where they were going and what would happen. In her arms, she felt him shudder. The longer he held his silence, the more she doubted if he was even capable of speech.

Agata stopped before her own home and said, 'I have some clothes that my boys outgrew, if you're wanting some for him.'

'I'd be grateful.' Elena met her friend's gaze. 'And I am glad you brought me to him.' Though she hardly knew the child, if she had come only minutes later, he would have been dead. She cringed at the thought of it.

Agata nodded. 'I'll bring the clothes soon while you take him home and give him a meal. You might also ask for help from Ragnar tonight.'

Though she faltered at the idea of asking him, she recognised that she might indeed need help. Ignoring the woman's suggestive look, Elena said, 'Thank you for the clothes.'

She continued walking back to her own home, but there was no need for Agata to send for Ragnar. He was already there, waiting for her. When he spied her holding the boy, a questioning look came over his face.

'This is Matheus,' Elena said. 'He's going to be my son now.'

At the incredulous look in his eyes, she sent Ragnar a warning look. 'We will talk more after he's had a meal and I've tucked him in to sleep.'

Chapter Fourteen

Ragnar opened the door for Elena, wondering why she'd gone back for the boy. But then, it was clear that this child had been hurt before, from the multiple bruises on his skin.

It was like looking at a younger version of himself. And when she met his gaze, he knew precisely why she'd brought him back.

'Where are his parents, Elena?' he asked quietly.

She sent him a narrowed gaze that told him she'd reveal more later. The determination on her face was that of a mother lioness, ready to defend her newest charge. Gently, she lowered the boy to stand, but he backed away from both of them.

Elena let him be and she turned to Ragnar. 'Will you warm some water for me? Agata is going to bring over some new clothes and I want to see about any other bruises he might have.'

The boy was shaking hard, his face pressed against one of the walls as if he wanted to fit inside it. He was terrified, unable to express himself.

Ragnar knew exactly what that felt like. But he had a

feeling Elena had underestimated Matheus. She wasn't prepared for a child who had been violently hurt. But he put aside his doubts for now.

He lifted the heavy iron pot and brought it to fill with water. Agata came by a moment later and handed Ragnar the clothes. Beneath her breath, she murmured, 'His mother tried to drown him. Elena saved the boy's life.' With a conspiratorial smile, she added, 'She'll need your help this night.'

The boy had nearly been murdered? His blood turned to ice and when he stared at the child, he realised that Matheus's wet hair and sodden clothing had nothing to do with bathing.

Elena had saved this child. Just as she'd tried to save him, when his own father had beaten him.

Ragnar took the clothes from Agata, thanking her, and lifted the heavy pot with his other hand. He moved without thinking, his mind caught up in the horror of what this boy had endured. After he hung the pot over the fire to heat, he gave the clothing over to Elena. Although it was likely the clothes would be too large for the boy, they were clean and better than the wet rags he was wearing now.

When Elena reached out and touched the boy's shoulder, he let out a howl and began crying hard. A moment later, his sobs turned into screams.

There was a steel calm beneath Elena's expression, as if she'd expected this. 'Bring me some of the warmed water with soap and a cloth.'

Ragnar didn't argue, though he suspected this would only be the first incident of many. The boy was now curled up into a ball, his shudders overtaking him.

Though he didn't know how Elena had taken Matheus away from his parents, he didn't blame her at all. He only wished he'd been there to confront the man and woman who had done this to a child.

He gave Elena the soap and a cloth, dipping warmed water into a small wooden bucket. 'Do you want me to stay or go?' He suspected the boy might lash out at her if she tried to touch him.

'I would be grateful if you'd stay,' she said. She walked over to the boy, ignoring his crying as she sat down a short distance away.

'You've had a terrible day, Matheus,' she said to him, dipping the cloth in the water. But as she spoke, she caught Ragnar's eyes. He saw the compassion in her and the gentleness in her voice drew him to stand closer.

He'd come back to her, his body aching from the fight earlier. One more competition would bring him enough silver for a boat. When he glanced down at his hands, he realised that they were still stained with his opponent's blood. He didn't even know if the man was alive.

He'd tried to kill a man today, while Elena had saved a child. The contrast between them was so great, Ragnar was tempted to leave them at this moment. But he'd made a promise to stay.

'I want to help you,' she said to Matheus. And though Ragnar knew the words weren't meant for him, he sensed that she'd wanted to do the same for him, when he was an adolescent. But some wounds couldn't heal.

The child behaved as if he hadn't heard a word that

was spoken. When Elena reached out for his hand, she washed his palm and hand with the cloth. His crying quieted, as if he'd never felt warm water before. Though Matheus didn't look at Elena, he reached out for the bucket and touched the surface of the water. An expression of startled awe came over him.

'It won't hurt you,' she said again, reaching for his other hand. Gently, she washed his skin while he experimented with touching the water and submerging his hand.

In Elena's sea-green eyes, Ragnar saw a woman who had waited all her life for a child. The boy allowed her to wash the dirt from his face and hands, and when she brought over the clean tunic, Matheus touched the soft wool as if he'd never felt such a texture before.

'Will you bring him some food?' Elena asked Ragnar. 'I think there's some bread and meat left over from this morning.'

He washed the blood from his hands first, his mood sombre. While he gathered the food, he kept his gaze upon the pair of them. Elena's hair was matted, but there was a new softness to her face. She watched over the boy, as he played in the water. And in this moment, Ragnar realised how very deeply she'd wanted a child.

Her husband should have found someone for her to foster, long ago. It might have bridged the rift between them, if she'd had someone to look after. Everything about Elena had focused inward, shifting her attention to caring for someone else. But although she had given the boy nothing but kindness, not once had the child looked at her. All of his attention was focused on the textures of the wool and the water.

Ragnar brought over the rest of the bread, along with some cold mutton and boiled eggs. Elena sliced a piece of the meat and offered it to the boy. When he stared at it and only held it, she had to put it to his mouth before he tried a bite. Once he tasted it, his expression transformed again. Ragnar half-expected the child to begin devouring the food, but instead, he tasted each bite as if he'd never eaten anything like it.

He could see Elena struggling to hold back tears. She, who had wanted a child for so long, would have given this boy everything. And yet the gods had given Matheus to parents who would sooner kill him because he was different.

When at last the boy had his fill, she guided him up to her own bed and tucked him under a blanket. Matheus began crying again, curling up on his side. He kicked off the blanket, his bare feet hanging off the edge. Elena tried to put the blanket over him again, but he fought it, as if fearing she would smother him with the wool.

'It's here if you want it,' she told the boy. But though his sobs had quieted, it was clear that he would not sleep for a while.

Ragnar didn't know what to say. Elena's demeanour held such worry, but she didn't approach the boy, granting him space.

He knew he should leave now. But something held his feet in place. Without warning, Elena turned and embraced him, burying her face against his neck. 'Thank you for being here. It helps.'

'I haven't done anything,' he protested. But he couldn't stop himself from bringing his arms to her waist, idly stroking her spine. The light scent of her hair smelled of soap and an herb he didn't recognise.

She never failed to take his breath away. He rested his mouth against her hair, wanting to kiss her. And yet he forced his hands to remain where they were.

'You've given me support,' she admitted in a whisper. Eyeing the boy, she added, 'I can't imagine why anyone would want to kill a child.'

Ragnar thought back to his own father and the beatings that had come from a man half mad with grief. Fermented brews had become his father's comfort and he'd often forgotten about his son. There were no reasons for the violence; only a sense that Olaf had been lost in the moment.

'You were good with the boy,' he said. 'Matheus will come to trust you in time.'

She shrugged, drawing back to look at him. 'I want to believe that. But he's never known what it is to be safe from harm. It may take a very long time for him to believe that I want to give him a home.'

She was likely right in that assessment. But an idea occurred to Ragnar, one that might quiet the boy's weeping. 'Wait here,' he suggested. The boy might not trust either of them yet, but there was another way of granting him comfort.

When he returned, Elena was startled to see a squirming puppy in Ragnar's hands. The dog was milky white in colour and his ears flopped against his face.

'This might help,' he offered. He went to sit upon her bed, still holding the pup in his hands. Matheus rolled over. When Ragnar placed the animal beside him, the boy's tears ceased and he curled up with the animal.

It was exactly what the child had needed, though Elena knew Ragnar wasn't aware that the boy had lived with a dog. Her heart softened at the sight of the pair of them together and she was grateful that he'd brought the puppy.

'Where did you get him?' she asked Ragnar.

'There was a litter born a few weeks ago. I traded for one of the pups.' He came to sit across from her at the table. In time, the boy fell asleep and only then did Elena begin to relax. Her mind was spinning with confusion, for everything had happened so fast.

Even so, she didn't regret saving the boy. He would have died if she hadn't thrown the door open and stopped the woman. And now he belonged to her.

The interior of her house was warm from the fire and Ragnar brought over some of the leftover meat and bread. 'You haven't eaten.'

She couldn't have imagined eating—not after all that had happened thus far. 'I was distracted,' she admitted, thanking him for the food. Ragnar broke off a piece of the bread and handed it to her. The slight touch of his hands was another distraction. She found herself aware of his firm mouth, remembering how he'd kissed her.

Without knowing why, she reached for the bread and broke off another piece, feeding it to him. Her fingers brushed against his mouth and he caught her hand.

A warning look flashed in his eyes, as if he wanted her to stop. His entire body went rigid and a swirl of hunger caught her.

Elena thought of her conversation with Agata earlier. *If you've the desire to take him to your bed, that's your choice.*

'I should go,' Ragnar said.

She didn't want him to. But when she stood and approached him, she grew aware of the fresh bruises upon his jaw and the scabs upon his knuckles. A pouch was fastened at his waist and she knew what had happened.

'You were fighting today.' She stood before him and touched the fresh wounds. He didn't deny it and if she spoke a word against it, she suspected he would go.

Elena pulled her stool beside him and the weight of silence hung between them. She leaned her head against his shoulder, fully aware that he had no desire to be here.

'There was a time when I could tell you anything,' she said, keeping her voice low. 'When we were younger, I always went to you. Not to Styr.' She reached out to his hand and said, 'I don't like the way you're so angry with me now.'

When he didn't answer her, she laced her fingers with his. For a long moment, neither spoke. But eventually, he let go of her hand and his arm curled around her waist. 'I'm not angry with you.'

'Let it be the way it was,' she whispered. 'I won't ask anything from you, I promise.'

But don't go, she wanted to say. The thought of him leaving her was an invisible blow, a wound that would never heal.

She didn't know what her feelings for Ragnar were. After the end of her marriage, she'd reached out to him in desperation and discovered that beneath the need for human comfort was something more.

Feelings that had been there for years, buried deep.

In his arms, Elena was too afraid to speak, for fear that he would go. A single misstep might send him away and the thought made her bereft.

'What are you going to do with the boy?' he asked.

'Take care of him as best I can.' So long as Matheus was fed and protected, he would be fine.

'Fostering a child isn't easy alone,' Ragnar warned.

'I know.' She stood and went to stand over the boy's bed. Matheus was curled against the puppy and the new clothes Agata had given him were too large against his bony frame. The urge to embrace him came strong, but she only smoothed his dark hair. In spite of his troubles, he'd already taken a piece of her heart.

Ragnar came to stand behind her and she took comfort in his presence. 'I'm not fostering him, Ragnar,' she corrected. 'I'm adopting him. He has nowhere else to go.'

She turned to face him and his dark green eyes stared into hers. 'If that's what you want.'

It was. Her mind was in turmoil, for her life had turned upside down in a matter of hours. She didn't know what would become of her, but she intended to be this boy's shield, to keep him safe from the world if that was what was needed.

Elena let out a breath and went to gather furs to make a pallet upon the floor. Ragnar was watching and she stood a short distance away before she unfastened the brooches at her shoulders.

'What are you doing?' he asked in a low voice.

She didn't answer, but removed the outer apron, leaving her gown in place. When she turned back to him, she said softly, 'Take off your armour. There's no need for it.'

He removed the chainmail and set aside his sword. But in his eyes, she saw wariness, as if he expected her to demand more from him.

Elena went over to the furs and curled up on them. 'Sleep beside me, Ragnar.'

She waited, wondering if he would join her. When he held back, she rolled over to her back. 'I won't ask more of you than that.'

He sat upon a low stool, watching over her. 'If I lie beside you, *søtnos*, I'll demand more than you want to give.'

Chapter Fifteen

Ragnar's days fell into a pattern, but there was a new restlessness. He'd continued to guard Elena and Matheus, but although she cooked meals for him and he slept in her home at night, he didn't touch her. Instead, her proximity was a slow burn to his senses.

She asked nothing of him except that he stay with her. At night, she lay upon the pallet and talked to him long into the night until he longed to kiss her into silence.

He hadn't touched her, but that didn't mean he didn't want to. The hunger and need to possess her grew stronger with each day until he was driven to fight more. Anything to release the physical demands within him.

This morning, he accompanied Elena and Matheus into the marketplace, but he was well aware of the eyes upon them. He had made many enemies, both the men he'd defeated and those who had lost wagers. Ragnar kept his hand upon his sword hilt, never taking his eyes off the unseen threat.

When Elena and the boy had finished with their purchases, he stopped on the way back to watch the fighting. Two men circled one another, wearing light armour and wielding battleaxes. The shorter man was faster, while the larger opponent swung his axe as if he intended to behead his challenger. Ragnar had defeated both of them in earlier matches.

Matheus was stopping to pet a cat who was weaving in between his legs. Elena released the child's hand and turned back to Ragnar. 'Let's go back.'

He sensed her discomfort and regarded her. 'I almost have the silver I need. If you've changed your mind about returning to Hordafylke…'

She looked stricken at his words and shook her head. 'I haven't.' Then she guided Matheus away from the cat, leading him back.

Ragnar stood behind them, guarding the pair as they returned to the dwelling. Elena kept the boy's hand in hers, while he kept his palm upon her spine to show that he was their protector.

When they reached the bridge, Elena stopped suddenly, glancing behind her. 'Do you sense that we're being followed?'

Ragnar shook his head, but there were so many people in the crowd, it was impossible to tell. 'Even if we are, I won't let any harm come to you.' He took a glance behind them, but nothing struck him as out of the ordinary.

'There was a man I saw in the marketplace earlier. He was watching Matheus, and I thought I saw him again just now.' She moved closer to Ragnar's left side, still holding the child's hand. 'Stay beside me,' she bade Matheus.

With her other hand, she reached for Ragnar's palm, but he put his arm around her shoulders instead. If they were being followed, he wanted it clear to others that she was under his protection.

He guided them back from the marketplace, past the quadrants of longhouses. The scent of peat smoke lingered in the air and he marked the faces of the people passing by. Still, there was nothing to suggest a threat.

When they reached Elena's dwelling, Ragnar held out his hand. 'Wait here first.' Before he allowed them to enter, he searched the interior. Again, there was nothing out of place.

The boy knelt down while the puppy scampered forwards, licking Matheus's fingers. Ragnar closed the door behind them and Elena appeared relieved to be home.

He studied her a moment while she put away the food and drink she'd purchased at the marketplace. Though her behaviour was ordinary, he sensed that she was upset.

He decided to steer their conversation back towards the boy. 'Matheus seems to be adapting well.'

She nodded, lowering her voice as she moved closer. 'But he never looks at me. Sometimes I wonder if he even knows who I am. And he doesn't like it if I try to hold him.'

Ragnar supposed that was due to the abuse the boy had suffered with his parents. 'What else have you learned about him?'

She motioned for him to sit down. Although she told him about Matheus's likes and dislikes, he sensed that Elena was holding back more.

'He likes to draw patterns in the dirt,' she finished. 'Each night he makes a new picture for me.'

As if to illustrate her words, the boy bent down to the earthen floor and began tracing lines with a stick. Each line was even with the previous one and Ragnar realised that Elena didn't care that Matheus was unlike the other boys, nor did she feel he had any less value. Instead, she saw beyond his problems and found his strengths.

The dark yearning for her caught him like a fist. If she belonged to him, he'd reach across the table and kiss her hard, drawing her back to their bed.

'Why are you looking at me like that?' she whispered, tucking a strand of hair behind one ear.

Because he wanted more from her. Not just a smile or a stolen moment together. He wanted her at his side, though he knew he didn't deserve her.

He gave her no answer, but stood up when he saw a shadow cross the window. Although it could have been anyone passing by, his instincts rose up. Ragnar stood and went closer, his hand upon his sword hilt.

'What is it?' Elena asked.

He didn't know, but he strongly suspected it had to do with Elena's earlier fears that someone was following them. 'Wait here,' he commanded. 'And bar the door behind me.' No one would threaten them—not if he could help it.

He opened the door and hastened to follow a man who was walking quickly towards a throng of people. The figure had no distinguishing features—from the back, his hair was a dark blond and he wore no colours to set him apart. But the fact that he was hurrying was reason enough to pursue him.

Ragnar pushed his way through the crowd until he caught up to the man. 'Wait,' he ordered, catching him by the arm.

The man stopped, a questioning look on his face. 'I don't know you.' His words were spoken in a calm tone, but his eyes shifted, as if searching for a means to escape.

'No, but you stopped at my house. I want to know why.' Ragnar didn't let go of the man's arm, waiting for an explanation.

The man glanced around him for a moment and shrugged. 'I didn't know it was yours. I only wanted to look in at my son.'

His son? Ragnar tensed, studying the man's features and realised that they were similar to Matheus's. 'Your wife tried to murder him a few days ago,' he pointed out.

The man's face set in a line. 'So I heard. He's not good for much, but my blood runs through his veins. I wanted to see how he was.'

Although it was a father's right to ensure his son's welfare, Ragnar didn't trust the look in the man's face. He didn't appear at all remorseful over his wife's actions. 'He's well enough.'

With that, Ragnar started to walk away, but the man called out, 'If we allow you to keep Matheus, we deserve compensation in some form.'

So this was the man's reason. Ragnar turned back, keeping his temper shielded. 'We saved his life. You'll get no compensation from us.'

A sly look crossed the man's face. 'I could accuse the pair of you of kidnapping him. It would be my right, as his father.'

'And I could accuse your wife of attempting to drown him,' Ragnar countered. 'Let the boy go and be on your way. If you wanted to be rid of him, you are. And he's better for it.'

'I want gold,' he said. 'A body price for the son I've given up.'

Rage boiled inside Ragnar. How did this man dare demand coin in return for a child? He closed his hands over the man's throat and slammed him against the wall of a house. Slowly, he closed off the man's air, lifting him off the ground. He waited until the man's struggles diminished, before he dropped him.

'There. You can have your miserable life as compensation. But if you come anywhere near Elena again, you'll lose it.'

One week later

Blood was streaming from Ragnar's temple and his jaw was swollen. Every muscle in his body ached, but he'd won his prize of silver. It was enough.

'What's happened to you?' Elena demanded, when he came inside. The boy was in the corner, playing. Before Ragnar could give her an answer, she predicted, 'You fought again, didn't you?'

'And won.' He tossed a heavy leather bag on to the table. Over the past few weeks, he'd earned a reputation as a ruthless fighter. He'd defeated every last opponent until now there were few who would challenge him.

'I don't know why you've come to me,' Elena shot back. 'Were you wanting me to heal your cuts and bruises, after I asked you not to fight?' She tossed a linen cloth at him. 'If you won't listen to me, you can heal your own wounds.'

Ragnar leaned in close, dropping his voice low. 'You're not my wife, *søtnos*. I don't have to answer to you.' He took a step forwards and she retreated. 'I fought because I wanted to.'

'I thought you said you had enough silver for the ship. Or was it not enough for you? Will you keep fighting until they bring your broken body back to me?' Her cheeks were crimson and she looked as if she wanted to strike him.

'I intend to make my fortune, regardless of the means.' Though it meant pushing his body to the limit, he no longer cared.

'Silver doesn't matter to me,' she argued. 'It never has.'

'It mattered to your family,' he pointed out. He remembered all too well the way her father had looked down on him. And although Ragnar's skill in fighting had improved, his wealth had not. He was hardly more than a mercenary, living by his sword.

'And you think that I judged you the way my father did? You think I'll want you more if you have more silver?' Her face turned incredulous. 'What kind of a woman do you think I am?'

'One who deserves a good provider.' Elena's outburst took him by surprise, for he hadn't meant to imply that she was greedy.

'All you want is to be rid of me,' she accused.

'You've been fighting for silver these past few weeks, because you're trying to send me back to Hordafylke.'

His anger exploded. 'I've been fighting these past few weeks because if I don't, I'll hurt you.'

She stilled, confusion clouding her face. 'You would never lift a hand against me, Ragnar.'

'You're wrong.' He moved forwards, pressing her back against the wall. With his voice low, he said, 'You tormented me every day of the past five years when I watched you go to his bed. And after you shared mine, I've thought of nothing else since.'

She averted her gaze and he murmured in her ear, 'Every night, I sleep away from you because if I don't, I won't be able to keep my hands off you. You're a hunger I'll never be able to sate. And fighting takes the edge off.'

Her breathing had grown unsettled and he moved away from her, knowing he'd frightened her. He shouldn't have come, especially since the raging desire hadn't abated at all.

'Wait,' Elena whispered. She reached again for a cloth and dampened it with water, washing the blood from his temple. He held steady, noticing the green of her eyes and the softness of the lips he wanted to claim. Right now, he didn't want to remain patient. He wanted to seize the moment and take what he wanted.

She dipped the cloth in cool water again and began sponging at his other cuts and bruises. The touch of her hands was gentle and she stood so near, his arousal was almost painful.

'I don't want you to die,' she said, rinsing away the blood at his temple.

'I wouldn't have died, Elena.' He couldn't believe the dismay in her voice. She'd seen Styr and him sparring all the time.

'But you could have been killed,' she insisted. 'And you will die, if you continue fighting for no reason at all.' She tossed the cloth down on the table, and her shoulders rose with the heat of her anger. 'I asked you not to.'

'Do you think I'll hide behind a woman's skirts with no means of earning my way?' It had hardly been a fighting match at all. He'd easily defeated his opponent but had left the man alive.

'Do you even care about your life?' she demanded.

He sobered and reached out with his knuckles to caress her face. 'Do you?'

The stricken look on her face caught him low, in the gut. In her eyes, he saw fear and worry, revealing her feelings. 'Yes,' she whispered. 'I care a great deal about you.'

In silent response, he leaned in and rested his forehead against hers. God help him, he didn't know what to say or do now.

When Elena touched her hand to his heart, he stole a kiss, claiming her mouth. She kissed him back and he tasted fear upon her lips. Not only fear for his safety, but a slight tremble of what was happening between them. But now was not the time to act upon it. Not with the boy here.

Ragnar glanced around at the house. The interior of Elena's home, normally immaculate, was in complete disarray. The bedding was unmade and there were dishes still on the table. He'd paid no heed to his surroundings until now and her cheeks flushed. 'I'm sorry about the mess. We were…busy working on the walls today.'

Young Matheus was smearing mud into the wicker crevices. He gave no indication that he'd heard any of their conversation.

Ragnar leaned in and asked, 'Have you seen any sign of the boy's father since last week?' When she shook her head, he added, 'I've asked some of our kinsmen to help me keep watch over this house. I don't think he'll return.'

But although he spoke the words to reassure her, he still didn't trust that the man would leave Elena alone. Matheus's father was far more interested in personal gain than his son's welfare.

'I hope not,' she whispered. 'And besides that, you're here.'

Her words sent another fierce ache within him, to take her down upon the pallet and claim her. He was itching to touch her, to palm her breasts and taste them until she arched in ecstasy.

By the gods, he needed to leave her before he gave in to the dark needs.

To change the subject, he asked, 'How is Matheus?'

Throughout the past hour, the child had continued to spread even amounts of mud into the cracks. He appeared content in the tedious task, his eyes staring at the crevices as if he saw something else there.

Elena moved behind the boy. 'He is managing as well as I could expect. Today he started filling the cracks in the walls, after I showed him how. He's been working on it all day.'

When Ragnar bent down to see the child's work, it was clear that the boy was locked upon the task.

'I've never seen anyone with such a strong focus,' Elena said. 'He does such good work. I think we may be able to find a trade for him, if he has a kind master to show him what's needed.'

She leaned down and asked, 'Matheus, are you hungry?'

The boy gave no answer, gliding his hands over the mud. Ragnar went to stand before him and the child never ceased from his undertaking.

'Come and eat with us,' Ragnar offered gently. But when he extended a hand, Matheus flinched.

Elena shrugged apologetically. 'He sometimes doesn't respond when I ask him to stop.'

It wasn't at all a good sign, if the boy was disobeying her. But perhaps there was more to it than she'd said. 'Does he understand your words?' Ragnar asked.

Elena shrugged. 'Sometimes. I don't know what has meaning to him and what doesn't. He's calm when he has a repetitive task to complete.' She didn't seem too concerned by it.

'And what if there's danger?' he asked. 'If you call out to him and he disobeys you, he could be hurt.'

Elena sobered at that. 'I would hope that he'd obey me in that instance.'

Hope wasn't strong enough. He worried that Elena's hesitation to discipline the boy might cause problems. 'You can't let him decide when he wants to obey you,' Ragnar warned her. 'If you are to be his foster mother, he has to learn.'

The boy stood against the wall, peering outside

through the crevices. The evening light was fading, but he stared at the sunlight, his hands frozen against the wood.

When he touched the boy's shoulders, Matheus jerked at the contact and let out a scream. The child's fingers curled into the wet mud and he began to fight when Ragnar tried to pull him away.

He squirmed and kicked his feet, as if trying to return to the wall. It took hardly any effort to restrain the boy, but when he brought the child to Elena, she appeared uneasy.

'Let go of his hands,' she pleaded. 'You're upsetting him.'

Ragnar continued to hold the child's hands firmly, but kept his voice calm. 'If you keep allowing him to do as he pleases, whenever he likes, you'll have a terrible child on your hands.'

Gently, he let go of the boy, but the moment he did, Matheus ran back to the wall, his eyes fixated on the outside sunlight. He smeared at the mud and then his screams quieted, almost as if he'd seen something.

'Wait here,' Ragnar told Elena, reaching for his sword. He stepped outside and walked around her dwelling, but there was no sign of anyone there. Ragnar shielded his eyes against the setting sun, searching for a glimpse of an intruder. But when he could find nothing, he saw no choice but to return.

The boy was right where they'd left him, his hands pressed against the wood. Elena was trying to coax him away, but Matheus refused to leave.

It was possible that the boy simply wanted to go outside into the sunlight. Ragnar lifted the child into his arms and brought him over to Elena, paying no attention to the boy's whining. 'Bring a basin of water. He should wash the mud from his hands before he eats.'

She poured water into a wooden bowl and brought over some sand to scour his hands. Ragnar could tell from her expression that the boy's dismay was bothering her deeply.

He ignored Matheus's protests and dipped the boy's hands in the water, rubbing them with sand. All the while, the child kept screaming and fighting.

Elena's face appeared even more worried. 'You're frightening him. Please…just let him go.'

'He has to learn that he cannot get whatever he wants, simply by screaming.'

Elena's soft heart was going to get her into trouble if she wasn't careful. From the way she was glaring at him, she believed he was being too hard on the child.

'He's endured so much. I don't think—'

'Dry him off,' Ragnar commanded. 'And then we'll give him something to eat.'

When she tried to dry the boy's hands, Matheus shoved her away. Elena stumbled backwards and Ragnar caught her before she could fall. Seconds later, the child ran to the wall and began screaming again. Over and over, he cried out, howling at the top of his lungs.

The stricken look on Elena's face revealed that she'd never expected the boy to lash out at her. She'd rescued him, giving him a home and food to eat. Likely she'd believed Matheus would love her for giving him all the things he needed.

But this had gone too far.

'Wait here,' Ragnar commanded, picking up the

child. The boy needed to calm down, to understand his boundaries.

'Do not beat him,' Elena argued. 'I know he's been disobedient, but—'

'Did I say that was my intent?' Ragnar cut her off and opened the door. It irritated him that she would believe he would beat a child who hardly understood anything of what was happening. The thought appalled him, that she would accuse him of such a thing.

You fight for silver, a voice inside reminded him. *There is blood on your hands. Why wouldn't she believe you capable of harming an innocent?*

He kept the screaming boy upon his hip. 'Come with us, if you don't trust me.'

She faltered. 'I do trust you. But you've never been around younger children.'

From the tone of her voice, he guessed her true fear—that he would be the same as his father, unable to control his temper. Olaf had beaten him regularly, with his fists and sometimes a wooden staff. Elena knew it, just as everyone else did.

It sobered him, for the last thing he would do was raise a hand to a child.

Ragnar continued walking away from the houses and towards the shoreline. He walked down the wooden docks until they reached the furthest end, away from the ships. With a glance behind him, he saw that Elena had followed at last.

He took the boy to an isolated part of the beach and sat upon one of the large boulders. He held the boy tightly in his arms and the boy's screaming eventually dwindled to sobbing. The cries calmed when the boy began staring at the rhythmic waves surging against the sand.

Elena trudged through the damp sand and came to sit beside them. She said nothing at all while Ragnar held the boy. It was strange to have a child in his arms and for a moment, he wondered if this was what it meant to be a father. To know that this small person depended on you for everything—food, shelter and protection.

'I'm sorry for what I said.' She reached out to touch Matheus's hair, but her eyes were on Ragnar. 'I wasn't thinking when I spoke.'

'I'm not my father,' he reminded her.

'I know that.'

But in her voice, he sensed a trace of unrest, as if she were uncertain what he was capable of.

She had brought a loaf of brown bread with her and broke off a piece, handing it to him. Ragnar took it and gave it over to the child, who devoured it. They held their silence, sharing the loaf between the three of them while the waves continued to roll across the shore. Matheus seemed to slip into a trance and eventually Elena spoke.

'You were right. I shouldn't have let him have his own way. I just…felt sorry for him after what his mother tried to do.'

He understood that. Her compassion was one of the reasons he'd been so taken by her, so long ago. 'Being a mother to him means giving him what he needs. Not what he wants.'

She moved to stand behind him, resting one hand upon his shoulder. 'I'm not very good at this.'

'You will be.' He drew her around to his side, keeping an arm around both of them. For a moment, he held her close and she tensed but didn't pull away. Eventually, her shoulders lowered and she leaned her head against him.

'Thank you for being here. And for helping me.' She tilted her head back to look at him and he inclined his head to acknowledge her remark. When he didn't take his eyes from hers, she lowered her gaze.

'We should go back. He'll be tired and I really need to clean the house.' She started to reach for the boy, but Ragnar stopped her.

'I'm not Styr, Elena. I don't care what the house looks like.'

'Neither did he,' she admitted. 'It was a habit of mine, because I thought it was a way I could take care of him.'

'Just sit a moment with us,' he urged. He wanted her to enjoy the quiet rise and fall of the sea. Though she was reluctant, he brought her beside him.

'You make me nervous in your arms,' she whispered against his ear.

'Why is that?'

She turned her face against his chest, but gave him nothing more. He sensed that if he pressed her, she would make up an excuse that wasn't the truth.

'You don't have to take care of me the way you did him,' Ragnar said.

She drew back and in the moonlight he saw that her face held confusion. 'I know you aren't the same as Styr. What frightens me is all the ways I feel different around you.'

To distract herself, she smoothed Matheus's hair, though her eyes were upon him.

'Styr should have given you a child to foster.'

'He offered to,' she admitted. 'I refused, saying that I only wanted a child that I bore.'

It was obvious that she'd changed her mind. But before he could ask why, she admitted, 'I thought a child would bring us closer together the way a foster child wouldn't. I thought Styr would love me if I could conceive a child of his blood.' Her hand stilled upon Matheus's hair. 'But in the end, it didn't matter. Nothing I did or said would make him love me.

'What I did that night when I lay with you… It wasn't fair. You were right,' Elena whispered. 'I *was* using you, even if I didn't want to admit it to myself. You deserve more than that.'

He heard the regret in her words and that wasn't at all what he'd hoped for. Despite her ended marriage, he didn't believe she was over Styr. And as much as it frustrated him, he still felt as if he stood in the shadow of his best friend.

By the gods, he was a fool for being empty-headed enough to let himself dream of her. And for what? A woman who was tangled up in her own battered dreams and marriage to a man who hadn't loved her.

'I'm grateful that you've stayed with me during these past few nights,' she whispered. 'I didn't want to be alone.'

He'd remained there to guard her, and while those nights might have brought her comfort, they'd only brought him frustration. Only last night she'd sat upon a stool, washing her face and hands. He'd watched her tie back her hair, the water droplets sliding over her skin.

She tempted him the way no woman ever had. But he wanted to give her so much more than a life like this. She'd been brought up in a large home with cups of silver and wealth that Ragnar could only imagine.

He couldn't give her that now...but if he fought to earn more, he could. In her eyes, he saw the future he craved, the woman he'd dreamed of.

Elena stood and tried to take the boy, but Ragnar kept him in his arms. 'I'll carry him.' He stood up from the boulder, shifting Matheus so he could continue staring at the waves.

With the boy against his shoulder, he led her back home again. And he made a silent vow to himself that one day, he would have Elena Karlsdotter.

Or die in the attempt.

Chapter Sixteen

Elena opened the door to her home and Ragnar passed Matheus to her. His head lay against her shoulder as she balanced the boy against her hip. When they entered, the darkness of the interior was broken only by the soft glow of coals on the hearth.

'Put the boy to bed,' Ragnar ordered. 'I want to look around outside to make certain it's safe.' His hand cupped her chin and he leaned in to her ear. 'Bar the door behind me and I'll return soon.'

Heat prickled across her skin at the words, but Elena gave him no answer. She closed the door and lowered the bar, her thoughts in a tangle of confusion right now. She'd apologised for seducing Ragnar, when the truth was, she wasn't at all sorry. She'd revelled in the lovemaking, perhaps because it had been so forbidden. The feelings he'd conjured inside her had been overwhelming and Elena admitted to herself that she'd never felt like that with Styr.

She couldn't put a name to her feelings for Ragnar, for while it had only been a few weeks since she'd divorced her husband, her heart knew that it was different with this man.

She'd always been close to him in a way she hadn't been with Styr. She could voice any thought, any fear, without feeling foolish. Comparing the two of them, she preferred Ragnar—and that knowledge frightened her. It was happening too fast and she couldn't tell if her reactions were born of lust…or of feelings that had always been there with a man who understood her in a way Styr didn't.

The flare of an oil lamp caught her attention and Elena froze. 'Who's there?' The hair on her scalp stood on end and she shifted her grip to the dagger at her waist.

'You're not going to take my son from me,' came a voice from the far side of her home.

Elena turned in horror to see Matheus's father emerging with a blade in his hands. She'd been too trusting, never suspecting that an intruder might already be inside.

'Leave my home,' she ordered, raising her voice louder in the hopes Ragnar would hear. She didn't dare let go of Matheus, for fear that the boy's father would try to take him.

'You're going to pay me for him,' the man insisted. 'With gold or—' his gaze passed over her breasts— 'by another means.'

She lowered Matheus from her arms, shielding him with her own body. In his ear, she whispered, 'Go and fetch Ragnar.'

Instead of fleeing, the child went to sit in a corner, running his fingers over the crevices in the wood. He had retreated inwardly, not looking at her or his father. Likely he didn't understand what was happening now.

God help them both.

'Ragnar!' Elena cried out. She started towards the door, but the man gripped her wrist and jerked her back. Clamping his dirty hand over her mouth, he said, 'Your man won't be coming for you. My friends have seen to that.'

Elena tried to scream, but his palm muffled any sounds she made. She fought against him, kicking and twisting her body. He clouted her against the ear and she saw stars, the room blurring all around her.

She struggled to remain conscious when she dropped to her knees. There was a spear on the far side of the room, if she could only reach it. The man kept his hand over her mouth and she couldn't shout to Matheus or anyone else. Though she tried to bite down on his fingers, his strength made it impossible. He reached for her skirts and her rage erupted.

No. She would *not* allow this man to rape her or make her a victim in her own home. Tangling her feet in his, she used her body weight to knock him backwards. The momentary assault freed her voice and she cried out for Ragnar, screaming as loudly as she could.

The man scrambled to his feet, but Elena brought a stool down upon his head. She lunged for the spear. When she seized it, the man reached for Matheus instead.

A white-hot anger controlled her now and she didn't care whether this man lived or died. Elena gripped the spear, wondering how she could wield it without hitting the boy.

'Do you even know how to use that?' he taunted.

'I'll pierce your heart with it,' she responded, tightening her hold on the weapon.

'Why would you want my son?' the man demanded. 'He's lacking in brains and his mother should have killed him at birth.'

'If he means so little to you, then you should be glad that I've offered to take care of him.'

'Not until I have my price.' He gripped the boy's throat and Elena saw the terror in Matheus's eyes. Though the boy couldn't speak, he understood the danger. His face was white and his expression pleaded with her for help.

'I've been watching you over the past few days,' the man said smoothly. 'Waiting for the right moment to slip inside. When *he* wouldn't be there.'

His gaze moved over to the wall where Matheus had been smearing mud. The boy's violent screams suddenly made sense. He must have caught a glimpse of his father tonight, when he was trying to block out the crevices in the wood.

Where was Ragnar? She couldn't understand why he hadn't broken the door down after she'd screamed. And what did the man mean, *Your man won't be coming for you*? Was he dead? Had others attacked him?

Elena glanced over at the door, but it was still barred. Though she didn't want to take her eyes off the man, she had to get help.

In one swift motion, she darted towards the door and raised the bar, throwing it open. To her relief, Ragnar was already moving in, his sword drawn. *Thank the gods.*

Blood was streaming down his face and though she didn't know what had happened to him, he was alive. Elena moved to the side but was taken by surprise when her attacker let go of Matheus and seized her instead. She was helpless to move when the point of the spear jammed against her throat.

'You're going to leave her to me, or I'll kill her before you can take another step,' the man warned Ragnar.

Elena couldn't breathe, but in Ragnar's eyes she saw a man bent upon murder. He didn't look at her, his gaze focused upon bringing down their enemy. Matheus was behind them and she couldn't tell if he was out of harm's way or not.

Ragnar kept motionless, but he never surrendered his drawn sword. Instead, he held it, poised to strike. His other hand moved to a pouch at his waist.

'Was it silver you wanted?'

Elena couldn't see her attacker's face, but his grip tightened upon her. 'Throw it to the ground and leave.'

'I'll only leave when she comes with me. And the boy.' Ragnar's voice was deadly calm, his eyes hard.

'That won't happen.'

Elena sensed the madness in his words, that this man would not give up his claim upon the boy. He might insist upon payment, but it wouldn't end with coins. He would continue to make demands, endangering the boy. There was no reasoning with him.

She closed her eyes, knowing Ragnar would strike him down. Her life was at stake, but if he didn't act, this man would kill her after he'd finished with her.

Do it, she begged silently.

She kept her eyes squeezed shut, waiting for the inevitable strike.

'No!' she heard Ragnar yell. Her eyes flew open and a gasp resounded from her attacker. The point of the spear thrust and Elena cried out, feeling the harsh pain against her throat.

Seconds later, the man fell to the ground. Blood poured from his back and she turned to see Matheus holding his father's own blade. Tears flowed down the boy's face and his hands were shaking as he dropped the knife.

By the gods, not this. Matheus had killed his own father to save her.

'It's all right,' Elena murmured to him. 'You can put the knife down. I'm all right.'

The boy obeyed, sobbing as he threw himself into her arms. It was the first show of affection he'd ever given and she wept against him. She'd never known that he would defend her or recognise that she'd wanted to help him. She kept speaking words of comfort, soothing him as she held Matheus close.

He understood that she wanted to keep him safe, that she wanted to be a mother to him. Though she'd only had him a short time, he'd known that she would not harm him. Her heart broke for the suffering he must have endured at the hands of his parents.

But it was over now.

Ragnar stood by the door, his sword still in hand. She raised her wet eyes to his, but there was tension in his expression. He walked towards them and Elena stood straighter, still holding Matheus against her.

'Are you all right?' he asked, tilting her chin back to see the cut.

Elena nodded. 'It's not deep,' she reassured him. But he found a cloth and used it to wipe the blood away.

'He could have killed you.' His voice was heavy, while his touch remained gentle. Elena went motionless, caught up in the way he was staring at her. She breathed in the scent of him and the urge came over her to bring his mouth down to hers.

'No, he couldn't have. You were there to defend me,' she said.

But when she tried to embrace Ragnar, he held back from them, keeping a stoic distance. Something was troubling him, but he wouldn't say what it was. Did he blame himself for the attack? Neither of them could have known that Matheus's father had slipped inside while they were gone. She didn't fault him at all.

But seeing a dead body on her floor didn't make the idea of staying here appealing. Not only did this house hold the memories of her failed pregnancy and ended marriage…but now there was death as well. She wanted to start over, some place where she could make a new beginning.

'I don't want to stay in Dubh Linn any more,' she confessed to Ragnar, opening the door to go outside. With Matheus's hand in hers, she led them both away from the man's body. 'I want to leave this place.' She hardly cared where it was, so long as there were no memories of the past and Ragnar accompanied her. 'Can you still get a boat?' She held Matheus at her side and the boy buried his face against her gown.

'In the morning, we'll find a ship,' he promised.

'Thank you,' she breathed. 'And…for tonight, I want to stay somewhere else. Matheus shouldn't sleep here—not after what happened.'

'You can stay with our kinsmen,' he agreed. 'I'll find a place for both of you.'

Ragnar brought her back to his house, opening the door for both of them. Every nerve was on edge, his mind blurred with the fear of losing her. Seeing the spear against her throat had sent him over the edge. He'd been ready to cut down her attacker, the unholy rage filling him up.

But the boy had struck first.

Ragnar hadn't seen the child cowering behind his father and when he'd swung his sword, the sudden movement had come so fast he'd barely managed to stop the blow. Ragnar's sword had sliced through the man's ribs and nearly taken the boy's head off when Matheus had struck with a blade.

His only consolation was that Elena didn't know. She'd had her eyes closed and had no idea how close the boy had been to dying. No words could have consoled her if the worst had happened.

He said nothing to her, but inwardly, he was disquieted by what he'd done. He'd been uncontrollable and he didn't trust himself at all right now.

Several of his friends were playing games and drinking, while others nodded to Elena in greeting. Ragnar brought her to a pallet on the floor against one wall and she set Matheus down, tucking him in while she sat beside him. The boy was trembling and she ran her hand over his hair to soothe him.

Her gentle motion calmed the boy and Ragnar realised that the child was coming to accept her. Though he would never be like other boys, Elena would be a good mother to him. She would love him for who he was, no matter that he was different.

Ragnar retreated from them and asked a kinsman to help him dispose of the body. He didn't want her home marred by that.

After it was done, he returned to his own home. He would have to face the *jarl* and pay a body price, but for now, he would stay with Elena and the boy.

Inside the house, she sat beside Matheus, watching over him. Ragnar let them have a private moment together while he centred his own thoughts. But even while he sat on the far side of the room, he never took his eyes off her. Long strands of reddish-gold hair spilled over her shoulders, while she leaned back against the wall.

He saw her hand pass over Matheus's shoulders and her green eyes caught his in silent thanks. She didn't know how close she'd come to losing this child at his hands. It haunted him even now.

Elena lay down beside the boy, but she remained restless and didn't sleep. After several minutes of tossing and turning, she got up from the pallet and crossed the room towards Ragnar. He remained with his back to the wall, waiting for her to speak.

In the darkness he could still see the scrape beneath her chin where the spear had penetrated her skin. It bothered him to know that she could have died this night. Life was a fragile thing, severed at any moment.

And perhaps that meant taking command of what he wanted, living each day to its fullest.

'I couldn't sleep,' she whispered. 'Not alone.'

Her hair was tangled about her face, her green eyes luminous. He wanted to kiss her, to feel her body pressed near to his. But he was still shaken by what had nearly happened to the boy.

Elena took his hand and led him away from the others. The men were fully aware of their presence, but no one paid them any heed. She reached out to his cheek and stood on her tiptoes.

'I just…want you to hold me for a while.' Her arms wound around his neck and she stepped forwards until he felt the softness of her breasts pressing against him. Ragnar hardened instantly as her female scent caught him with a flare of desire. 'I was so afraid.'

He breathed in the scent of her hair, knowing he had no right to hold her. And yet he couldn't move away. Not yet. 'I will always keep you safe, Elena.'

'I know,' she murmured. She pulled back and rested her forehead against his. 'I hold a lot of regrets inside me,' she admitted. 'I never thanked you for saving my life when we were nearly taken captive.' She stood on her toes and pulled his face down to hers, kissing him.

It took all of his willpower not to ravage her mouth, claiming her the way he wanted to. He let her take what she wanted, allowing the kiss, but not overpowering her.

'I never told you how grateful I was that you protected me on the island.' She slid her hands to rest upon his heart, kissing him again. The innocent touches were igniting his lust, provoking him to lose control. When she touched her tongue to his mouth, he opened to her offering, deepening the kiss until she broke away.

'And I never told you how thankful I am that you never left my side. Even after Styr and I divorced.' She ran her hand through his hair, adding, 'I couldn't have endured those first few days without you.'

Although she had put her marriage behind her, the mention of Styr was like frost against his desire. He knew that her husband had shared her bed, that Styr had known her intimately. And it provoked a jealousy beyond any he'd ever felt before.

He wanted Elena to know who *he* was. And he was not Styr.

Ragnar took her face between his hands, plundering her mouth. He kissed her hard, running his hands over her body. Teasing the swell of her breasts, down her waist, until he grasped her hips.

She was breathing harder, but she was giving back to him everything he wanted. Her hands were moving beneath his tunic, touching his bare skin, a moan escaping her when he nipped her ear lobe, tasting the soft skin and arousing her.

'Beautiful Elena,' he growled as he took her mouth again, thrusting his tongue against her own. Her arms came around his neck and he didn't doubt that she wanted to share his bed tonight. The thought made his shaft harden at the thought of penetrating her wetness.

He wanted her to respond to his touch in a new way, to be tempted in ways Styr had never shown her.

You're not good enough for her, came the voice of doubt inside him.

He wouldn't let himself believe it. Instead, he kissed

her hard, trying to blot out anything except her touch. He wanted to memorise her features, learning her with his hands. The raw craving—to take her body beneath his and join their flesh as one—was shocking.

When her hands moved to his leggings, he captured them. 'No. Not yet.'

Her face flushed and she started to move away from him. 'I'm sorry. I shouldn't have—'

'I'm not finished with you, *søtnos*.' He held her captive against the wall, kissing the soft underside of her chin, just above her wound. Her weight sagged against him as his hands moved up her bodice, his thumbs finding the tips of her breasts.

'I let you take me that night, but you've no idea what it means to share my bed.' He pinched the tips lightly, watching as she closed her eyes, her hands digging into his shoulders.

'If you want to be lovers, I'm going to drive the memory of Styr out of your head. I won't have him intruding on what's ours.' To underscore his words, he reached beneath her skirts, touching her bare thigh. Though he stroked her skin, he kept his palm below her intimate opening.

She tried to shift against him to bring his hand against her, but he kept it in place. Her green eyes flew open and she pulled his mouth down to hers.

'Say my name,' he demanded. 'Look at me and know who's touching you.'

'Ragnar,' she said in a throaty voice. He sensed how deeply aroused she was, for he was aching as badly as her. But he'd learned, long ago, that the greatest fulfilment came from the greatest longing.

He'd been given a second chance with her. And if it meant casting his own spell over Elena, tempting her until she could no longer think of anything but him, so be it.

Chapter Seventeen

'Take me somewhere,' Elena asked softly. She wanted Ragnar desperately, but not here. Not surrounded by so many.

'Unless you want to go back to your home, this is all we have,' he admitted. They were shielded from view and Elena didn't doubt that no one would interrupt them.

He moved to whisper against her ear. 'Can you be quiet?'

The thought of making love to this man a second time, while other people surrounded them, was both terrifying and stimulating. Elena nodded and Ragnar removed his tunic and chainmail corselet.

She was transfixed by the sight of his muscled body. His brown hair was tied back with a thong and he had leather braces on both arms. When he caught her staring, a slight smile played upon his mouth as if he wanted her to remember the stolen touches from the last time.

His hardened muscles were ridged and she ached to touch him.

With this man, she had never felt unworthy. Instead, he stared at her as if she were as necessary to him as the air he breathed.

'I shouldn't have married Styr,' she confessed, her hands resting against his chest. 'I was so taken by him when I was a girl, I never saw the man he was.'

Ragnar's face tightened, as if he didn't want to hear any of this. And yet, she needed him to know it. This man had been her best friend and she *had* sensed something between them long ago. He filled up the spaces within her in a way Styr never had.

'Styr cared about you,' he said at last. 'He wanted to keep you safe. When we were at Gall Tír, he made me swear to protect you.'

'He liked me well enough, for an arranged match.' Elena traced her hands over the hard flesh of his abdomen. 'But it was never right.'

She let her hands fall away, wanting him to know the truth. 'Do you know how awful it was, trying to mould myself into a woman he could love? I did everything I could to change myself, but it never worked.' The bitterness in her tone was harsh. 'And then I couldn't even give him children.'

'Don't do this to yourself.' He caught her by the arm. 'We don't need to talk about it.'

He didn't understand and she took a breath, gathering her courage. 'I wanted you to understand that…it was never a good marriage. Even in the beginning. I could never talk to him the way I talk to you.'

'He was blind to what was in front of him,' Ragnar said. He pushed her back against the wall and when he trapped her hands, she inhaled sharply. 'But I'm not.'

In his eyes, Elena saw the open yearning. It reached into her, past the heartache of a husband who had never been able to love her. She'd tried so long to change herself to be the woman Styr wanted. And here was a man who didn't want her to change at all.

'Perhaps *I* was the one who was blind to what was in front of me,' she said.

And it was true. She'd sensed all along that Ragnar had feelings for her, though he'd been careful not to show them. 'Or am I wrong?'

He framed her face with his hands. 'What do you think, *søtnos*?'

His words gave her a boldness she'd never imagined. She pulled him down to kiss him, but instead of the familiar, soul-stealing kisses he'd claimed before, this one was softer.

It was an awakening, a sense that she'd known this man for so many years…and yet she didn't know him at all. Her breathing quickened and the rush of arousal that filled her was one she'd never before experienced. There was no guilt or remorse. Only a new beginning.

He was learning her, tracing his hands over her hair and face. And when he bent to her throat, she leaned back, shuddering as his tongue flicked against her pulse.

She pulled back to look at him and for the first time, she realised how much Ragnar had come to mean to her. He'd stood by her when she'd been taken captive and they'd managed to survive. He'd been there for her during the worst of times.

Yet she wanted to know him better.

His hands were moving over her, gently loosening

the laces of her gown. But she didn't want a hurried night of lovemaking—at least, not now. She wanted to slow down, to open her eyes to the man before her. To know him, the way he'd known her all these years in secret silence.

'Slow down,' she whispered, stepping back. There was a fleeting look of surprise on his face, but she touched his bare chest, caressing him.

'I always admired you, even when I was a girl,' she admitted. 'Even if I was already betrothed to Styr... I enjoyed watching you.' She traced the outline of his muscles, where skin and sinew joined to a harsh pulse at his throat. 'You moved like no man I'd ever seen before.'

'I wanted to prove myself,' he admitted. 'Fighting was all I knew how to do.'

'There's more to you than a sword and a shield,' she said. 'You are a man of honour and courage.'

'None of my thoughts were ever honourable towards you,' he said, his tone turning deeper. 'I never gave voice to them, but I imagined taking you away from Styr. Capturing you and claiming you.'

'I wanted you to claim me,' she admitted. 'That night when I dreamed of you. When I forced you to touch me.'

'You didn't force me to do anything I hadn't already imagined.' He reached out and drew her face to his, staring down into her eyes. 'I don't care what Styr ever said to you or what he thought. You're perfect in my eyes and always have been.'

A soft ache caught her heart, for no one had ever

said that to her. She felt a yearning to show this man that he had nothing to prove. That she did care for him.

They were shielded by the wooden partition, but she was fully aware of the others nearby. Ragnar knelt down to the hem of her skirts, lifting them as his hands moved over her bare calves. He slid his palms over her thighs and hips, until he removed the gown and she stood naked before him.

Her breasts tightened and Ragnar laid her clothing down on the ground. Although she was shy, afraid that someone would interrupt them, she wanted this man.

Before she would let him lay her down, she stopped him. 'I want to see you.' Her eyes rested upon the bulge of his erection.

Ragnar untied his leggings, until his naked body was revealed to her. She was fascinated by the differences in him. His legs were thicker, his body honed like a sharp blade. And she knew well enough what it was like to have him inside her.

She lay down upon her clothing, feeling more nervous this time. Her mind spun with fears, even though she knew he would not hurt her. She had lain with him before and it had been thrilling beyond anything she'd known.

But even with him, she had not become pregnant. Her courses had come and gone, and she was left to realise that lovemaking would not be about creating a child. She had to let go of that dream and find happiness in another way.

When she reached for Ragnar, he took her wrists and laid them above her head, lifting her breasts towards him. With his voice low, he said, 'The last time, you took your pleasure from me, for your own desires. Now I'm going to take mine.'

He covered her erect nipple with his warm mouth, sending a jolt of arousal flooding through her. With his tongue, he swirled and suckled her, making her want so much more.

Ragnar took one of her hands down and brought it between her legs. 'Put your fingers there and don't move your hands.'

She didn't understand at first what he meant, but when he kept the pressure there, he bent to her other breast. A startling shimmer of pleasure rocked through her.

She started to touch herself, but he stopped her. 'No. Keep your hand there and don't move it.'

He lifted one of her legs up, bending her knee and touching her skin. He claimed her mouth, his tongue twining with hers. The raw sensations were coursing so fast, she imagined that the pressure of her fingers was his hard length. She was wet for him, wanting to have him joined with her.

To encourage him, when he freed her left hand, she reached for him, circling his shaft with her palm. He kissed her harder, hissing when she began moving her hand up and down.

He pressed his hand atop hers, his fingers dipping into her wetness. And although it brought her pleasure, she fought against the rush of sensation, almost afraid of the way he was making her feel. It was happening too fast and she bit her lip hard.

'Don't scream,' he whispered against her ear as he thrust inside her body with his fingers. The command made her want to cry out and she couldn't believe how violent her feelings had become. His thumb edged her hooded flesh while his fingers caressed inside her. The sensations built up within, until she was trembling.

Ragnar shocked her when he immediately pressed his rigid length between her legs. The pressure of his thick erection drew an unbidden moan from her lips. It felt so good with him there and the shimmering pressure took hold again.

Then, finally, when he sheathed himself inside her, she let out a sharp gasp.

'Don't cry out,' he breathed against her mouth. 'I don't want you thinking at all. I only want you to feel me inside you and know that no one will come between us again.'

By the blood of Freya, she had never felt so aroused. But that was what Ragnar wanted. He was trying to force away the memories of her first husband, putting himself in their place.

He held himself deep inside and with his mouth, he began giving attention to her breast again. He circled the tip, biting gently while his hips moved in a rhythmic circle.

'All these years, I saw the two of you together and I imagined him doing this to you.' He withdrew nearly all the way before plunging deeply, connecting their bodies. 'I wanted to kill him for touching you.'

She was wet and desperate for more. 'Don't bring Styr into this,' she demanded. 'This isn't about him.'

He quickened the rhythm, using shallow thrusts to press against her. She couldn't stop the spasms of arousal that took hold, and though she wanted to force him closer, she knew that he would not cease his assault upon her senses. She locked her legs around his waist, but Ragnar overpowered her, pulling out until she was quivering with a greater need.

'I don't want you ever to think of him again,' he said quietly, until she grew even more tense, not knowing what he would do. His mouth kissed her stomach, while his hand touched her soft curls.

Ragnar cupped her bottom and touched her intimately, dipping his fingers into her wetness. Her fingers dug into the ground, gripping the earth as he tormented her with the pressure of his thumb against her hooded flesh.

She was coming apart from the inside. Though she could hardly bear what he was doing, she understood why. He wanted to torture her, taking vengeance against her body for having had another man before him. He was going to continue touching her, until she was wild with need.

And the more she fought against the sensations, the stronger they grew. Molten heat clawed inside her as the shimmering excitement mounted harder.

Without warning, Ragnar grasped her hips and thrust his shaft inside her again. The abrupt sensation sent her flying over the edge and she dug her nails into his shoulders as he spun her off into a release so hard, she couldn't stop the tremors. He rode her deeply, their bodies slick with sweat, until she was no longer able to grasp a single thought. The instinctive, animal urges commanded her now and she gripped his hips, forcing him to penetrate her hard and deeply.

Every part of her convulsed against him as yet another release tore through her. She was liquid and primal, and he withdrew and turned her on to her hands and knees, thrusting again inside her as his hands filled with her breasts.

By the goddess, she was so overcome by lust, she could do nothing except surrender to him. He was commanding her, dominating her in every way as he pounded into her.

'Enough,' she pleaded and at last he released his seed into her, his body jerking until he collapsed atop her.

Ragnar remained buried inside, his body covering hers. And now that it was over, she questioned whether he'd made love to her because he cared about her…or whether he was trying to prove that he was a better man than Styr.

The familiar hilt of the sword rested in Ragnar's palm. The clouded air was heavy with the anticipation of battle and the promise of rain. His enemy stood before him, yet another warrior he'd faced with the promise of silver. The man's face was obscured by the mist and when Ragnar struck out with his sword, the metal bit into a wooden shield. Seconds later, a sharp sting sliced through his upper arm and blood spilled over his skin.

His muscles strained as he slashed and swung, but his energy began to drain from the wound. And when he reached into his reserve of strength, calling upon all that he had, his weapon struck the killing blow.

When he removed the man's helm, he saw the face of Styr.

Horror filled Ragnar when he saw his friend's sight-

less eyes, his body covered in blood. A raw cry tore from his throat but the body blurred, shifting and transforming into the body of Matheus. The child lay lifeless on the ground, blood spilling from his heart.

'Ragnar!'

The nightmare vanished, but when he opened his eyes, he saw that he was holding a dagger pointed at Elena's throat. He dropped it immediately, stunned to realise that he'd raised a weapon to her.

'You were dreaming,' she said softly.

He'd nearly hurt her in his sleep. Somehow she must have touched him and he'd reacted out of instinct, seizing his weapon.

'I could have hurt you.' The knowledge struck him to the bone. Never in his life had he thought he could harm Elena. But the dream revealed a truth he couldn't deny. In the midst of fighting, when he was lost in the haze of battle, nothing would stop him from killing.

Not the face of his friend or a young child. Not the face of Elena. He drew up his knees, covering his face with his hands to let go of the terrible dream.

Last night, after he'd made love to her, they had both dressed again and slept beside Matheus. He hadn't slept that soundly in months.

'You wouldn't have hurt me,' Elena said gently. But when Ragnar dared to look at her, he saw that the boy was inching away. Matheus traced his fingers over the surface of the wall, as if he didn't trust him. Given how close the boy had come to being beheaded, that wasn't surprising.

Ragnar exhaled slowly, rising to his feet. 'I should go and see about the boat.'

Elena stepped in front of him. 'Wait.' Her arms came around his waist and she embraced him hard. It was likely meant to reassure him, but though he squeezed her in return, he couldn't help but remember what he'd done.

You're not trustworthy. You could have killed her without opening your eyes.

'I'm going to take you back to Hordafylke,' he said. 'Some of our kinsmen may come, but we'll likely need a crew to sail with us.'

'I already told you, that isn't where I want to go.'

'It's where you'll be safe.' He turned his back to go outside and wasn't at all surprised when she followed him.

'Am I a child now, who needs to return to her parents?' she demanded. Her green eyes flashed with anger. 'What makes you believe I'll go there willingly?'

'You don't have a choice.'

'And when did you decide you wanted to be rid of me?' Her face darkened with embarrassment and she took him by the hand, leading him back inside his house. The interior was dark, but she was right—this wasn't a conversation he wanted to have with so many around them.

She gripped her hands into fists at her sides. 'Was it that bad last night when I shared your bed? Are you so eager to leave me now?' Her face was crimson and he couldn't believe she'd think such a thing.

'No.'

Elena picked up a cloth and dipped it in a bucket of water. Without thinking, she began scouring the table.

'I don't think you need to clean just now.' He took a step back, planning to return to the waterfront. 'Not when we'll be travelling soon.'

She threw the wet cloth at him and it struck him in the chest. 'I don't understand you at all. Last night, I thought we could…be together. That you cared about me.'

His chest tightened, and it took an effort to hold his silence. Though he wanted to be with her, to love her as he had all his life, he didn't trust himself.

'Were you using me last night?' she whispered. 'Were you trying to prove yourself better than Styr?'

The words enraged him. 'No.' He unsheathed his weapon and tossed it down on the table. 'But I was caught up in you.' He reached to the nape of her neck and guided her to the centre of his house. 'This morn, I remembered who I am.' He pointed down to the earthen floor. 'I'm a warrior who kills, Elena. And the other night when Matheus's father died, I nearly struck down the boy.'

She went pale at that, as he'd wanted her to.

'Your eyes were closed,' he went on. 'You didn't see when I raised my weapon to kill the man. I swung hard, just as the boy came up behind him. I nearly killed Matheus when I tried to slay his father.'

'But you didn't,' she said, a moment later. Her voice was barely above a whisper. 'You held back your weapon.'

'I might not have.' He wanted her to be afraid, to understand that he had not been in control of himself. One misstep, and the boy would have been dead.

'Stop it,' she said. 'Just stop.' Elena moved forwards

and grabbed his tunic with both hands. 'You would never hurt me or Matheus. Not in a thousand years.'

'My own father died at my hands, when I got angry,' he pointed out. 'I couldn't stop myself then.' Though he'd never intended to harm Olaf, there was no denying that the man had died only days after their fight.

'He didn't die because of you.' Elena relaxed her hold upon him and forced him to look at her. 'He was drinking too much and he was weak of heart.'

But still Ragnar blamed himself. Though his father had beaten him often, he knew the man had been torn apart by grief. Olaf had numbed the pain by drinking too much mead and he'd lost the man he'd been.

His father's blood ran within him and Ragnar couldn't know if, one day, the battle lust would turn him against those he loved.

'You cannot blame yourself,' Elena said. 'I trust you with my life.'

He reached out to touch her face, tangling his hands in her hair. 'But I don't trust myself. Even this morning, I could have hurt you without knowing it.'

She covered his hands with her own, her eyes bright with tears. 'You're wrong. I see the man you are. And I intend to follow where my heart leads.'

She leaned up to kiss him, but Ragnar pressed his mouth against her forehead. 'Not this time, *søtnos*.'

Though it tore him apart, he would endure the heartache of losing her, if it meant keeping her safe. He'd become a man he didn't recognise, a fighter who had taken too many lives.

He let go of her and opened the door, only to see Matheus standing outside it. In his arms, the boy held his puppy. For the first time, he met Ragnar's gaze steadily.

'Go inside,' he bade the boy. 'Your mother needs you to help her pack your belongings for the journey.'

Chapter Eighteen

Elena held herself together by strength of will, though she was furious with Ragnar. How could he think she would stand back and let him go? Her heart was bleeding at the loss of this man who had been with her from the very beginning.

She should have known that the easy friendship she'd found with him was what she'd needed all along. And when she'd pushed past friendship, he'd taught her that she wasn't as cold as she had once believed. With Ragnar, every touch stirred her senses, making her yield to his pleasure.

There was more at play here, more he hadn't said. But she knew that when she'd startled him from sleep, his reaction had shaken him.

It didn't bother her, for she'd known he would never hurt her. Neither did his confession about Matheus cause her any concern. He had stopped his sword the moment he'd spied the boy.

But she was so confused about what to do now. Matheus was chasing his puppy around the room and, for the first time, she heard him laugh. The sudden burst of joy caught at her heart and when she neared him, the boy threw his arms around her waist.

It was exactly what she needed right now. His small embrace broke down the barrier of tears she'd held back. Elena swung him up on her hip, striding away from everyone else. This boy, her adopted son, had taken a large piece of her broken heart and had begun to mend it. Though she might never bear a child of her own flesh and blood, she still had him. And for now, it was enough. She held him close, weeping silently.

She needed time to think, to sort through the confusing emotions that plagued her. Her footsteps led her towards Agata once again, needing the woman's friendship and advice. She set Matheus down, holding his hand while the puppy trailed behind them. He found a gnarled stick upon the ground and handed it to her as if it were a blossom of heather.

'Thank you,' she told him, leaning down to the boy. In answer, he wiped the wetness from her cheeks.

By the gods, this child was an answer to her prayers. She hugged him again, so grateful for his quiet presence. He was a gift she'd never expected. A son, not from her body, but one who was, none the less, a part of her heart.

'We need to convince Ragnar to stay with us,' she told him solemnly, not knowing whether or not the boy understood. 'I am going to talk to Agata for a while and you may play with her children.'

The boy's expression never changed, but she took his hand in hers and continued walking towards her friend's house.

* * *

'Ragnar is going to leave,' Elena told her friend. 'He's decided he wants me to return to Hordafylke, to stay with my family.'

Agata's gaze turned pensive. 'Isn't that just like a man? Believing he knows what's best for a woman.' She handed Elena a cup of mead and added, 'Has he been unkind to you?'

She shook her head, explaining what had happened with Matheus and herself this morn. 'It's as if he believes he has no right to be happy with me. I don't know how to convince him to try.'

'Do you love him?' Agata asked.

Elena grew quiet, afraid to think of it. Her head warned that it was far too soon after divorcing Styr. She had no right to love someone else.

And yet…Ragnar had been there beside her from the beginning. He'd saved her life upon the island and had fought to protect her. The thought of never seeing him again went deeper than the loss of a friend. She couldn't even imagine the pain and loneliness.

'Yes,' she whispered. 'I do love him.'

'Then fight,' Agata urged. 'Stop thinking the way a woman would and think in the manner of a warrior. Don't allow him to command you.'

An idea took root within Elena, one that was not at all something she would have considered in the past. But she wanted this man and wasn't about to stand in the shadows and let him dictate her life.

She told Agata her plan and the woman brightened. 'It's perfect, Elena.'

'He'll be so angry with me.'

'If he cares at all about you, that won't matter. In the end, he'll be glad that you brought him to his senses.'

She hesitated, so afraid that it wouldn't work. Before she could voice a protest, Agata intervened. 'You already know what to do, Elena. Now give me Matheus to watch over and go do what you must.'

He didn't go to the waterfront, as he'd thought he would. Instead, Ragnar found himself back near the fighting matches, watching the men as they struck hard at each other with their fists. The roar of the crowd and the cries of men wagering on the match filled his ears, but he held back.

One of the fighters could hardly be more than seven and ten. Lean and untested, the young man reeled when the older man struck him across the jaw. Ragnar held steady, watching. It was as if he were viewing himself, years ago, when his father had hit him.

He'd been punished for anything and everything. And when men like Elena's father had claimed Ragnar wasn't good enough for his daughter, it had been easy enough to believe. If his own father saw him as worthless, why wouldn't anyone else?

But Elena had never seen him in that way.

The young boy was on the ground now, his shoulders hunched over as the blows came. Ragnar's fists tightened with the desire to interfere, though he knew he could not.

Elena had tried to save him from this. She'd never once treated him as less than a man. And when they'd been stranded together, he'd discovered what he'd feared all along—that the attraction to her went far deeper than he'd ever imagined.

He knew he was a poor substitute for Styr, but last night, she had given herself freely, wanting him. She'd granted him a taste of immortality in her arms, a glimpse of the afterworld.

The honourable path was to let her go, to take her home again. But the warrior within him wanted to damn the consequences and claim Elena for his own. He wanted every night in her arms, seeking only to worship her.

Dimly, he was aware of others watching him. They knew how many matches he'd won and several glared at him for the wagers they'd lost.

'I know you,' one said. 'You're one of the fighters.'

Ragnar's hand moved to his sword, eyeing the man with wariness. 'I didn't come here today to fight.'

'But you will,' came another voice. 'You murdered my brother Vakri and stole his son.'

The crowd of people had fallen quiet and the earlier fighting match had ceased. The young man stumbled away, his face and hands covered in blood.

'Vakri tried to kill my woman. I defended her life and took his.' Ragnar unsheathed his sword. 'I will pay the required body price, when judgement is passed.'

The man unsheathed his weapon, his dark eyes holding the promise of vengeance. From behind him, Ragnar saw others surrounding them with their own weapons at the ready. They were men who had lost silver, men who wanted their own retribution.

'I don't want your silver,' the man said, gripping a battleaxe. 'I want your head.'

* * *

Elena had finished preparing her home, but there was no sign of Ragnar. Although he wouldn't like what she'd done, she hoped to convince him to stay with her. She would no longer be the quiet, meek woman to stand aside and do what she was told.

No, she was a Norsewoman with power of her own. The blood of warriors ran through her veins and she would stand up for what she wanted.

But the longer time went on, the more worried she grew. What if he had already left? Although he'd said he would escort her away from Dubh Linn, something might have happened.

When there came a knock at her door, she opened it, only to see Agata standing there. 'It's Matheus,' she said, her face mirroring Elena's fear. 'He slipped away and we can't find him.'

Fear roiled inside her, that someone else had taken the boy. Elena seized a blade to arm herself. 'And what of Ragnar? Has anyone seen him?'

Agata shook her head slowly.

Freya help me, Elena prayed. Terror mingled with determination to find both of them. She didn't know what had happened, but she wasn't about to stand by and weep.

To Agata, she ordered, 'Find Hring and tell him to bring several of our kinsmen to help me search.'

She prayed that no one would harm Matheus or Ragnar. It didn't matter that he was not her sworn husband. He belonged to her in every sense of the word, just as Matheus was her adopted son. And by the gods, she intended to fight for her family.

* * *

The haze of bloodlust possessed him as Ragnar swung his blade. He was surrounded by men who wanted him dead, but he would not go down without taking several with him.

He let the wrath consume him, transforming him into an instrument of Death. His sword bit into flesh, but he heard no screams. He was lost in the moment, unaware of anything save raw instinct.

A blade sliced his arm, but it was only a scratch to him. There was no pain, no sense of anything, except the need to survive.

Until he saw the boy.

Awareness jolted back into him when he saw Matheus walking alone to the centre of the fighting ring. The boy continued moving towards him, heedless of the fighting.

'Get back!' Ragnar ordered, his voice hoarse as he cried out. But the boy did not understand his words, as each step brought him closer.

Soon Matheus would walk in the midst of the fighters and his life would be forfeit.

A renewed surge of purpose filled Ragnar, as he cut down one man, then the next. He held up a hand to Matheus, willing the boy to stay in place. He seized a shield from one of the fallen men, swinging his sword wide.

He kept his gaze fixed upon his enemies as he took slow steps towards the boy. 'Go home,' he ordered. But once again, the child did not heed his words. Instead, he ran forwards to Ragnar and stood beside him, facing the men.

Thor's bones, the last thing he wanted was a child caught in the middle. But then it occurred to him— he'd ceased fighting the moment he'd seen Matheus. The battle lust had not taken away his awareness the way he'd thought it would.

He drew the boy behind him, handing him the shield. 'Hold this and don't let go.'

The presence of Matheus did nothing to deter his attackers. Instead, the man who had named himself Matheus's uncle had a thin smile upon his face, as if he'd been waiting for a distraction like this.

'You can't win,' he said smoothly. 'There are too many of us.'

'Tell that to the men who are already dead,' Ragnar countered. He raised his sword and the blade was covered in blood.

'Lay down your weapon and we'll let the boy go,' his enemy said.

But there was no trusting a man like this. He would say what he wanted to and the lies held no meaning. If Ragnar dared to set down his weapon, he and Matheus would die.

One slashed his battleaxe towards the boy and Ragnar spun, deflecting the blow. Though he knew the odds were not in his favour, he would do all that he could.

And then he heard Elena's scream.

Chapter Nineteen

Elena rode hard, a spear in her hand. Though she had never used the weapon before, her true advantage was being on horseback. She saw Ragnar cutting down the men surrounding him while Matheus hid behind a shield.

A white-hot anger filled her up as she rode towards the men. She ignored their weapons, screaming at the top of her lungs while she guided the horse into the fray. The animal trampled one of the men and Ragnar lifted up Matheus, handing the boy to her. 'Take him and go!'

He intended to sacrifice himself for both of them. Elena understood that, even as she held the boy in front of her.

'Now!' Ragnar commanded, just as another man struck.

But Elena gripped the boy with one hand, wielding her spear in the other. She saw another man attacking and she drove the spear forwards, watching it splinter as a sword struck the wood.

'Get on!' she called out. Ragnar started towards her, but his path was blocked by another man.

He met her gaze steadily, nodding for her to go without him. Instead, Elena held her ground. She had come this far and she wasn't going to abandon him to die.

She let out another scream, diverting the man's attention, but the horse reared up at the sound, causing her to lose her balance. Elena grabbed for Matheus, holding him tightly before she took the brunt of the fall from the horse. She landed on her back and all the breath was driven from her lungs.

Panic filled her, but she managed to scramble away, still fighting for air.

She found Matheus and was grateful to see him unharmed. Ragnar stood a short distance away, his last enemy upon the ground.

To the witnesses, he stared hard. He cleaned his sword and sheathed it once again, daring anyone else to attack. No one did.

When he reached Elena's side, she hugged him tightly. Matheus came and took his hand. Ragnar ruffled the boy's hair and said, 'I'll teach you to fight if you wish to learn, son. But this wasn't the right place for it.'

'Come with me,' Elena said. 'Please.'

'I need to see about the ship. Later,' he promised.

But although they were safe now, she didn't want him to go. She didn't want him believing that she would be better off without him, hundreds of miles away.

Elena mounted the horse, and Ragnar lifted Matheus up in front of her. Let him believe that she was going to remain obedient, then. She had another plan in mind and it was time to see it done.

Three other men arrived at that moment and she rode

towards them, reminding them of her orders. Hring sent her a knowing look and smiled. 'As you command.'

Her kinsmen had taken Ragnar by surprise, after they were away from the fighting area. They'd bound his hands behind his back and he was hooded. From the muffled sounds beneath it, Elena suspected they had gagged him as well.

He was going to be terribly angry with her. Furious to the point where he would be ready to tear her apart. While she ought to be frightened, instead, she imagined how she would ease his fury, seeking to soothe the angry beast.

'Bring him in,' her kinsman Hring ordered. He raised an eyebrow when he saw the chains Elena had arranged. Though she ought to be embarrassed, she said nothing.

'Do you want him unbound?' Hring asked.

Elena shook her head. 'Put the manacles on his wrists. I'll cut the ropes when I'm ready.'

Another kinsman snickered and she glared at him. But they obeyed her, chaining each of Ragnar's wrists. The long chains were attached to the beams of her house, so he could not escape. She had sent Matheus to spend the night with Agata and her friend had promised to look after him.

Ragnar was on his knees and, from the tension in his muscles, she sensed that he was seething. But she fully intended to change his furious mood.

This strong, virile man was her captive. And she would do whatever she wanted to him.

A heady sense of power filled Elena and she moved

in closer. 'I'm going to cut your ropes now. Don't move, or the knife could slip and cut you.'

She sawed through the rope, and when the bonds fell to the ground, his hands could now spread open. Ragnar tested the chains, pulling them until they were taut. His arms strained and the bulge of his muscles entranced her.

She removed the hood and saw that he was indeed gagged. 'I'm going to take this off.'

His green eyes glittered with fury and she suddenly questioned if this had been a good idea at all.

'Then again…I think I should leave it for a moment,' she said. 'So you'll listen to what I have to say.'

His glare was so dark, it was smouldering. Elena took a breath and faced him. 'I know this might seem offensive to you. I know that you're angry with me for using our men against you.'

In response, he gripped the chains tighter, trying to break them. Agata's reassurance that this would help her to win him back was suddenly appearing questionable.

'I was afraid if you left me, I'd never see you again,' Elena continued. 'And whether you believe it or not, I *do* care about you.'

She was nervous, standing in front of him, so she pulled a low stool over and sat. 'When I was a maiden, I was blind to anyone but Styr. I always thought you were handsome and kind. You were someone I could talk to about anything. Never once did you make me feel awkward or bad about myself.'

Ragnar was listening now, though it was clear that he still didn't like the chains or the gag.

'I thought I should love a man like Styr, because my father chose him for me. We all thought he would be the leader and he was handsome and kind to me. But I know now that Styr didn't...' She paused, searching for the right words. 'He wasn't interested in me. I could have been his little sister, for all he cared. But you were different.'

Suddenly feeling shy, she gathered her hair over one shoulder. 'I think I always knew you loved me. But I didn't know my own feelings until last night.'

She moved in so close, his face was a breath away. With her hands, she reached behind his head, resting her fingers against the tie of the gag. 'I know this was a desperate move. But I didn't want you to go without knowing that I love you. All these years, you were the man who stood by me. The man who loved me for the woman I was—not the woman I thought I should be.'

She untied the gag, tossing it aside. He didn't speak, but his eyes held a fire that she feared.

'I would have done anything to be a mother and I let it consume me.' She reached out to touch his shoulders. 'I judged my worth on whether or not I could bear a child.'

She moved her hand down to his heart. 'I want a man who loves *me*,' she insisted. 'A man who won't grow frustrated with me or ask me to change who I am.'

'I never asked you to change. Not once.'

Elena felt her breath growing tremulous and she drew her arms around his neck. 'I know.'

Ragnar pressed his hips close and she drew a sharp breath at the junction of his hard length against her softness. 'Why did you take me as your captive, Elena?'

She steeled herself and took a deep breath. 'You wouldn't listen to me earlier today, when I told you I wanted to stay with you. Caragh Ó Brannon took my husband captive in this way and she won his heart. I hoped...that I might do the same.'

'Unchain me,' he demanded. From the dark tone of his voice, she didn't think that was a good idea at all. He would only leave.

Instead, she removed her shoes, standing barefoot before him. Then she unclasped the twin brooches holding her apron in place, setting it aside. Last, she removed her gown, until she was naked before him.

His expression grew shuttered, as if he didn't want to look at her. But neither did he look away.

She came closer and loosened his tunic, moving her hands over his hardened chest. 'I don't think I am meant to have children. At least, not children of my blood.'

She lifted up his tunic and wrapped her arms around him, her breasts against his chest. His skin warmed her and she loved the feeling of hard against soft.

'With Styr, I always felt that if I didn't become pregnant, I wouldn't please him. With you, I don't worry about it. It seemed like you only wanted to be with me. The way I want to be with you now.'

His anger had not diminished and she strongly suspected it was due to his imprisonment. She moved her hands down his tight backside, then around the front to where he was heavily aroused.

'A child was never as important to me as you are,' he admitted.

A dizzying rush of relief filled her and she stepped

back, letting him see her smile. 'I love you, Ragnar. And I want to be with you, sharing whatever lies ahead.'

He studied her for a long moment. 'I've loved you for as long as I can remember. But I was afraid that I would be the same man as my father. That one day, my love of fighting would change me into a person who might hurt you or Matheus.'

'You would never harm me,' she insisted. 'I trust you with my life.' And she saw in his eyes that, for the first time, he believed it.

'Take off my chains,' he commanded. 'I want to touch you.'

Instead, Elena knelt below one of his hands, placing her breast within his palm. An intrigued expression came over him and when he teased the erect nipple, she reached over to help him remove his leggings. His tunic still hung loose against the chains, but she took his shaft in her palm as he touched her. The shudder in his breath excited her as she stroked him, revelling in the power.

'I can't take off the chains,' she confessed. 'I don't know how.' An unexpected laugh broke free and she asked, 'Should I call the men back?'

'No,' he growled. 'Not while both of us are naked. But since you didn't consider this, I think you should obey my commands.'

She stepped back, biting back her smile. 'It seems to me that you're the one in chains. Perhaps you should obey my commands instead.'

A wicked look crossed his face and he added, 'Since I can't use my hands, I'll have to use my mouth, *kjære*.'

She blushed, fascinated by the idea of this chained

man using his mouth upon her body. When she drew close again, he bent down to take her breast in his mouth. He licked the nipple, sucking hard until she felt the wet spiral of need spinning within her. She touched his hair, closing her eyes as the sensations gripped her.

He punished one breast, then the other. An idea occurred to her and she broke away for a moment, bringing a stool for him to sit upon. Then she straddled him, holding on as he continued to nip at her breasts. The new position brought her intimate flesh directly against his hard shaft and she caught her breath as the proximity brought a new pleasure.

With her hips, she edged against him, using the pressure of his erection against her wet folds. It was a delicious torment and she started to stand up, intending to sheathe him inside her. But to her shock, Ragnar dropped down to his knees. With her legs spread apart, he used his mouth against her intimate opening.

'Don't move,' he commanded and the vibration of his voice against her flesh evoked a new sensitivity.

'I don't think I can remain standing,' she admitted, as he delved into her secret places, tasting and sucking at her tight nodule. Her body was reacting violently and her knees shook as he used his tongue to arouse her.

'If you do, it will be worth it,' he promised. 'Use your hands to touch your breasts while I taste you again.'

She felt shy but obeyed, stunned when the shimmer of pleasure tore through her. She jerked with shock, her breath coming in short gasps as he drew out her need. She was so very close to the edge, her entire body was trembling. And when he sucked hard, using his tongue upon her hooded flesh, she bucked and came apart. Elena grabbed him to keep from falling, but she couldn't stop the tide of release that took her under.

She helped him to sit back on the stool and mounted him, so grateful to be joined with his flesh. He was unable to touch her with his chained hands, but she moved up and down, loving the sensations of him sheathed inside her.

'Turn around,' he ordered. 'Reverse it.'

She'd never tried such a thing, but if it would please him, she didn't mind changing the position. When she raised herself off him and turned around, he drew his knees together and she straddled him, sinking down so that she took him in deep. The friction was different as she rose up and she found her rhythm, plunging and riding him.

His shaft kept bumping against her in a new way and she convulsed as the pressure continued to build. Higher and higher it intensified and she cried out as she peaked again, her body shuddering upon his.

'I love you,' she admitted, riding out the crest of the wave as she continued to let him pump against her. 'I always have.'

Ragnar thrust inside her as she sat against him and, when she heard the shift in his own breathing, she quickened her pace. She was achingly wet for him, her body accepting his in the wild lovemaking frenzy. And finally he jolted against her, straining with the chains as he let out a shout.

'I love you, Elena,' he said, pressing a kiss to her shoulder.

She lifted slightly and turned around, wrapping her

legs around his waist. The intimacy of being with him was wonderful and her body felt satiated in a new way. 'Don't leave me,' she pleaded. 'Stay.'

'Only if you wed me.' He kissed her chin, nibbling a path down her throat.

'Yes,' she whispered. 'And especially if our nights together are like this.'

His hips moved against hers, and at the intimate touch, she felt another surge of desire rising.

A smile holding the promise of temptation was his answer.

Epilogue

'He's looking at me,' whined the eight-year-old girl. 'Make him stop.'

Elena exchanged a silent look with Ragnar, who was hiding his amusement. Beata was one of five children they'd fostered, besides Matheus. Though none of them was of her own blood, she loved them. Some days she felt more like a shepherd than a mother, herding the children, feeding them and dressing them.

She sent the five-year-old boy off to play with his older foster-brother and took Beata by the hand. 'He meant no harm. I imagine he was looking at the embroidery on your apron.'

Beata rolled her eyes. 'He's a boy. They don't care about embroidery.'

'Brothers and sisters were born to fight with each another,' Ragnar intervened. 'You'll learn to ignore his faults, one day.'

'That will be a *long* time from now,' she pronounced, before adding, 'Matheus is my favourite brother. At least he doesn't talk.'

Elena resisted the urge to answer, but she was grateful that her other foster children had accepted Matheus so readily. He was growing taller and, though he'd never spoken, he'd been apprenticed to a shipbuilder. His attention to detail and his willingness to complete the repetitive tasks no one else wanted had earned him respect.

When she was alone with her husband, she yawned and he came over to take her into his arms. 'They will fight more tonight,' she predicted. 'But I love them in spite of it.'

'You were right,' he admitted. 'You were born to be a mother.'

Her hand passed over her swollen middle and his hand covered hers. This pregnancy had taken her by shock, after so many years of being childless. She'd fully believed she would never bear a child, particularly after she'd learned from their kinsmen that Styr and Caragh now had children of their own. Never had she imagined that the blessing would come to pass.

Now, only a few months remained until she would hold their own child in her arms.

'I pray that the gods will keep you safe when this one is born,' Ragnar added.

She leaned back to look into his green eyes. 'They will, though I never expected I would bear our own child.'

'The gods rewarded you, because you took care of the children no one else wanted,' he said.

Elena tightened her arms around him. Over the years, she'd taken sickly children, some who could hardly walk or run, and one child who had been born without sight.

'They are a blessing to me,' she admitted. 'Each and every one.'

But the greatest happiness was not the love surrounding her each day. Nor was it the settlement they'd built, a dozen miles north of Gall Tír. It was the man who had given her a love beyond any she'd ever dreamed of. It was his steady presence at her side and knowing that he loved her even through the worst of times. She'd given up on having children, only to be surprised by this pregnancy at the least expected moment.

Ragnar kissed her and the familiar affection brought a warmth to her heart. Her first marriage had been born of duty and the dreams of a young girl's heart.

But the man she was meant to love was standing here now. And she intended to do so for the rest of their lives.

* * * * *

REQUEST YOUR FREE BOOKS!

 HARLEQUIN® HISTORICAL:
Where love is timeless

2 FREE NOVELS PLUS 2 **FREE GIFTS!**

YES! Please send me 2 FREE Harlequin® Historical novels and my 2 FREE gifts (gifts are worth about $10). After receiving them, if I don't wish to receive any more books, I can return the shipping statement marked "cancel." If I don't cancel, I will receive 6 brand-new novels every month and be billed just $5.44 per book in the U.S. or $5.74 per book in Canada. That's a savings of at least 16% off the cover price! It's quite a bargain! Shipping and handling is just 50¢ per book in the U.S. and 75¢ per book in Canada.* I understand that accepting the 2 free books and gifts places me under no obligation to buy anything. I can always return a shipment and cancel at any time. Even if I never buy another book, the two free books and gifts are mine to keep forever.

246/349 HDN F4ZY

Name _____ (PLEASE PRINT) _____

Address _____ Apt. # _____

City _____ State/Prov. _____ Zip/Postal Code _____

Signature (if under 18, a parent or guardian must sign)

Mail to the **Harlequin® Reader Service:**
IN U.S.A.: P.O. Box 1867, Buffalo, NY 14240-1867
IN CANADA: P.O. Box 609, Fort Erie, Ontario L2A 5X3

Want to try two free books from another line?
Call 1-800-873-8635 or visit www.ReaderService.com.

* Terms and prices subject to change without notice. Prices do not include applicable taxes. Sales tax applicable in N.Y. Canadian residents will be charged applicable taxes. Offer not valid in Quebec. This offer is limited to one order per household. Not valid for current subscribers to Harlequin Historical books. All orders subject to credit approval. Credit or debit balances in a customer's account(s) may be offset by any other outstanding balance owed by or to the customer. Please allow 4 to 6 weeks for delivery. Offer available while quantities last.

Your Privacy—The Harlequin® Reader Service is committed to protecting your privacy. Our Privacy Policy is available online at www.ReaderService.com or upon request from the Harlequin Reader Service.

We make a portion of our mailing list available to reputable third parties that offer products we believe may interest you. If you prefer that we not exchange your name with third parties, or if you wish to clarify or modify your communication preferences, please visit us at www.ReaderService.com/consumerschoice or write to us at Harlequin Reader Service Preference Service, P.O. Box 9062, Buffalo, NY 14269. Include your complete name and address.

HH13R

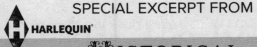
You are cordially invited to
Blythe Gifford's Royal Weddings, a brand-new duet.
In this first story, SECRETS AT COURT,
Anne of Stamford is hiding something that could
bring the English royal family crashing down.
And Nicholas Lovayne, the man charged with
uncovering the truth, could threaten everything
she holds dear....

Beneath the table, Anne wove her fingers tightly together and closed her eyes, giving prayerful thanks to God that she had stopped herself before she'd told this man everything he must not know.

What a weak, spineless woman she had become. Just a few days of being close enough to touch a man, close enough to dream, and she had forgotten who she really was.

"Anne?"

Now. I must look at him as I always do. I must give him no reason to question.

She opened her eyes, only to see Canterbury's crowded streets again, full of pilgrims with wounds visible and invisible. Turning her back, she faced Nicholas. "Forgive me. Being here, surrounded like this, I was...overcome."

Her lady and her mother and the secret. That was all that stood between her and those wretched creatures.

His hand, she realised, still cradled her shoulder, and he squeezed it, a gesture that seemed more intimate than any kiss they had shared. "I am sorry. This I cannot make right."

Simple words that nearly undid her. When had anyone ever

told her such a thing?

Her fingers met his. "You are a kinder man than you think, Sir Nicholas Lovayne."

To her relief, he straightened, breaking the intimacy. "And you are a gentler woman than you show, Anne of Stamford."

No, she was not. She was a woman who knew something that must be kept from Sir Nicholas Lovayne at any cost.

A smile now. "All will be as it must." She waved him away. "Go. You must not worry."

You must not become curious or suspicious or ask more questions.

For keeping that secret had been, simply, the reason for her life. Now she would keep it for another reason.

She would keep it so that the caring she had seen in his gray-blue eyes, caring she had never seen from another person, would not turn to abomination.

And as he left to make arrangements for the beds and the horses, she gazed after him, choking on truths she dared not speak.

I am not the woman you think I am. I am a woman whose life is based on a lie, and I hope you never discover the truth about me.

Don't miss
SECRETS AT COURT
available from Harlequin Historical March 2014

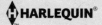
HARLEQUIN®

HISTORICAL

Where love is timeless

COMING IN MARCH 2014

The Fall of a Saint

by Christine Merrill

Honorable—and handsome to boot!—Michael Poole, Duke of
St. Aldric, has earned his nickname, "The Saint." But the *ton*
would shudder if they knew the truth. Because, thrust into a
world of debauchery, this saint has turned sinner!

With the appearance of fallen governess Madeline Cranston—
carrying his heir—St. Aldric looks for redemption through a
marriage of convenience. But the intriguing Madeline is far from
a dutiful duchess, and soon this saint is indulging in the most
sinful of thoughts…while his new wife vows to make him pay
for his past.

Available wherever books and ebooks are sold.

HH29776

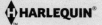

HISTORICAL

Where love is timeless

COMING IN MARCH 2014

At the Highwayman's Pleasure

by Sarah Mallory

CAPTIVATED BY THE DARK RIDER...

Embittered by injustice, Ross Durden leads a double life:
gentleman farmer by day, roguish highwayman by night.
He has sworn to right the wrongs of the past, but danger lurks
around every corner—not least when he sets eyes on the beautiful
daughter of his sworn enemy.

Celebrated actress Charity Weston is no stranger to disguises
herself. But when a darkly daring masked man steals a kiss, she is
drawn into a web of intrigue even *she* could never have imagined.

Available wherever books and ebooks are sold.